T0065098

THE I IN EVIL

THE I IN EVIL

Accepting and Embracing the Monster You Are

Ken W. Hanley

Skyhorse Publishing

Skyhorse Publishing books may be purchased in bulk at special discounts for sales promotion, corporate gifts, fundraising, or educational purposes. Special editions can also be created to specifications. For details, contact the Special Sales Department, Skyhorse Publishing, 307 West 36th Street, 11th Floor, New York, NY 10018 or info@skyhorsepublishing.com.

Skyhorse® and Skyhorse Publishing® are registered trademarks of Skyhorse Publishing, Inc.®, a Delaware corporation.

Visit our website at www.skyhorsepublishing.com.

10 9 8 7 6 5 4 3 2 1

Library of Congress Cataloging-in-Publication Data is available on file.

Cover design by Rain Saukas

Print ISBN: 978-1-63450-310-5
Ebook ISBN: 978-1-5107-0098-7

Printed in the United States of America

For people who can read. I couldn't have written this book without you. You know who you are.

Contents

Chapter I

I Am Monster, Hear Me Literally Roar

I'd like to tell you a story, and please, *don't* stop me if you've heard this before. In fact, the only acceptable reason for you to stop reading is if you are frozen in fright. This should be the only reason for you to stop reading any book in general, but especially this book, since this book is scary and about monsters who are also very scary.

A man walks into a therapist's office and says, "Doctor, I have a problem. I'm depressed because the world is harsh and cruel. I feel all alone in this threatening world, and my future is vague and uncertain."

The doctor, who may or may not be technically licensed, responds, "Well, I think the treatment is simple. You know the great clown, Pagliacci? Turns out he's in town tonight and he should be able to pick you right up."

The man, who the doctor now realizes is covered in full clown makeup, bursts into tears. "But doctor . . . I am Pagliacci!"

The doctor pauses. "If you're Pagliacci, then what happened to my three o'clock, Mr. Robinson?"

The man, wiping the tears from his face as if second nature, stares up at the doctor. "Why, he's dead, doctor. *They're all dead.*"

At this point, the doctor realizes that the blood-red, fourteen-inch, knife-like outline bulging out of Pagliacci's pockct is not his disfigured, mangled penis but instead exactly what he has suspected all along. The doctor looks at his quill pen, knowing that this day would come sooner or later.

While Pagliacci struggles to pull the giant goddamn knife from his pocket, the doctor leaps across his impressively large oak table. The doctor buries the quill pen into Pagliacci's throat as the great, murderous clown swings his knife wildly at him. As blood splatters across the room with cosmic indifference, Pagliacci falls to the ground, turning into a cold shell of a man in mere seconds.

Of course, the doctor composes himself fairly quickly; after all, it wasn't the first time someone had tried to kill him, and the sight of a mangled human corpse had become anything but shocking thanks to prior experiences. The doctor weighs his options on what he was going to do with Pagliacci; after all, the amount of blood soaking into the carpet was most certainly going to cost him his security deposit, but he couldn't just throw the body out the window after a previous "heated exchange" with the head of the sanitation department.

Further complicating the matters was that the doctor's "lawyer" couldn't come through with a "reliable solution" to the Pagliacci problem. The doctor knew he couldn't carve up and dispose of the body on his own, as there was not enough room in his briefcase to fit an entire body, and the building's elevator was on the fritz. Rather than take a frankly offensive number of trips up and down stairs with leaky body parts in his fine brown leather briefcase, he decided to take the easy way out and call the police.

Luckily, ignoring his dirtbag instincts actually worked out for the doctor, literally: Pagliacci was a wanted man, and more than a few states were willing to pay top dollar for his apprehension and/or death. After taxes and lawyer fees, the doctor ended up netting nearly $125,000 for sending Pagliacci on a one-way trip to Helltown. And not only that, but the doctor was able to even milk a little fame out of the affair, as more than a few news outlets wanted to talk about Pagliacci especially considering the doctor's tumultuous formative years.

But Pagliacci had the last laugh after all. Even though the doctor's quick wits and heroism stopped a cross-country crime spree that had become known as "The Therapist Murders," he knew his time treating humans had come to an end. After all, humans are unpredictable and the doctor did not want to be murdered before he became too old to enjoy life, as one is wont to do.

And then there was the whole murder trial that started after the doctor skipped town dressed as a woman and was caught stealing a pallet of ham sandwiches at a Sam's Club. Unfortunately, the authorities were a little more than skeptical of his 100-percent-legitimate plans to attend an upcoming Shelley Winters convention, and his dead-eyed stare and calculated choice of words didn't do him any favors either. Luckily, his defense that "I killed the guy but it wasn't no murder" was all he needed to evoke reasonable doubt, and the doctor was soon back on the streets to practice his "craft."

So, on advisement from his "lawyer," the doctor decided that he would forever trade in his role as a therapist for a career as a motivational speaker. After all, motivational speaking doesn't require any education or training; in fact, just about any idiot can be a motivational speaker. But the question remained: who out there in this world of ours needs reassurance but isn't human?

After an unsuccessful attempt at branding himself as a motivational speaker for feral and rabid dogs, which essentially drained all of his sweet murder money, the doctor turned his sight to the one place no other self-help guru had before: the shadows. The doctor knew about the existence of monsters from a young age, as his father groomed him to inherit the family business of hunting down and killing these creatures of the night. But the doctor had always seen these monsters as misunderstood beings, an opinion that created a decisive rift between his father and him that'd never quite been patched up.

If you haven't been able to piece this together, that doctor and the man writing these words are one in the same. That's right: most of my life has been in one way or another a living nightmare, which makes me all the more suited to help monsters to improve themselves. I'm a practical thinker, a man of the people, and most of the emotions that would otherwise prevent me from communicating with these creatures have long since died.

So who, or rather, *what* are these so-called monsters? Unless you are a monster yourself, you likely don't know the answer to this question, as if you did, you would be dead. And as far as my knowledge of monsters goes, dead people still cannot read books, unless they are ghosts. However, if you are dead, or know of someone who is dead, I must mention that the cover art on *The I in Evil* has been specifically designed as an exquisite coffin garnish. Furthermore, if you know a large number of the recently deceased, we could offer a great bulk deal so that every coffin has a personally signed copy of my book buried with it.

But to answer my own question, monsters are creatures who live beyond conventional logic and prey upon the weaker of the human race. These creatures include vampires, man-made creatures, mummies, lycanthropes, gill-men, and other supernaturally enhanced beings of lore. Of course, little video evidence exists of these monsters, who have been misrepresented by the media in a fashion not unlike O. J. Simpson, Oscar Pistorius, or other athletes whose names start with the letter O. In reality, these monsters are just as afraid of you as you are of them, although they're admittedly more likely to do something very terrible to calm their fears.

For instance, think of the vermin that live inside of the walls of your home. Do they mean to irritate you and ruin your living space? Of course not; those disgusting little critters are only interested in cohabiting a shared environment and staying relatively laissez-faire about your lifestyle. But instead, we lure them into traps, poison them, or hunt them down to kill these frightened, desperate creatures for simply following their nature. Monsters are much like, but not exclusively like, those vermin, and would choose not to hurt people at all if they had a choice in the matter.

Now that's not to say monsters aren't dangerous. After all, they kill people all the time for seemingly no reason. So much blood has been spilled senselessly, often times consumed or used as part as some terrifying ritual, by monsters whose fleeting thoughts of casual violence would shame even the most wild imagination. But think of it this way: modern art is pretty terrible too, but we don't cast artists into the dark recesses of the night, do we? These monsters have just as much right to be rehabilitated as any modern artist, and that's a fact no doctor can refute.

Furthermore, monsters have only earned a reputation for their most horrific crimes through secondhand accounts from time periods in which the greatest advance in medicine was a stick you would bite down on during amputation. For all we know, there might be a very good reason that monsters have lashed out at humanity and treated us as prey instead of equals. And since there are no recorded monster attacks on video, there's no concrete way of knowing just how harsh and frequent these attacks might be. For all we know, monsters could be humane in the way they killed their victims, and could have used every piece of their body like whatever Native Americans did that back whenever they did that.

As we see in our very own penitentiary system, there's hope for redemption with every monster, no matter how many people they kill or consume, or how much pleasure they appear to have in the process. After all, if a dog excretes on a fine rug, most people do not chase the animal into a windmill and burn it to the ground. Instead, we're taught to show the dog his excrement and let him know that it's the wrong thing to do. By keeping the verbal part of that process, I hope to condition these horrifying abominations to become full-fledged members of society and, God willing, teach these monsters to organically shove their faces into their own shit when they do something shitty.

On the other hand, if you *are* a monster and you are reading this, then I would like to formally welcome you to the first day of the rest of your life. Unlike people, you can trust this book. I have personally made sure the pages of this book were printed on an extremely expensive non-flammable, rubberized wax paper, free of silver, garlic, moondust, and any other harmful substances. I've also had every copy personally blessed by my good friends over at the Church of Satan, making this book 100 percent certified God-proof.

Now, that doesn't necessarily mean this book is safe in any way, as contrary to popular opinion, Satan and his minions can essentially possess anything, including monsters. In my research on monster culture, I've seen or at least heard unconfirmed reports of vampires, mummies, gill-men, dogs, cars, computers, air conditioners, and more things falling under demonic or satanic possession. And from what I can tell, it sucks and you would likely prefer not to have that happen to you.

It's hard enough to find a decent exorcist nowadays, let alone one willing to work on a vampire or a wolfman. Despite what you might see in films, the exorcism game is more or less a racket for the older members of the Catholic Church to retain employment and seem important. Most of the time, they don't even know where they are, and feel that reading a book and throwing water on someone whose brain is melting on the inside is God's will. Poor old bastards.

On that note, if you are a human reading this book and my motivational tactics do not dissuade any of your homicidal tendencies, I'd suggest you line every inch of your house with copies of this book. Therefore, any sins you commit in your residence, legal or otherwise, will escape the sights of the Almighty and give you full deniability at the pearly gates. It's a worthy investment for an eternity of reasonable doubt, and God's court is much more harsh than Earth court, believe you me.

Furthermore, if there are any monsters out there in service to the dark lord and want to even the odds, I wouldn't dissuade you from buying hundreds of copies of *The I in Evil* and leaving them in every hotel room you'd encounter. By pairing every Holy Bible, and in radical cases, the Book of Mormon, with a copy of this book, you'll be balancing religious equality in the lives of hundreds of thousands potential patrons of these hotel rooms. Also, if you want to buy even more copies and leave them in random mailboxes, I wouldn't oppose that action either, especially once monsters begin moving into nice neighborhoods.

I should also clarify that the random mailboxes in which you should be leaving my books should be in nice neighborhoods. These fucking things don't grow on trees, and outside of monsters buying this fucking book, I can't have books given out like charity to poor neighborhoods that can't pay it forward, emphasis on the word "pay." So get it together, monsters, and use your fucking brain(s) to sell me some more books.

But back to my monstrous friends, I'd like to thank you for taking the leap to better yourself. I can only imagine the suffering you've gone through from the years of insomnia, social anxiety, and residential displacement, as well as the suffering you've inflicted on others for reasons that frankly aren't my business. But by coming with me on this journey towards self-enlightenment, you are telling the world that you will suffer no longer. You are ready to look to the people around you and say, "I am Monster. Hear me literally roar."

Now, I'm not a fucking bullshitter, okay? If you wanted to be fucked around, or shit on, or have your shit fucked on, then I recommend you return this fucking book and pick up some Dr.-fucking-Phil shit. I'm here to speak the truth and to unfuck your shit, so leave your fucking shit at the fucking door and get your shit together before you fucking read the rest of this book, got it?

That said, I want you to know that I care about you. I care about the things you do and about the monster you are (or, if applicable, the person you used to be). I care about your future on this beautiful little orb we call Earth. And I especially care about preserving the goodness within you now and building on that goodness to achieve happiness.

Of course, the amount that I care about you also is somewhat dependent on what exactly you do to achieve that happiness. If your version of goodness is to drain an entire family of blood so no one is left to mourn, or to strangle a boat full of fisherman for profiting off of the death of a species, I can't necessarily support those acts. I *could* accept a vampire levitating someone across the street or a wolf-man helping to round up loose sheep. Don't be too hard on yourself though. Any step away from eating their flesh is a baby step in the right direction, so if that leads you to happiness, I'm sure mankind will meet you halfway.

But in order for that care to mean anything, I need to know that the monster within you wants to change. After all, stubbornness isn't an innately human quality, and if my words are perceived as disposable by your rotten, abnormal brain, then they will be no good to either of us. You need to truly believe that the monster you are on the outside does not represent the monster you are on the inside. And hopefully, my words will help them meet in the middle, around your abdomen or solar plexus, probably.

Now, there is one universal truth I must address before I begin working with you monsters individually: you must let go of your grudge against mankind. That is your first internal obstacle, and likely the one that drives you towards your most unbecoming behavior. But for a second, imagine things from humanity's point of view: if you knew you existed, wouldn't you want to hunt you? Of course, you would.

If you could admit that you hate yourself more than you hate mankind, then the process of moving on and healing will become so much easier. My words are meant to reach your dried-up monster heart, and remove the scars that humans made on your vulnerable psyche. If you are ever to help yourself grow beyond your means and reach your petrifying potential, you need to allow me to reach you and help you change for the better. After all, this book is as useful to a monster who can't be reached or changed as a dick on a snowman.

Actually, there is also another universal truth worth addressing. Don't look up monster slash fiction on the Internet. There are some things even the darkest of souls should never bear witness to, unless that's your thing and the idea of gill-men sex gets you harder than Medusa's optometrist.

Oh, you know what? There's a third universal truth that I should share: no matter what, the ends justify the means. Whether shining the light of positivity and goodwill on the darkness of the underworld, or writing a self-help book to pay for the multitude of debts following a post-trial breakdown spending spree, the eventuality of results should serve as motivation enough to do any and all unethical, immoral, scandalous, disrespectful, violent, deplorable, reprehensible, reckless, antisocial, misanthropic, vicious, selfish, and malicious acts along the way. As kings, innovators, and people who exercise can tell you, the light at the end of the tunnel is all that matters, and whatever you do in that long, dark tunnel is fair game.

If you are a man-made creature, also known among humans as "Frankenstein's Monster," then I'd like to congratulate you. After all, with brains that are miswired or outright idiotic, reading a book of this capacity is as difficult as chasing a boat in the arctic on foot. Nevertheless, you are a prime case for behavioral repair and I hope my words can help elevate you from simpleton to charleton.

Furthermore, I'd like to remind you that you're not nearly as freakish as your counterparts, likely since you were created by man and man rarely makes completely boneheaded mistakes. This author has met many eloquent and thoughtful man-made creatures, and outside of harboring a wealth of anger and self-pity, they've all been relatively normal in conversation and overall behavior. In fact, the only thing that can get super off-putting about your kind is when your parts don't necessarily sync up in terms of looks and mechanics, and that's often more of your creator's fault than yours.

If you are a mummy, I'd like to congratulate you as well but unfortunately, my "public school" educators never responded to my requests to learn Egyptian. But if you have either learned English, have hired a translator, or are somehow American, then you will find much to cherish in this book. After all, the treasure you've been cursed with immortality to protect pales in comparison to the treasure that can be found in your mind. And if my words are successful, hopefully they'll awaken the mummy in your head, ready to kill any negative influences that dare invade it with its metaphorical hands.

Likewise, I find that mummies are quite adept at learning and communicating their concerns to others; in fact, most people who have been killed by mummies were at least *aware* that the tombs they entered may have been cursed. But at the end of the day, curses are just words (but not necessarily curse words) and words don't really mean shit thousands of years later. So perhaps after you've given this book a proper read, you might be able to amend your hieroglyphics to let future archaeologists know that the only reason a dried-up skeleton hand isn't wrapped around their throats is *The I in Evil*.

Are you a werewolf? If you're reading this in your human form, please put the book down and revisit it at the next full moon. Once you've changed into your beast-like form, you will be ready for the enlightment I can provide. Now, I will start by asking you to sit. Sit. Now, stay. Stay. *Stay*. Now, *learn*. That's a good boy.

Also, considering how difficult being a werewolf can be, this author even made sure your particular chapter has plenty of information for your family, rommates, and even wolf pack, if that's how you roll. This author never feels that a dog can get too old to learn new tricks, especially if these tricks save them the embarrassment of pulling their cock out of a pool of lamb's blood once a month. Also, since your curse is ultimately the most punk rock of all the afflicted creatures addressed in this book, this author figured you might need all the help you can get to help control and adapt your animalistic sensibilities.

If you're a vampire, you likely think you are better than this book, and humanity in general. But while it was easy for us to coexist in the prior millennia, the times have changed and you must accept it. With social media and the Internet making vanity and hypersexuality more commonplace than ever, the classist viewpoint of the vampire has gone out of style. Yet with this book, I can look to give you motivation to better yourself and once again give you the esteem that someone who hunts and eats human beings deserves.

To be fair, this author might have found the greatest amount of emotional investment with vampires, as all vampire readers may remember my previous book, *Blood-Drinkers in the Mist*. For that book, I spent three years observing, studying, and living with vampires in their natural habitat, watching them do everything from draining their victims completely of blood to hypnotizing their familiars to jerk off in front of one another. It was a taste of hedonism that would make the Babylonians feel ashamed. And knowing just how fragile the ego and mentality of a vampire can be, hopefully my book will provide them with as much solace as it hopes to provide humility.

If you're a gill-man, I'd first and foremost ask you to keep your book or electronic reading device in a well-sealed plastic bag. I actually don't know if you can read or not; I don't understand the vision or biology of gill-men. To be completely honest, this entire chapter was written as a shot in the dark, more or less. But if you can read, then I am absolutely, 100 percent positive that my words will inspire great confidence and will give you the strength to be a better gill-man.

And if you're a gill-man, you can at least take comfort in knowing that you're the most biologically natural monster of them all. Rather than being deformed, cursed, or crafted into your monstrous exterior, you were simply an evolution of man and fish birthed from God's own dark, sick humor. In that sense, you can at least know that you are supposed to look and act in the way that you do, and that may make accepting your flaws and changing that much easier. Again, I really hope you can read this, although if you paid for this book, I guess it doesn't matter at the end of the day.

Also, if you didn't pay for this book and instead pirated an e-version online, I want to congratulate you because if I have the time to write a stupid self-help book for monsters, I will certainly have the time to hunt you down and take my deserved money out of your cold, dead hand. I will also make sure that your death is not as swift and easy as it was to download this book; I will likely bring a couple of my monster friends and let them work out some of their more undeniably negative behavioral issues. And if not, I'm more than capable of doing the job myself, and making sure that the next self-help book I write is written in *blood*, and I know who is going in the acknowledgements . . . literally.

Back to business, this book is also meant to help criminally insane scientists and doctors, some of the few actual monsters that are also humans all of the time. After all, we both know the human shell you exist within is merely an inconvenience of mortality and limitations, all of which your brain will likely survive after its expiration. You are clearly insane with delusions of grandeur and a God complex that strikes fear in those around you. Unfortunately, none of those qualities are compatible with your paternal responsibilities with your creations, and that's something we definitely will have to work on.

Also, I anticipate that we will have to go over some of the basics of communication since mad geniuses seem to not understand how to talk to others. One might rush to believe that they might have a disorder that would prevent them from understanding or conveying emotions in a proper fashion, but upon closer investigation, it seems that they clearly know what they're saying and are being intentionally suspect. By ending every sentence with an ominous sense of foreboding, people will instantly pick up that you are being malicious, and that's a really terrible approach to establishing and maintaining relationships.

I also must calm any suspicions right now that this book will not provide an equal opportunity for monsters of a female disposition. I firmly believe that the same methods and words that work for Frankenstein's monster and Dracula will also work for their brides. It's 2015, and even the archaic cultural pathologies of these monsters must accept that the lines between man and woman get blurrier by the day. Hell, I wouldn't be surprised if Dracula himself hasn't worn a dress at some time or another. After all, it's the ultimate act of biological empowerment; in a perfect world, men and women alike would all wear dresses.

In addition to that sentiment, this author feels that he has further right to dish out self-help motivation to female monsters because he has become aggressively familiar with his feminine side. This author intimately understands the many aspects of womanhood, such as the side that can't take the stress of life and indulges in comfort food or can't take the stress of life and contemplates drowning children. And for monster women, I understand exactly how it feels to be paired with someone who drives you to murder and isolation, as does every human with an ex-wife. Though that statement seems misogynistic, it's actually more feminist than anything, because any marriage with someone you hate is an arranged marriage in spirit, and those are way more uncool for women than they are for men.

And while many people in the motivational speaking, medical, and psychological care communities have repeatedly denied the existence of ghosts, I am not one of them. Yes, that's right: I believe that I am the first motivational writer to expressly pen literature intended for the spectral undead. I believe that ghosts can still learn to be better people even after crossing the physical threshold, and I believe that we can also learn much from ghosts. So if you are a ghost, and you are reading this right now, I must insist that you find a way to contact me so we can speak privately. I want to know your secrets. All of them.

If you're not a ghost, do me a kindness and please disregard the entire last paragraph. After all, ghosts would never know the secret to immortality, and I wouldn't assume they would know in the first place, let alone capture and study them to find out. I mean, that'd be against every intention I have for this book, and I wouldn't cannibalize those intentions for something as frivolous as becoming a God among both men and monsters. That's simply ridiculous and I won't waste another word on it.

But if you are a ghost, all I'm saying is that it would be nice to be included on some of those ghostly secrets at the end of the day. After all, ghosts barely qualify as monsters, and their need for self-help may go beyond the simple advice-column hooey that can be applied to the mummies and wolfmen of the world. And I'm willing to go that extra mile to make sure that ghosts can haunt their premises with a clean conscience and strong resolve, and all I ask for in return is you do me a favor and reach out to me so that we can get this whole "secret underlying motivation" schtick all cleared up.

I would also like to take this opportunity to thank any psychic medium or séance instructor who may be helping ghosts read this book. While I may be a shameless opportunist who would much rather see the ghosts pay full price for the audiobook version of *The I in Evil,* I do understand that reading is a difficult task for ghosts and that purchasing books is an even more difficult task. So thank you for being a conduit for these spirits and allowing them to experience my words in the way that any paying customer deserves.

Now, it has occurred to me that, for one reason or another, human beings may still be reading this book, and that's okay. I believe that humans who cannot find solace in the advice of colleagues, family, friends, and other self-help books will find the answers they're looking for only in this book. And for humans looking to be more understanding of monster culture, I appreciate that you're taking the first step with my book; as they often say, the first option is always the best option. But for those reading this book with darker or more malicious intentions, I have some words I'd like to share with you.

Firstly, if you're a doctor or professional in the motivational sector, back the fuck away from the book. If you remember correctly, I was silenced by the bigwigs at the National Medical Associates Convention when I forcibly took the microphone from musical guest Don Henley and called dibs on treating the monster community. Well, whether you like it or not, dibs is still in effect and according to my "lawyer," it's also legally recognized. So go ahead: steal my idea. You wanna see if I'm litigious? I'll bleed your wallet like a stuck pig, you degree-carrying motherfucker. Then we'll see who is "discourteous and shameful."

Secondly, to all the amateur Van Helsings in the world who want to use this book to better understand their prey, then maybe you should take a look at yourself, then buy another copy of this book since *you're* the real monster with actual problems. Think about it: these monsters are trying to better themselves for humans as well, and you want to take advantage of them? That's the mindset of a real piece of shit, and hopefully, when mankind and monsterkind sit side by side at the table of brotherhood, it will be you who is living in the shadows waiting to be slaughtered by some other asshole in a duster.

Thirdly, if you're a skeptic and you don't believe in monsters, that's fine. After all, I've been accused of many things during my life, such as fraud, animal cruelty, alimony evasion, and starting a riot. I've even been accused of murdering the great clown, Pagliacci! But if there's anything I am not, nor have I ever been, it would be a liar.

Monsters exist, and that's just a fact that the world needs to catch up on in order to better themselves. Monsters who are reading this right now know that they exist, and I'm sure the government knows monsters exist as well. There are doubters out there, but they have not walked into the darkest shadows of the night, and they sure as shit have never danced with the devil.

Remember the president who was in a wheelchair? Remember when he said the only thing we had to fear was fear itself? Read between the lines: he was talking about monsters existing, and he was assuring us not to fear them because they're meant to be understood and helped. By disavowing their existence, not only are you hurting monsters, but you're doubting the word of the wheelchair-president-guy who killed Hitler. Therefore, you're implying that you would rather see Hitler still in power. Shame on you.

The fact is I believe in helping others, even those who might not arguably exist. And who am I to tell an entire race of people who might not exist that they do not need a confidence boost? I would not spend all this time writing this specific book if I didn't think my words of wisdom could help those in the monster community. So believe me when I say: monsters are real and they are everywhere, and they can purchase this book at their local literature retailer.

Now, I know that by offering social and psychological help to monsters, I am putting myself at great risk as well. Some anti-monster nationalist groups will be keen to label me a "monster sympathizer," which puts me at risk of harassment and even assassination. Others will be quick to call me an opportunist, making a quick buck off of an underprivileged and underserved monster population. But I've never found myself to be one for labels: I'm just trying to give monsters the same treatment that I expect myself, and I'm also trying make a lot of money.

I also know that some monsters are not seeking the help of a man who couldn't help people or even feral dogs get their shit together, since monsters are a whole different ball game. Obviously, historically speaking, humans haven't necessarily earned the trust of the monster community, and vice versa. And then there's the militant sections of the monster community, the ones that organize sit-ins in castles, pyramids, and the moors, who actively hate any human that reaches out to the monster community.

But as a motivational speaker, it's my job to believe words can change the world. To this day, if you yell "fire" in a crowded movie theater, the lives of the people in that movie theater will change forever. But to yell "fire" at the monster community, the reaction would be devastating. Someone could even be killed.

The reality of the situation is that, as we stand, monsters and humans don't mix. By asking monsters to join our society with open arms, this book will pioneer a whole new school of thought altogether. Laws will be written, educational institutions will be demolished, and children will be brainwashed to believe that monsters have always been a part of the equation. Monsters will no longer look at people only as things which they can kill or frighten at will, but also things that they can talk to, become friends with, and hire to do their taxes.

But if humans and monsters are going to break bread at the table of brotherhood one day, there needs to be a mutual sense of trust, and there's no better place to start than with my words here. After all, no one else is champing at the bit to be the unofficial ambassador to the dark side, and much fewer monsters have ever tried to derail my life in the way humans have. Besides, if I were ever to be targeted for murder as I have been in the past, I would appreciate the intimate approach that monsters have, which humans lack.

From the monster perspective, this author is likely the most trustworthy human they'll find to help them find themselves, considering I have no active religious affiliations and my misanthropy levels are at a seasonal low. Much like monsters, I mostly operate at night at my own discretion, and our mutual fascination with death makes us mentally connected. Also, I assume monsters and myself share the same funeral etiquette, and have similar approaches in terms of reporting our income to the federal government. And lastly, I might be in possession of key materials that, according to occult scrolls written throughout centuries, could bring upon the apocalypse to mankind and monsterkind, which pretty much means they have little choice but to trust me not to use it.

The I in Evil is meant to be a stepping stone for monsters to finally receive the self-help they've fought so hard for. After all, it's hard to help yourself when you spend your life focused on the destruction of others. But even though they're set in their ways, this book will help monsters accept that they are, in fact, monsters and embrace that they are, in fact, monsters. In fact, by finally having this handy tool, these monsters might even realize how similar they are to people after all.

Also, I'd like to clarify that by monsters, I don't mean those awful humans that are labeled as monsters by the media or history textbooks, such as those super-weird serial killer types or those creepy rapist characters. If you like to torture and kill people and fuck their refrigerated corpse for weeks on end, there's very little I can offer you in terms of self-help, especially because it seems that you're perfectly content doing your own thing. And if you're a rapist or child molester or any kind of sexual criminal, there's probably an institution or mental wellness center that might be able to help you once you're out of jail. However, if you're either a serial killer or a rapist and you're in prison, you might as well use *The I in Evil* as reading material, as long as it keeps you from killing or raping anyone, you fucking ghouls.

I'd also like to state that this book is also not meant for monster cosplayers either, although I'll certainly take their money. I mean, you don't have the shared experiences that vampires, man-made creatures, or even the odd outliers like cat-people and swamp-beings do; you only pretend that you do since the human race left you high and dry a long time ago. That's not necessarily a problem, and if my book makes you feel closer to the real thing, I'm not going to discourage you. But I will say I wouldn't be caught dead in any of the monster communities dressed up as one of them while holding this book, unless you want your first monster interaction to be your last.

I guess what this author is trying to say is that whether you're a man or a creature from any color lagoon, there will always be the opportunity to sink low. If things aren't going well in life and you're on a downward spiral, you'll find yourself at rock bottom, dodging a clown with a knife jumping around your "office" with nothing but a quill pen to save your life. It's these introspective moments that remind us that we're all in this rat race together, and if we don't all try our hardest to run uphill, the world is more than willing to let us tumble down.

So take a look around you. Whether you see man, monster, or otherwise, they're all connected. You see, everybody's brain doesn't work, at least not as intended. Every single living thing on Earth is crazy to some degree, and they all have severe problems that they can't overcome themselves. Men and monster alike both need that little push towards self-actualization, and thankfully, writers like myself step in to do just that.

That's the beauty of self-help, and it's a beauty that monsters like you will see for the first time. Technically, I'm not saying or doing anything that you can't say or do for yourself. The fact is, though, you won't say it to yourself because you've always thought of yourself as an abhorrent freak of nature. Self-help books change that entirely, as I write the things you're supposed to say to yourself. I recommend reading this book out loud, so therefore, you *are* saying them to yourself. As five little Jacksons might say, it's easy as A-B-C (or possibly 1-2-3 or even potentially do-re-mi)!

There is one concept that most motivational speakers/ writers forget about until Bob Dylan comes on the radio: the ever-changing nature of time. Much like people, some monsters can change overnight while other will go through eternity while not changing one iota of their being. And if there's anything that institutionalized conditioning has taught me over the years, it's that if you keep telling someone something over and over again, eventually they'll stop listening to their doubtful inner voices and submit to your teachings.

Considering the nature of many monsters, time is the main difference between human and monster, with the former having too little in their lifetime while the latter having too much time. But if a human or a monster reads this book over and over and over in their spare time, the revolutionary ideas on display will slowly but surely ingratiate themselves into their brain to change them for the better.

Time provides the building blocks for which man and monster can better themselves, specifically by reading my book and burning its messages into their thoughts on a primal level. And when your life comes to a close at the hand of God or some weirdo with a silver-tipped sword, you will not be remembered as the monster who razed the Earth and all of its inhabitants, but rather as the one who tried to change the world for the better by bettering him/herself.

Now, I know if you're told that you're evil your whole life because you scare people, murder people, and eat people, you just might believe that you are in fact evil. And believe me, I understand that logic; for the first seven years of my life, I thought my name was "You" because it was the only name my father called me. But you're not evil, just as much as I'm not You. I'm me, and you are a monster. And starting now, that's not a bad thing.

Chapter II

Stigma, Not Stigmata

Whether you are some entitled piece-of-shit child or an old, irrelevant bag of bones, it's not hard to see that one of the biggest problems facing our society today is stigma. Stigma, for those of you who are slack-jawed assholes too lazy or ignorant to pick up a fucking book, is a preconceived disapproval of certain people, such as nerds, geeks, or dorks, who operate or distinguish themselves outside of normal societal expectations. Stigma is often applied to outcasts, people with alternative lifestyles, or, in some cases, just plain weirdos. But even if you're some stinky, shitty, garbage hipster, there's no group that has faced a stigma as vile and ferocious as monsters.

Based solely on the stereotypes of a select few trouble-makers in the monster community, monsters as a whole have faced stigma, whether it be looks of fear, screams of terror, or disparaging remarks on the Internet. But while monsters have their problems, so do humans, and we all should know by now the many faces that stigma can wear. It could be a woman tugging at her turtleneck sweater in the face of a vampire, or people averting their gaze from the scar-ridden bodies of a man-made creature, but stigma hurts monsters where they're most vulnerable: on the inside. Literally, that's where they're most vulnerable, especially gill-men, because they have scaly bodies impervious to small blades and bludgeons.

Hell, monster stigma isn't even something you might notice necessarily, but it is a part of everyday life. There are myriad words in our vernacular that people use all the time but have unmistakable ties to degrading monsters, including (but not exclusive to) "creepy," "kooky," "mysterious," "spooky," and "altogether ooky." To us, they might be words one might use to describe quality television, but to monsters, it's essentially terminology ripped straight from H.P. Lovecraft's *other* writings.

Even worse might be how much as a society we continue to encourage such stigma, even in light of the wonderful steps we've taken to empower our youth, repair race relations, and eradicate domestic abuse. Do monsters occasionally get out of line? I'm sure there are a couple of villages that might think so. But does that warrant making light of their unfortunate situations in our theaters, on our apparel, or on our breakfast cereal boxes? I mean, *Hotel Transylvania* is basically a minstrel show in the guise of a children's film with anti-monster imagery that would make the terrifying ghost of D.W. Griffith blush.

Even though my father wasn't the perfect man, in some states more than others, he did teach me two valuable lessons: "don't make two phone calls in the same county" and "never judge a book by its cover." By taking in these words of wisdom, not only have I avoided reading many shitty books, but I've been able to have an inherent empathy for all of God's creatures, living or otherwise. With that clarity in mind, I find it important to make steps in eliminating monster stigma and discrimination in all of its forms.

Of course, the first step in ridding the world of monster stigma is to lure these monsters a reasonable distance out of the shadows and show them that they have support. If you're reading this book and, for some odd reason, you're not a monster, please go back to the store, buy another copy, and leave it in a nearby patch of darkness. If the place where you bought the book was closed, you can look for the local twenty-four-hour book emporium, or stay up all night drinking coffee and definitely not doing drugs until the store re-opens in the morning.

If you bought this book online, why not order six or seven more copies and go on a darkness dropping spree? If you consider it a public service, take it off your taxes. It's all legal, and if some fucking government cocksucker tells you that you're intentionally fucking up your tax statement, call him a liar, ask for his name and tell him he's a dead man. That'll show 'em, every last one of 'em.

Now, if you're a monster and you're reading this book, you've hopefully figured out by now that we want you to come out of hiding. Will it be difficult? Probably; monsters like yourself, after all, are pretty scary. But once you're out in the open, you will see that it gets better, and a local citizen will show you the way to the monster wellness center.

But what's that? There is *no* monster wellness center?! Sadly, I'd believe it. For all the luxuries we afford to alcoholics and rape victims and suicide survivors, it looks like monsters are left to fend for themselves in this cruel fucking society. Where are the monsters to go when the world has turned its back on them?

Luckily, in the pursuit of bettering monsters and making the world aware of monster stigma, I have been hard at work to develop the world's first monster wellness center. With the help of two congressmen, eight former professional wrestlers, and twenty-three generous freelance construction workers from what I assume to be Spanish-speaking countries, the Ken Hanley Center for Monsters, Ghouls, Etcetera Wellness is on track to open in 2016, all funded by federal tax dollars as well as a lucrative licensing agreement with Hot Topic.

At my institution, monsters will begin societal integration by working with fellow monsters and human volunteers to improve themselves and gain crucial life experiences. Furthermore, we'll offer free therapy sessions and job consultations. We will have thirteen rooms available for monsters (or ghosts) who have fallen on hard times. But most importantly, the entire building is made out of military-grade bulletproof glass, to show the world that monsters will not succumb to social stigma and that they're here to stay. After all, it takes a great deal of transparency to make monster stigma a thing of the past, and what's more transparent than an entire standing structure made out of glass?

Now, I am sure I will have been accused of profiting off the misery and degradation of monsters with this book, just as I am sure I will be accused of using my monster wellness center improperly, probably thanks to the liberal news media that looks down upon charging admission for humans to view into a big glass monster prison from the outside. Did I type and spellcheck "prison?" That's strange; I clearly meant to type "monster wellness center" again. Well, you get the picture.

Nevertheless, I've seen a world without monster wellness centers, and it's not pretty, especially because monsters themselves aren't pretty to begin with (despite what a multitude of message boards might tell you). Monster equality demonstrations in the past have often had weak results, where the best case scenario is for perplexed onlookers to think that the Halloween parade has come early. The alternative outcome, of course, is that monster stigma takes control of the crowd, which would almost always end in riots.

The most infamous of these poorly received demonstrations is clearly the Million Monster March that took place in Thelma, Tranyslvania in 1968, in which thousands of monsters congregated to stand against monster discrimination. Their message was to end scare-gregation and anti-monster legislation, including a critical bill that made it illegal for the dead to come back to life, was a powerful one, and yet their critical opposition made for an intense showdown between Transylvania's peacekeeping militia and the monsters. Of course, violence erupted: peacekeepers beamed giant ultraviolet lights on the demonstration and unleashed dozens upon dozens of cats to break up the march. The monsters reacted in the only way they knew how: the vampires went into a frenzy, while the cats tried to eat gill-men, were chased by wolfmen, and sent the mummies into hysterics.

"It happened all in a flash," said eyewitness Robert Boris Pickett. "They did the mash. It was a graveyard smash. It was a monster mash."

Any way you look at it, the Million Monster March did as much help to the monster community as it did to harm it, bringing to light the presence of these creatures. To some, it showed that monsters had organizational skills, that in and of itself is a terrifying concept, even if it was technically a step forward. To anti-monster radicals, it confirmed their notions that monsters are hostile creatures, hellbent on the destruction and consumption of human beings. And even neutral parties agreed that monsters probably shouldn't be screaming and roaring during school hours, as it would distract children from learning about whatever bullshit they taught in 1968, like math or something, maybe?

While there were a few successful monster awareness demonstrations after that, most notably "Occupy Fleet Street," most would end in further "mashes" or, on select occasions, "big battles" in which monsters would scale buildings and break whatever they found on their way up. But the stigma was just too much for many monsters: it sent them back into the shadows and left them vulnerable to various Van Helsing family members and the semi-frequent raids by Busters of Ghosts. But ask yourself this: if someone came into your home and tried to kill you, wouldn't you have the right to rip them limb from limb, and maybe feed upon them while they were still alive for a week or so?

However, if you're a monster and you're reading this, know that you are not alone, and that for some humans out there, monster culture is more hip than horrific (yes, even mummies!). These people embrace monster culture with open arms because, unlike actual people, they don't have real friends and are residing in their own living hell called adulthood. They also know what it's like to be an outcast, banished to their parents' basements, much like most man-made creatures, although the reason for their punishment usually correlates to the amount of incessantly played metal music and concomitant lack of hygiene.

Without being too dramatic, these people essentially worship monsters as gods, obsessively watching monster movies, and adorning their image on their apparel and denim jackets. Sometimes they will even dress up like monsters outside of annual Halloween parties. Most of the time, they know the ins and outs of monster culture and are proud of it. They have studied the dark arts, read genu-inely terrifying literature, and even go as far as listening to scary noise music, whatever that is. They are the closest things monsters have to human allies in the effort to end monster stigma, and also will have some very interesting fan fiction that you might want to read, especially if you're a *really* lonely monster.

It's these monster lovers that you will also have to rely on when taking the first steps to assimilate into society after defeating monster stigma after we presumably beat it nearly to death before burying it alive. Well, actually, a better way would be to lure stigma outside of its house late at night, and then hit it in the back of its head with a lead pipe. Then we'd drag stigma into the backyard and drown it in a kiddie pool.

Then we can wrap stigma's body in a thick plastic sheet, submerge it in wax and then drop it in a swamp, where it'll remain hidden until the hot summer water melts the wax and leaves the meat for the 'gators.

Or maybe we can tell stigma we're taking it to a really cool party where Jenny Grady is there, and word around town is that she has the hots for stigma. But little does stigma know that not only does Jenny Grady think stigma is a fucking clown, but there's no party at all. Unless your definition of a party is a dark basement where we light stigma on fire, break its bones, dismember it and place its remainders in a safe, to which only we know the combo. That is everything except for the head and hands, which we drain the blood out of and keep in a dry, odor-suppressing box, which is then placed in a safety deposit box under an assumed identity.

In any case, stigma is fucked, and if we're going to make people forget about it, our greatest allies will be monster lovers. However, identifying them is a whole different story, as monster lovers and monster poseurs (who we'll get to in a moment) can be hard to differentiate, especially because they're so sexy with their bad boy lifestyles and hair dye. After all, you can't just look at either group and go, "Oh, that giant man is covered in scars and has a green complexion," or "that wolf looks like it's walking on hind legs and wearing ill-fitting jeans without a shirt" because they'll clearly never be "one of you." So to find out the true nature of a monster lover, as well as their loyalty to your monsterdom, it might take as long as several hours, and even then, you might want to rip their jaw from their skull just to be sure.

Now what are "monster poseurs," you so stupidly ask? Actually, do I really have to answer this stupid fucking question? Do you have the Internet wherever you creatures hide? Can't you burrow under a McDonald's or a Starbucks and use their Wi-Fi? I just don't understand how you found out or got this book if not for the Internet. Do you guys have book store familiars? I wonder how many library cards carry the name "Renfield." . . .

In any case, monster poseurs can be one of many things, but for the most part, they are people who pretend to be pro-monster when they're really monster-indifferent or, in extreme cases, secretly anti-monster. They will normally dress and adopt the stylings of monster lovers to fit in with the crowd, but when push comes to shove, they probably don't even know the lyrics to Alice Cooper's "Feed My Frankenstein" and likely have never seen any of the sequels to *Frankenstein* (including *Bride of*). Sometimes, you can tell by their T-shirts that try too hard to get recognition for their horror fandom, or perhaps obnoxious tattoos on their inner wrist, the most obnoxious place for tattoos. They're really shitty people with a part-time interest in a subculture that they know little of, and yet act like they're Captain Horse Cock of the HMS *Weekend of Horrors*.

However, sometimes monster poseurs can have a much more sinister agenda, whether it be as petty as stigma-fueled "monster shaming" or as terrifying as undercover monster hunting. While I've always said that the only shame I am okay with Seamus O'Shanahan, my former "Medication Consumption Advisor," monster-shaming is as rampant as ever, with websites like *Monsters of New York* and *Fuck No Monsters Tumblr* providing less open-minded humans with their fair share of easy laughs at your monstrous exteriors. Some monster poseurs will use monsters for their own gain, including at heavy metal festivals, or they are given to producers behind the popular direct-to-video scum films *BEASTFIGHTS*, where down-on-their-luck vampires will punch out each other's fangs for a vial of virgin blood.

But the worst kind of monster poseurs will always be the monster hunters, who provide alleged monsters with sympathy to get close enough to persecute and kill the monsters who fall for their traps. Fortunately, most of the monster community has become savvy of these shithead extraordinaires, often being able to see through their generic monster affiliations. Usually, you'll be able to pick up on their myriad awful monster tattoos and actual silver jewelry to separate them from the real deal. In fact, any overt pride is usually a telltale sign of a monster hunter, as any monster will tell you pride is a learned trait among their ilk.

However, some monsters slip through the cracks and find themselves entangled in the spider web of a monster hunter. Not literally spider web, unless they are Spider-Man or, even worse, spider-collectors with a wealth of time on their hands. Nevertheless, these monster hunters are fucking assholes of the highest order, and are among the top tier jerks who are really making things hard for monsters to join society.

While there is not enough documented evidence to prove their existence, I've got the word from some anonymous former-wrestlers-turned-governors-turned-conspiracy-theorists that there might even be government-commissioned monster hunters roaming the streets of America today. As a part of Operation Sleeping Fish, these alleged creature cleansers are equipped with state-of-the-art technology and tactical training, justifying their kills with a "cleaning up the street" mentality that "protects citizens" against "violent criminal enterprises of non-human origin." And there are even rumors that these murderers even post pictures of their kills on their Facebook, Twitter, and Instagram profiles, like those limp-dick fuckfaces who still go on safari despite it being 2015.

[Ed. note: Operation Sleeping Fish does not exist. The United States government does not have a vested interest

in the destruction and genocide of most monsters. They furthermore do not condone violence against monsters. Also, if Operation Sleeping Fish was real, any soldier within the operation would not be active on social media.]

And then, there are the independent monster hunters out there who, despite what films would like you to think, are actually shockingly ineffective. In fact, just by going after these monsters, these imbeciles are not only putting the monster community at risk but are also making things incredibly inconvenient for the human race as well, considering their amateurish actions will likely leave them eviscerated in a pile of shit, piss, and grue that someone else will have to pick up. It doesn't matter how many movies you've seen or books you've read about the occult, or if you carry the Bible on your person all the time, you are *not* ready to take on these monstrous motherfuckers.

Even if you do happen to get a leg-up on these monsters, what do you think is going to happen? Do you think you're going to catch these monsters off-guard? Considering that monsters live almost exclusively in hostile fear and homicidal rage, there is no off-guard for these beastly beings; you're better off killing yourself in the comfort of your own home. You might even get in the way of the actual professionals, who are trained to take down these monsters but aren't trained to improvise around idiots running with a stake or pitchfork in the middle of the night.

I guess now is a good time to introduce all monsters to their most aggressive enemies, as you bought my book and I want you to continue to buy my books, so I might as well ensure your survival to see them printed (or at least until the pre-order date). Outside of the various angry vigilante mobs and the legions of monster hunters coming to kill you, there are equally damaging opponents who don't need a silver bullet or whatever kills the gill-man. No, these pieces of trash have their own ways of keeping down monsters in the court of public opinion, or in case of monsters who take small sums of money and refuse to provide goods, the People's Court.

Perhaps the worst offenders of propagating monster stigma for their own agenda would be the notorious Southbound Foxboro Church of Insane Jesus out in Heaven's Vegas, Arizona. Infamously known for protesting the funerals of Count Dracula, Victor von Frankenstein, and the voice cast for early *Casper The Friendly Ghost* cartoons, the Southbound Foxboro Church of Insane Jesus have literally rewritten the Bible to target monsters and their kin, hatefully steering any poor bastard who joins them into an unfulfilling life of religious dick-wagging and absurd publicity stunts. But perhaps what is most frustrating about the Southbound Foxboro folk is how strongly they emphasize that they believe in their bullshit. They built their church entirely out of silver, and set booby traps around the premises that essentially turns their entire church into kindling at a moment's notice.

But the Southbound Foxboro Church of Insane Jesus doesn't just stop there when it comes to their hate. Southbound Foxboro, who among other things believes that rain is a result of God itself being composed of ice, has made it their mission to target the innocent civilians who support monster culture. Amulet stores from around the country have been targets of their seemingly arbitrary protests, as have gill-man sanctuaries, haunted houses, and abortion clinics where vampire brides pick up their dinner. While destroying the livelihood of these hardworking citizens, the Southbound Foxboro Church of Insane Jesus has also been suspected of participating in hate crimes around the Heaven's Vegas area, including burning religious effigies outside of low-income, mummy-populated pyramid parks.

And it's not like the issues with the Southbound Foxboro Church are an easy fix either, considering their paranoid and ironic sense of pride and self-awareness. The Southbound Foxboro Bible states that Insane Jesus was not killed on the cross, but rather was turned into a vampire, drawn and quartered by multiple werewolves, pinned to the ground by a man-made creature, and burned alive by a mummy's solar staff; also, his flames were frequently doused in water by gill-men, which prolonged his death by minutes. Out of fear of monsters doing the same to them, they're perhaps more guarded than even the most prepared monster hunter. Even the Southbound Foxboro Church's bus is shaped like a cross, making it one of the most dangerous street-legal vehicles imaginable.

If you're a monster whose ancestry traces back to the motherland of Transylvania, you might be familiar with the family at the head of the Southbound Foxboro Church of Insane Jesus: the Van Helsings. While it is true that Abraham Van Helsing respected his nemeses in the monster community, his son, Lucien Van Helsing, was much more fanatical. While the Kronos family took up the mantle of fighting monsters on the front lines, Lucien Van Helsing laid the groundwork for what would be the Southbound Foxboro Bible, inspired by what he believed were prophetic constellations but have since been theorized to be large quantities of horseflies on his bedroom ceiling. Lucien believed the strongest way to stop monsters was to deny them a place in civilized society, and organized a small following of dickheads to help drive thousands of innocent, not-intrusively-violent monster families out of their villages.

Lucien's legacy would later be carried on by his grandson, Hunter Van Helsing, who was the first of his family to settle in America. Hunter was much more voracious and ridiculous with his lies, telling his congregation that vampires were the reasons why their homes smelled like old people's skin and that dueling mad scientists were attempting to create land lightning to replace their tried-and-true system of coal power. As with most stupid fucking religions, people with nothing better to do began to believe him, and Hunter Van Helsing formally established the Southbound Foxboro Church of Insane Jesus towards the end of his life.

Yet there is no Van Helsing that registers higher on the "being a cunt" scale than the current leader of Southbound Foxboro, Red Van Helsing. Red's hatred of monsters and their kin makes his predecessors seem like monster-loving liberals in comparison, and his sentiments are shared by his thirty-three children, as well as his loving wife, Rasputina. In fact, Red's hate-mongering has even found its way into the digital age, as he developed the official Southbond Foxboro app which tracks and catalogs monster funeral dates and informs the user about acceptable, Jesus-approved lemonades.

Now I know what you're thinking: if monster hunters and bigots are such a problem for us, why don't we just kill all the humans and take over Earth? That's a good point, and since the numbers on monster populations aren't exactly transparent thanks to the frequently missing monster census workers, I can't exactly deny the notion for you. But if that does become the case, remember who was good to you, and who wrote this nifty book to help you all fix your fucking brains. That's right: I'm worth more alive than dead, even if you force me to write these books as your slave. I'll be your Uncle Person house human any day, my potential monster overlords.

However, should the thought of mutiny against the human race float across your mind, let me remind you all of a piece of horror history that cemented monster stigma in our culture in the first place: the Trail of Terror. While little evidence of the Trail of Terror remains in our textbooks, remnants of the era from anti-monster propaganda posters to frames of mostly destroyed newsreels can be found infrequently on auction sites, though many are refused by any museum that could take them. And even though monsters have often killed people throughout history, they were never forced into the shadows before the Trail of Terror.

For those unfamiliar, the Trail of Terror was a social and cultural movement against monsters following World War I, set in place by President Hoover in fear that the nation would be too weak to suppress a potential monster uprising. The destructive consequences of this movement were nearly instantaneous: vampires were abruptly forced into the sunlight by the national guard, man-made monsters were segregated from humans in almost all public settings and ghost constables took many benign spirits into custody. Meanwhile, public pools and baysides were chemically altered as a preventative measure against gill-men, while wolfmen fled the nation en masse following rumors of were-internment camps.

Indeed, the Trail of Terror was among the lowest point in monster history, and perhaps the most offensive part of it was the government's discrediting of said events in the years since. Most letters to congress by monsters go unanswered (although, understandably so when a letter just says "Argh" or "Boo"), while displaced monsters have since attempted to seek reparations for their suffering. And while the US government has gone out of their way to deservedly make good for survivors and descendents of traumatizing periods from throughout history, it looks like monsters won't be as lucky.

Nevertheless, monsters who have learned to live and deal with the stigma from years of discrimination have been able to find a silver lining to their story. Some monsters have successfully entered the American workplace and risen to prominence through hard work and dedication, while select humans have set up programs to help down-on-their-luck monsters find employment in the arts, the most arguably real of the workforces. And in certain situations, monsters who have embraced their stereotypes have even found jobs that help permanently eliminate other issues plaguing our country.

That's right: cities around the world are creating jobs for monsters who have simply given up trying to defeat monster stigma. As long as their capacity to terrify is used for the greater good, such as chasing the homeless off of their streets or volunteering to scare our veterans into a permanent psychosis so that they become the problem of privately owned mental institutions. Meanwhile, certain cities have set up public works projects that allow monsters to be out of sight and mind while building underground travel systems for when the above-ground world becomes a barren, irradiated wasteland. Frankly, some politicians don't care about how much it costs the taxpayers, as long as they don't have to explain to frightened children about monsters every day.

Now, is there a way to embrace society's norms and stereotypes on monsters while helping to eradicate monster stigma? It's a thin line to walk, but that's not to say that it is impossible. In fact, this author has met several ghosts who moonlight to scare people out of their homes for bank repossession, even though the ghosts are simply appearing and not actively attempting to frighten. Likewise, the gill-men community has been abuzz with rumors that the US Navy is recruiting their kind as a more effective alternative to those dolphins they trained to put bombs on submarines, satisfying their desires to kill with their presumably awesome undersea abilities.

However, I know that in defeating monster stigma, and improving the emotional and mental well-beings of monsters in general, there has to be some element of pride that may stop them from taking these "hand out" jobs. But there's nothing wrong with a bit of circumstantial charity when it comes to monsters with scarred or undead flesh, especially since bloated pride has often resulted in monsters' imminent doom in the past. And while coming out of the shadows and into society should not be a problem in the first place, it's better to come out in safety and roll with the cultural punches than to just scream and slaughter any bystander in your eyeline.

In fact, these "hand out" jobs can be the first step to truly assimilating into human society, as the accumulation of money is one of the most proven ways to ensuring respect from strangers. And when you have a lot of money, people don't care what you do or what you've done in the past; media scrutiny is often ignored by the general populace, and there are tons of murderers, rapists, and thieves who are among the wealthiest people in the world. I mean, just look at the late, great Vlad Dracula; sure, he can turn into a bat and drain you of blood in a matter of seconds, but would he have been nearly as imposing if he lived in a studio apartment? You be the judge, monsters.

However, just because a monster can game the system in the same way any motivated and reckless person can doesn't necessarily fix the larger problem of monster stigma. After all, a few successful individuals don't necessarily make up for the entirety of oppressed beings, and I've seen *The People vs. Larry Flynt* enough times to know a thing or two about oppression. And paying it forward is only a temporary solution, much like taking over a hot dog company and then giving hot dogs to the hungry, only to realize they don't have an ice cold soda to go with it and thus making all your efforts null and void. Monsters need to look out for their own, and in doing so, there needs to be change on both a societal and individual scale.

The first major way the human race can accommodate the needs and desires of the monster population is by realizing that it's going to cost us a small percentage of the population. Likely, this means two to three hundred thousand people will have to be considered expendable, and that number is nearly negligible compared to the population of the entire earth, not to mention the number of people wasted needlessly by unchecked warlords in other nations who could be instead added to the cause. In fact, if the cadavers are fresh enough, the inclusion of monsters in our society may be an excellent source of synergy in terms of body removal and disposal.

In any case, even the most domesticated—erm, I mean sophisticated—monster is prone to a rampage once in a blue moon, and some of them even exclusively feed on human flesh or blood. However, if society can realize that shaving off a hundred thousand people here or there will allow monsters to live freely and contribute to our infrastructure, why wouldn't we make that sacrifice? Do we really need *every* baby? There's no better way this author can think of to lower the percentage of people contributing to global warming, the welfare state, and basic overpopulation than to allow monsters to run amok, doing what comes naturally to them.

And think of the good it could do for the monsters themselves! By giving them both freedom and the power to be themselves, there's a greater chance that monsters will also be more willing to indulge the other elements of society. And once they've got out their initial rage, monsters will be less likely to go on killing sprees in the future, much like a dog who is trained to follow a routine in exchange for treats, only this time these treats are "volunteers" "willing" to give their lives for the "greater good." And monsters will also have an increased sense of trust in the human race, something that our world as a whole does not have the best track record with. In fact, it might even be easier to trust monsters than it would be for humans, because (and here's an insider's tip) vampires, mummies, and man-made creatures have terrible poker faces.

Now this next paragraph is *for humans only*, so if you're a monster, just skip ahead to the following paragraph and whatever you do, don't look back. Okay . . . now that they're not reading, let's be frank here. Monsters are fucking gullible as hell. I just literally told them not to read something that was guaranteed to be fishy and I'll bet you all my book sales that they're not reading this. And if they're that dumb and open to persuasion, just think of what we could do with these numbskulls out in the open? It's a no-brainer . . .

Anyways, now that you've skipped the last paragraph, the most important part of eliminating monster stigma on an individual level is through cultivating respect. Despite the anti-monster sentiment plaguing pockets of society, no major figure in the world has publicly endorsed R-E-S-P-E-C-T for the monster population to find out what it means to them. People often forget that, at their core, monsters are essentially variations on regular people and reflect an incredibly on-the-nose commentary about the human condition paired with all the gruesome violence that we know and love. By giving them the respect we often give our fellow man (and having seen the Internet, I know how infrequent that can be), monsters and humans could connect on a much more intimate level.

For instance, think about what you would do in this scenario: You're in a dark room in a big, quiet house by yourself. Your flashlight begins to flicker and suddenly, SOMETHING JUMPS OUT AT YOU! Now, if that something turns out to be a human, mostly that exchange would be written off as a misunderstanding or a mean-spirited prank (presuming the person is not trying to actively kill you). But if that something turns out to be a wolfman, you're likely to run away, screaming at the top of your lungs until you find another human to protect you. I don't know what that sounds like to you, but to this author, that's got double standard written all over it.

Speaking of which, this might be a good time to promote my upcoming line of monster apparel, Double Standard Clothing. Whether it's T-shirts, baseball caps, decorative shoes, or extra-skimpy hot pants, these bad boys actually have the phrase "double standard" written all over them, and work well in the aforementioned scenario as well as in terms of giving some guff to the haters out there. And they come in all shapes and sizes, whether it's for the more slender frame for Frankenstein's Bride or the scaly physique of a gill-man. Keep an eye out for them in retail outlets that allow monsters on their premises in the coming months. . . .

But even if you skip out on my clothing line entirely (though, really, why would you?), just a basic greeting and respectful handshake could go the extra mile for many of these socially maladjusted monsters. Honestly, scaring people comes second nature to these creatures, and a little understanding and patience from the common man might be the vote of confidence they need to really start socializing with their non-monster counterparts. That is unless you're one of the people designated to sacrifice your life in the hopes of improving monster/human relations, in which you might as well be as disrespectful as possible in order to ensure yourself a quick, merciful death.

You don't have to be a rocket scientist to discover the potential benefits that can come from eliminating monster stigma, although being a rocket scientist will probably help you get to the conclusion faster, unless you're one of the more dumb rocket scientists. Just imagine how much crime around the country will decline when vampires, werewolves, and ghosts are wandering around the streets every night. Then there are the many obvious economic benefits, from the increased profits for late-night businesses to the number of new IDs and health insurance plans that will be purchased among the monster community. And plus, if the monsters can actually get out to the brick-and-mortar book stores before they close, more copies of this book will sell, which is more important than those other things combined.

Another upside to the death of monster stigma would be the wealth of information that we will learn about monsters. Aside from a singular interview with a vampire, there have been very few cases of monster interaction that have given us firsthand insight into their world and conditions, which is a part of why these monsters have been misunderstood for long. In essence, monsters are like the nerds of the universe: sure, they're fun to fuck around with because it's so easy and their culture is a borderline parody of reality, but at the end of the day, they can provide us with some important wisdom since we were too busy fucking around with them to pay attention to anything else.

Considering the unique nature of some of these monsters, just think of what can be learned once our prejudices and preconceived notions are taken out of the equation.

The immortality of vampires, the strength of man-made creatures, the regenerative qualities of werewolves, the unbreakable will of the mummies, the innovation of mad scientists, the emancipation of monster brides, the various physical powers of ghosts, or the gill-man's power to swim well can all be studied on a much more intimate and comprehensive level, and hopefully may bring more opportunities and possibilities furthering both mankind and monsterkind.

Furthermore, the disintegration of monster stigma will help ensure a better legacy for men and monsters alike, helping to repair thousands of years of violence and hatred from both sides. On the human side of things, we can start by rewriting textbooks, censoring monster novels propagating stereotypes, and by providing tax incentives for businesses that employ monsters. On the monster side of things, they can stop killing random people, give us all of their magical secrets, and help us pull our economy out of comically oversized international debt. From there, both humans and monsters alike will make sure to say and do nice things to one another in the interest of creating a better future for children, kid monsters, and whatever bizarre fucking hybrid that comes from people who fuck monsters. If you're one of the people/monsters who write that previously mentioned fan fiction, you'll probably know what they're called better than I ever will.

Truth be told, I've had my fair share of encounters with monster stigma especially during my youth, coming from my father, who was renowned monster hunter in his own right. While the media certainly painted a different portrait, especially in the interviews with all of those families, I knew that monster hunting was the only explanation for the sights I had seen. It's this familiarity with that specific brand of anti-monsterism that helps me understand what these monsters are going through, what with their repeated assassination attempts and the surprisingly plentiful message boards devoted to monster hate speech.

To be fair, this author never quite did fit in with the human race, giving me perhaps a greater mental connection to disenfranchised monsters. As a child, I often would respond to basic greetings and politeness with hostile shouting, eventually leading to irrational bouts of self-inflicted violence before my narcolepsy kicked in. Such behavior earned me such endearing nicknames as "retard" and variations on the nickname "retard." By the time my father pulled me out of school to go on his mysterious cross-country motel adventure, I had learned to take this criticism and take it as a badge of honor.

While "actual" doctors may have called my reactions a "coping mechanism," I'm sure the monster community knows that phrases such as that are used to make our natural adaptation skills less impressive. Luckily, I don't listen to doctors, and three tumors and multiple ignored psychiatric evaluations later, I'm showing them all how right I am by writing a self-help book for monsters. I'd like to see them write a self-help book for monsters. I'd like to see them write a book about anything; I bet most doctors can't even read. All they care about is body stuff and gross fluids and brain deterioration, not words that can change the world.

But back to the point: if living on the defensive is a key trait of monsters, then you might as well call this man a monster, as I understand the plight all too well. Much like monsters, I understand the perpetual absence of safety and companionship in this world, and how books like these, no matter how generally worthless, can sometimes be the reason vampires rise from their coffins every dusk. Additionally, I don't care much for people and often try to exist within their peripherals, which have lead to me being described as an outsider.

But perhaps it's the outsider's perspective that makes me (and monsters) essential to the world and to society. I'm the most suited to bring man and monster together to create a world that is like the bastard child of Moses, Charles Xavier, and Dr. Moreau, if they had a three-way for swinging, progressive geniuses.

Having personally lived through monster stigma firsthand, I can personally say that it must be destroyed in all of its forms. While I understand the safety of American citizens is key, propagating monster stigma should be punishable by torture. Prison is an environment that only propagates the worst side of the human race, and only makes monster stigma spreaders more bitter and resentful of monsters. However, torture gets results, and the association of monsters with pain will inspire more fear than hate, which is the lesser of two evils.

By ending monster stigma altogether, monster culture can finally be embraced by the world at large, allowing us to pick up on their mannerisms and routines as if they were second nature. Vampires, werewolves, and man-made creatures will no longer be seen as "creatures of the night," but rather "creatures of all the time," while Frankenstein and Frankenstein's Bride can finally make their union 100 percent legal, which might actually be okay in the eyes of the Catholic Church anyways. Who knows? Maybe the human race will become more tolerant of even the darker side of monster culture, like the rampant killing and the eternal damnation.

If you're one of the likely thousands of monsters reading this book right now, there's a good chance that all you know is doom and gloom because you've lived under the scrutiny and bigotry caused by monster stigma. Because you've hid for so long from mankind's unjustified wrath, you haven't been able to see the brighter things in life. More than likely, you probably have been so busy eating people that you haven't even tried pizza, which is a crime in its own right.

In fact, this author is willing to speculate that once monsters discover pizza, their entire way of life is going to change forever. Pizza is so delicious, no matter what you put on it, and you can get it in so many styles, whether it's thick Sicilian slices, or crispy thin crust pizza, or the deep dish pizza that's loaded with all kinds of flavorful, wacky shit. Hell, even if you're a stubborn or conservative monster, you can probably cook human flesh into pizza. Just thinking about it now makes me my mouth water for the most dangerous game as long as it's surrounded by melted cheese and zesty tomato sauce.

Pizza is an essential part of the human experience, and I'll be completely honest with you: even if monster stigma becomes a non-issue and society welcomes you with open arms, you'll still be excluded from the world if you don't like pizza. In order to function in society, you must eat pizza, and you must like to eat pizza. If a human tells you they don't like pizza, demand to see their phone, and if they refuse, it's because they're hiding evidence of their crimes and should be reported to the local authorities. And if a fellow monster says they do not like pizza, then do everything in your power to send them towards a populace that will accept them, like the middle of the fucking ocean.

In conclusion, there will always be many humans and monsters who retain their cultural prejudice; after all, the status quo is a tempting safe zone. But to evolve into a world where monsters can eat pizza and do other stuff as well, monster stigma needs to be killed and disposed of in a shallow swampland grave. If not for man, if not for monster, then for pizza, the only thing that really matters in this harsh and terrifying world. Pizza tastes good, and this is why I'm such a skilled motivational speaker.

Chapter III

You Are More Than the Sum of Your Parts

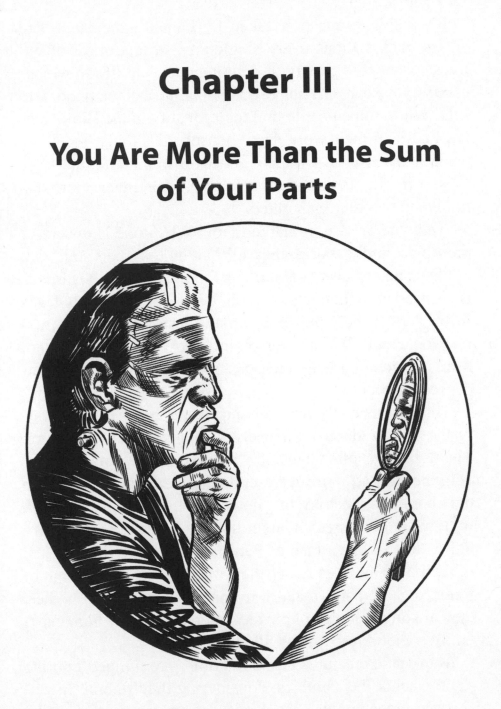

"**W**ho are you?"

It's a simple question asked by humans, monsters, and classic rock stations every single day. In fact, most of our lives are spent in pursuit of defining our identities in whichever way we can, chasing satisfaction like a crack fiend with E.D. While some people find their identity in the Bible, others find it in their workplace, household, family, or ethnic background. But as with any endeavor in this life, there are those who find their path to self-realization much more difficult and bloodier than others.

And who are we to blame them? When one is unsure of their place in the world, they fill that hole in their soul with anxiety and criticism; sometimes food, too. Their headspace is clouded with thoughts of doubt and fear, which only leads further down the rabbit hole of self-destruction or destruction in general. When a person hits rock bottom and cannot turn to anyone for help, their best intentions can lead to their darkest moments.

This is especially true for monstrous beings, specifically those who identify themselves as a man-made creature. These beings, often labeled "Frankensteins" among less-enlightened and more terse cultures, essentially operate in the emotional spectrum of a newborn child while consciously living in bodies much larger than the average man. Essentially, they're like a race of Paul Bunyons with the intellect of their big blue oxes. Since they are often constructed out of found organic parts, usually from freshly murdered bodies, they are often victims of physical stereotyping by humans as bulky, violent, resentment-filled monsters.

Man-made creatures also sometimes are lumped into the same category as zombies, considering they're both inconsiderate monsters who were raised from the dead. But the similarities between those specific monsters essentially ends there, as any zombie or man-made creature can tell you. While man-made creatures certainly aren't spring chickens and are also kind of dumb, zombies are living whilst brain-dead and lack the bloated sense of pride that man-made creatures seem to boast. Furthermore, man-made creatures and zombies have different modus operandi entirely: while the former feels entirely deserving of a better brain, it wouldn't dare try to eat one.

However, if you're a man-made creature and you're reading this, there's a certain mantra I would like to share with you. While you might not know what a mantra is, I certainly don't have the time or the desire to explain, so just take a deep breath and repeat after me:

"You are more than the sum of your parts."

I know you don't understand what that means just yet, but enlightenment doesn't happen overnight, so just be patient, okay? You may have been put together from the parts of reprehensible cadavers, mostly sick murderers and sweaty scoundrels with no sense of empathy or remorse, but you are nevertheless composed of your own flesh and blood. Just because you have the hands of a serial strangler does not mean *you* were the one doing the strangling, and to live with any baggage from your past life would be like the Dalai Lama feeling shitty for all the awful things he did before being annointed as the Dalai fuckin' Lama.

Not only that, but you have to remember that the murderers that you are made of were still people, and truth be told, they were probably better people than most humans who don't take responsibility for their trespasses. Sure, it's easy to confess your sins and crimes to your family or priest, but to say to the world, "Hey, what's up? I killed a bunch of people. What are you going to do about it?" That takes guts, and frankly, you should be a little proud of it, too. The world was made by conquerors, my simple-minded frankenfriend, not secret-hiding, two-faced jerks.

So what is the first step to solidifying your own identity in your monstrous form? Do you disavow your creator? Do you swear revenge on all of mankind for thrusting you unwillingly into existence? Or do you just decide to bide your time while you wait for scars and neckbolts to come back into fashion like vinyl and police corruption?

These overdramatic and trite concepts may appear to be the first rational steps to be understood in your mind, but to your heart and soul, they do nothing but reinforce pain set by societal standards. To find your identity is to find comfort in the balance of your heart, mind, and soul, and to do that, you must come to terms with what you are. You may be a monster on the outside, but that does not mean you must succumb to your most monstrous internal urges and do some seriously monstrous shit to others.

The first step to finding that comfort is to embrace the particular brand of monster that you are. In basic terms, you are not far removed from human beings, no matter how many people that you are sewn out of. After all, you inherited these pieces and all the flourishes within them in the same way that humans inherit traits from their parents, the difference being that your father literally gave you your flaws and deformities. But these traits give way to individuality and insecurity to both man and monster alike, which in itself gives way to the many different faces a man-made creature can wear. To be honest, it makes this whole "self-help" thing kind of a nightmare, but if the legal system has taught me anything time and time again, it's that I'm not the one to give up in the face of logical embarrassment.

The need to embrace your particular type of monster also extends to your gender identity, a subject that I feel is less needlessly controversial among monsters than it is man. To be honest, this author doesn't see the problem if a man-made creature wants to identify as a he or she regardless of organic gender, considering that the monster probably has parts of both genders stitched into them somewhere. Also, at the end of the day, if you can find clothing that will fit on your massive, disfigured body, then I think you should reserve the right to be whatever gender you so choose.

But if you're going to be comfortable in your skin, you need to understand that doing terrible, unspeakable things to people is not only an inherited trait, but a tradition of humanity. While guilt is an expected byproduct of said terrible things, it's also rarely our explicit intention, from which we've coined the term "crime of passion." Nevertheless, our hands usually spill blood at some time or another over the course of our lives, and as long as we refuse to take responsibility and find the slightest of reason to justify our action, then who is to say it's necessarily wrong?

For example, take all the crazy, fucked-up shit that has happened because of children of divorce or broken homes. An environment of a tense family living situation can be taxing on a developing psyche, and to make things worse, those people are genetically composed of two people who are repellent and adversarial to one another. In man-made creature terms, it's like stitching together a roadrunner and a coyote into a single entity, destined to despise its existence for all of eternity. Much like human children of divorce, man-made creatures may be more predisposed to depression, anxiety, anger issues, and reclusiveness, but to the world at large, it's not attributed to the internal struggle in each and every cell of their body, but rather that their home life was a Rubik's Cube of assorted emotional issues.

However, the reality of the situation isn't nearly as black and white as with humans; in fact, man-made creatures such as yourself may find that dynamic of content existence on a much more complex level since you have disadvantages that most humans will never understand. Most humans don't have the physical scars to match their mental scars, and while vanity isn't necessarily a man-made creature's forte, it's very hard to find a way to make non-matching skin tones and protruding stitch scars work in modern fashion sensibilities. Then there's the mental stress of being a perpetual outsider; unless your mad scientist creator is a billionaire, there's no way to make up for all the Christmases, birthdays, and Memorial Day weekends that your current consciousness has missed.

But the physical obstacles in finding your identity are not the highest hurdles you're going to have to jump, even if you were patched up out of the fattest royal family this side of Obesitonia. You may be new to this world and you may not even understand the lifestyle that you're living, but much like thousands of rap artists can tell you, the world is all too ready to chew up and spit out everyone who doesn't learn its ways. While more charitable humans may address your monumental stupidity as conditional or environmental ignorance, the majority of humans, and even possibly monsters you may not even know, will see it as willful neglect.

So after you've embraced what physically defines you as a monster, where do you go from here? Do you devote your life to destroying the lives of those who make you feel negatively? Do you proudly step out into the light and make your existence everyone else's problem? Do you rebel against your creator and join a biker gang or a bizarre secret society of swingers?

In short, the answer is no; doing any of that shit is bound to piss someone off, and will likely cause a domino effect of very bad things that will ultimately lead to your immolation. Instead, what you need to do is to figure out what exactly is so negative in your brain so that you can replace that shit with good vibes. You need to look in the mirror and go, "Sorry, bad emotions. My brain is liberated from your Nazi-esque grip of negativity. Walk away and die."

But in order to do that, we must reach within our deformed, decrepit hearts and find the strength to extinguish the fires within them. Luckily, as you may already know by now, fire is bad. Now, you need to know that I'm not literally speaking about your brains and hearts; please, don't attempt to remove your vital organs from your body. Although you're much harder to kill than the average human, you also shouldn't push your luck by reaching into your guts or skull and looking for metaphorical emotions. This also extends to your fellow man-made creatures; just because your creator bisected brains and body parts to create you doesn't mean you have the right to satisfy your own morbid curiosity.

While we're on this point, I'd like to talk to you man-made creatures and tell you that I am hereby relieving myself of liability on any homemade surgeries that you might think that I am suggesting. I don't care how easy your creator made it seem to be, or how much fun it looks, or the strength of your impulse control. Please, leave all anatomical adjustments and dissections to the professionals, and if you don't, destroy this book and disavow all acknowledgement of its existence, and then later, when the heat has died down, buy another one as penance for fucking up so bad.

But before we make any progress on that front, you need to identify what constitutes emotions of "hatred" and what constitutes "frustration" in your childlike brains. By focusing on the wrong fuel source for your endless anger, you're only going to waste your time and make yourself look like a foolish dipshit in front of your loved ones. So in order to understand the difference between hatred and frustration, you must learn the value of patience. Take some time out of your day right now to sit and listen to the world around you: examine the sounds, stare at the colors, feel this book in your hands, and relax.

Have you noticed how you're not doing anything? How about now? I bet you want to do something so bad. *No!* Don't do anything yet. Are you fucking crazy, man? Do you want to die, buddy? Do nothing. Still not doing anything? Exactly. This is a taste of patience, and you've passed the first test to know it firsthand. You're welcome.

If this moment of zen has sent you into a furious rage spurred on by upsetting confusion, don't destroy everything in sight just yet. Just because you don't understand what the world is doesn't make it your enemy; in fact, enemies are more likely to be those closest to you rather than a vague, oblique concept. Similarly, the traits of the world around you aren't completely shared either; for instance, this book weighs significantly less than a human being, although with your advanced strength, they probably weigh the same in your hands and are likely equally easy to break into pieces.

Once you've understood patience, your next course of action is to find a way to give that quiet time some substance. When I was young, there were plenty of times when I'd have to zone out from my surroundings, focusing on the voice in my head rather than the screams coming from the bathroom. But luckily, I was able to carry that driven focus into adulthood, fostering it like a kangaroo would an abandoned infant in the outback. And much like that allegorical kangaroo, I've raised that focus baby into a full-fledged mangaroo of confidence, concentration, and coherence; emotions that a monster like yourself might feel for the very first time.

Now, luckily for man-made creatures, it seems that almost every waking hour that you have is alone time, which should give you plenty of opportunities to get used to patience. Now, some man-made creatures are more contemplative in nature, especially if their creator gave them a brain that was worth a damn, and should adapt pretty easily to the quiet times. However, a majority of man-made creatures have been given the brains of grade-school flunkies, the criminally insane, or just plain-old weirdos, so you might want to use this alone time to center on skills you've already learned, like physical training or improvising boxcar jingle-jangles.

Yet perhaps the best method of learning patience to connect with yourself and society is to turn your anger into poetic relaxation, which will make you less likely to grab random strangers off the street and rip them in half like an old newspaper. It's no longer the 1990s, so random, violent outbursts of undirected anger are not in vogue anymore; instead, new age understanding, chi, and transcendental meditation are the cat's pajamas, a phrase that certainly will confuse and possibly scare you. So even if you take a fraction of your imposing physical strength and apply it to your yoga or whatever nonsense they'll tell you at yoga school, you'll probably find more things about yourself to love.

While we're on the subject, I might as well inform you that, as a man-made creature, you likely have no idea that there is an ongoing rivalry between self-help motivational writers and the yoga-friendly spiritualist crowd. I'm sure there's some asshole writing a spiritualism book for monsters, and that's okay, to each their own. But between us, spiritualism is a train full of lies, speeding down a one-way track of deception and impotency that will keep you from eating delicious red meats and say that evil is bad without even knowing it intimately.

Actually, I take that back; please go to yoga class and read all of their shit literature. If you want to reject all of my valuable teachings and go off for some false deity that lives in your diaphragm, then I'd rather you do so. Then, when those big dumb idiots trigger your insane rage with their scented, fair-trade candles, they can deal with being ripped apart limb from limb. Hard to recruit more yoga friends without your limbs, isn't it, yoga nerds?

One way of adding substance to your quiet time is to break down the reality around you and realize that there's nothing to fear. By looking around and seeing the things in your immediate area, you'll realize that there aren't any conspiracies or threats breathing down your neck, and you'll be more likely to not be a goddamned handful. Once you've conquered your fear, presumably holding its disembodied spine from atop a castle during a lightning storm, you'll be able to take even more pride in yourself over your already magnified sense of being.

"But, doctor, how can I have pride when my parts have collectively done so many bad things?"

Firstly, I am not a doctor, which I made explicitly and legally clear in Chapter One, although considering that your definition of a doctor is your creator, all is forgiven. Secondly, your parts are now under your control; no one can do harm with them except you and you alone, even though you still retain the right to blame others. Thirdly, if the guilt of the pasts of your body parts is keeping you from having a unique identity, you might as well take pride in repenting for their sins.

"Isn't pride a deadly sin?"

Firstly, I am not a religious figure, which I made explicitly and legally clear in Chapter One, although considering that your definition of a creator is a mad doctor, all is forgiven. Secondly, pride is only deadly when used for negative purposes, such in extreme cases of vanity and greed, which you won't have to worry about. Thirdly, pride is incredibly important to defining your identity, as pride is a factor within every choice in a happy lifestyle. Hell, there's even pride parades about people who have great lifestyles, like homosexuals and their kin.

By learning how to apply your pride, the philosophical antithesis to prejudice, to your life, you're going to be one step closer to becoming a functioning member of society. And that's why you bought this book, right? You want to mingle with mankind, correct? Or is this some sort of study guide so you can learn what makes us weak, so you can manipulate and decimate us as a species?

While I wouldn't blame you since I know I would definitely look for a brilliant poster boy for humanity in someone like myself, I would certainly dissuade you using this book as a way to perpetuate your hatred for mankind. This is especially true considering that, out of all the monsters out there, you're likely the most practical to integrate into society since no one has to worry about you turning into a wolf all of the sudden or being too committed to your pyramid. You're so close to being human adjacent that it would be a shame to suddenly whip out your monster dick and try to call humanity's bluff.

Honestly, the best way to serve your hatred against mankind is to do the one profession that destroys mankind the most: the legal system. By becoming a lawyer, you will not only prove to humans that you're not some big, monstrous dummy who looks like Gumby on steroids, but rather that you're an intelligent, refined creature who will either put humans through the hell of prison or take large sums of their money, to the chagrin of their victim's families. To a monster, it's a win-win situation; not only are you hurting *someone* in any scenario, but you're looking damn smart while doing it.

Furthermore, you'll find plenty of tools to serve yourself and your monstrous needs in the legal system as well. You can learn how to divorce yourself from your creator, which will be important if they have been a generally shitty parent to you and might cause problems down the line. You'll also be able to know your constitutional rights, and which loopholes will get you out of trouble in the future, should your monstrous side rear its ugly head. And lastly, you can become more educated on the prospects of citizenship, so that you can vote as a Monster-American and not have to rely on work visas and temporary licenses.

In any case, you have to realize that your hatred towards humanity is, at the very least, manageable, and that we can move on to replacing those negative emotions. For this next step, I'll need you to take another second so that we can differentiate what is "therapeutic" and what truly makes you, as a monster, happy. If you feel better after strangling someone or ripping out their heart for the sake of a petty grudge, it may feel good at the time, but it won't solve what is truly eating away at you. There was a saying in the Hanley household: "You can't fill the holes in your heart with blood."

So, what makes you, as a man-made creature, happy? What fills every inch of your surgically crafted being with ecstasy? Ecstasy? I wouldn't recommend that you pursue the use of illegal amphetamines, that's for sure. You'll either go to jail or, even worse, lose all of your bitcoins.

The easy fix for an unhappy soul would usually be companionship, yet there is more difficulty than ever to find your true identity while surrounding yourself with others. In fact, you're more likely to find yourself with the same inner turmoil, considering your identity would be an amalgamation of your influences. That's a proven fact, too: most humans who hang out with douchebags generally seem to be douchebags themselves. By being influenced by your friends, your inside self would ironically become a reflection of your outside self: a stitched-up facade covering up something naturally remarkable.

This sentiment also extends to companionship of the opposite sex; carnal desires, while healthy and awesome, do not have enough substance to create an entire identity. While time spent with the opposite sex won't actively hurt your identity, it may influence or sway your behavior to a point of dissatisfaction. Then there's the chance that you might find yourself wrapped around a woman's finger, and no, not literally, if you're thinking someone might stitch you to a woman's hand. Furthermore, when you are still unsure of your identity, rejection from the opposite sex could send you on a downward spiral back to your monstrous behavior, painting the streets red with blood just because your crush finds you as sexually attractive as a beehive covered with AIDS.

But I digress. In terms of happiness, you have to recognize the things in the world that you can personally connect with. Intuitively, why not find happiness in nature? Nature is both beautiful and terrifying at once; the only thing in life that offers the gorgeous beach and the endless pit of liquid horror extending past the shore. And of course, nature doesn't mean to be destructive and harmful; it's merely reacting to the surrounding environment. Sound familiar? It should, since that's what you do, you fucking psychopath.

So once you've taken in the comfort of nature or any other source of euphoria, you need to incorporate it into your thoughts. If you're able to control your own happiness, you will develop discipline as well as respect for yourself, and you'll learn to use what you currently perceive as disadvantages as tools. Even with your scarred, mutilated face, you'd be surprised how many societies and workforces could use a super-strong creature with low intelligence who is nearly impervious to pain. And that drive that would push you to get bloody, vicious revenge on your creator could be applied to rising up a corporate ladder, especially if you retain the clear sense of antipathy and disregard for others.

Speaking of all that, it's important that you address the role of self-esteem in your identity. As stated before, you are more than the sum of your parts, and just because parts of you are considered scary or disgusting doesn't mean *you* are scary and disgusting. After all, a man-made creature with confidence isn't the kind of creature that would allow himself to be chased into closed quarters and burned alive. No, a man-made creature with confidence burns down all potential closed quarters beforehand, and then demands that the angry mob not only make him/her one of their own, but appoint him/her their infallible leader.

Unfortunately, it will never be that easy; you're likely familiar with the criticisms hurled at man-made creatures, as well as the condescending tone in which they're referred. But you must remember that human beings are merely releasing the pent-up frustration in their own life rather than targeting your legitimate flaws; after all, we're all just walking, talking meat waiting to expire, even if you may personally be further down the line. Then you have to remember that bullying is the tool of the insecure, and no matter what verbal barbs they throw at you, you're undeniably bigger and stronger, and you can beat them up if need be.

While you might see the similarities in your intimidation of humans and their treatment of you, be assured that an assertive, borderline aggressive personality is what is needed to flourish in this day and age. Not only should you own your monsterdom, but make sure everyone else knows about it in a big, bad way. Don't just be a monster; be an alpha monster, and while you don't have to go around stomping people's ribcages in, you can certainly remind everyone that you have that power and are not afraid to do it at the slightest provocation.

But once you've embraced that side of your identity, the next step is to incorporate your newfound attitude into your physical appearance. Ill-fitting hand-me-downs that are black and dirty make you look like street trash. A wardrobe change befitting of a confident and glowing monster is likely long-overdue. Even more subtle changes, such as adjustments to your posture and facial expressions, are more likely to solidify your status as a socially comfortable monster-about-town, and likely to get you in favor with monster-friendly maidens. At the same time, you should never forget your roots; scars and body modification are naturally endearing and great talking points, which will work wonders for your newfound identity.

One completely underrated aspect when building a unique, personable identity for man-made creatures is establishing an accommodating sleep schedule. While little is known about the sleeping patterns of man-made creatures, what is known is that these creatures do need rejuvenation at some point in their day. For whatever length of time you must rest every day, make sure you rest consistently and relative to your daily routine; after all, I can only imagine how volatile your monster temperament will become once coffee is introduced to your system. If you're fucking up your sleep schedule, then how will you be able to share your new identity with the rest of the world?

"Wait a second. What if this identity is similar to the one of the murderer whose head I now adorn?"

First of all, if you're self-identifying as a murderer even after all the knowledge I've provided beforehand, perhaps the best chance you have at assimilation would be physically restraining yourself. Of course, we're not talking about restraint to the point of killing yourself or driving yourself crazy, but just the basic motions to show society you're willing to restrain yourself to spare them a greater problem. This would include tracking collars, shoes with heavy polystone soles, magnetized cufflinks and, of course, hats with remote-controlled sleeping agents in the brim.

Secondly, you can only be a criminal once a crime has been committed, which is a huge loophole when it comes to feeling guilt. Therefore, as long as you have the motivation to steer clear from murder in all of its oh-so-tempting forms, your identity will technically not be that of a murderer; in fact, you legally won't even be indictable for conspiracy to murder. However, if this concern sticks to your subconscious, there arc ways of circumventing your murder-adjacent emotions.

On the darker side of your emotional palette, you psychologically justify any murders or violent crimes by citing the numerous befitting physical traits that endorse such behavior. Therefore, to retain the identity you have worked so hard to establish, you must change that justification altogether. If your creator refuses to build you a bride, don't kill his wife;

instead, allow him to get married and allow them both to face a fate worse than murder: marriage.

In fact, thinking outside the box is an excellent approach to breaking any emotional barrier built by your past deeds; for instance, you don't need to apologize to anyone for the murders your parts committed previously, as anyone deserving of an apology is likely dead. And if someone does happen to recognize one of your parts as that of someone who caused them ill will, you have no obligation to explain anything since the other ninety percent of you had nothing to do with it. It would be as if a bank heist went wrong, one of the burglars killed a security guard, and then a mad scientist decided to kill all of the burglars and stitched them together into a single person; you can't blame the other burglars who kept their cool for the actions of the one loose cannon.

Speaking of, once you've assimilated into society, there might be a lot of temptation to move into a life of crime, and legally speaking, I'd prefer if you didn't. Now it's not that I don't understand why organized crime could use someone like yourself as an enforcer from beyond the grave, and it's not like I can't see the temptation of barreling through a bank vault like a giant anthropomorphic glass of absolutely generic fruit drink. But not only would you be doing a disservice to yourself by eventually being killed or sent to a secret monster prison that I know nothing about, but you'd also be doing a disservice to man-made creatures everywhere by reinforcing all the negative stereotypes and mythological lore about your kind.

While *The I in Evil* is specifically supposed to be a self-help book, I can't stress the importance of acting as a cheerleader for monsterkind, specifically your man-made kin. Man-made creatures certainly are associated with histories of violence, whether it's throwing children into large bodies of water, systematically wiping out entire bloodlines, or crushing people's larynxes with the simplest of ease. Therefore, any examples of good behavior and positive role models from the man-made creature community benefits all of your ilk and makes humans more trusting of you personally.

The next step to building your identity is to create a web of associations via visual cues, familiarizing your emotions with specific locations and learning more about your background. By doing this, you're likely to improve your admittedly simple mental well-being. This also helps you limit the number of emotional triggers that could revert you into full-on rampage mode, which will never end well for the man-made creatures in your neighborhood. Furthermore, it will help you get a sense of how humans relate to their own identity so that you don't accidentally go on a racist tear full of backhanded bullshit because you were raised in dark, dreary basements.

A better mental health will also help you in terms of communication with humans as well, considering you'll have less of a problem conveying your ideas to others and less of a reason to resort to violence out of humiliation. Communication is one of the biggest problems plaguing the majority of man-made creatures, especially those who choose to grunt and moan despite understanding the English language. While such verbal communication may make man-made creatures perfect assets on a porn set (especially considering their glorious monster-sized genitalia), it's not going to fly in the real world, especially considering the language barrier is bending day after day. You're certainly not going to learn the many various languages of the world in our constantly-shifting culture if your brain is erratic and scrambled from its post-mortem reanimation.

As I mentioned previously, visual cues are crucial to defining your tastes, which in turn inform your particular identity. If you happen upon a great scent or a piece of memorable music, actively associate said cue with a nearby visual as to retain that memory in a positive context. The simplest way to do this among humans is with food, although this author willingly admits that he knows very little about the sense of taste of a man-made creature. I mean, I'd assume it's the same as when you were alive, but who knows? A lack of ability to taste would certainly explain why man-made creatures have so often been accused of eating human beings, unless human beings are delicious and I've been missing out my whole life. Being at the top of the food chain, I can only hope we're delicious.

But by creating these visual cues, you'll create a mental bank of positivity that you can then associate with practically any experience, which will then root your identity in a better place than existential torment. This also helps retain your sense of identity when confronted with experiences that threaten to dull aspects of your personality, such as overbearing workplaces, gridlock traffic, and windmills set on fire by angry mobs. You'll also be prepared to survive in situations that are even nerve wracking to humans, such as small talk, family phone calls, and eating alone in public.

Another great way to build your identity is to actively learn more about yourself, even the unflattering aspects. In every body part of an unrepentant criminal that's sewn together onto your body lies an opportunity to discover more about your past, as well as reasons to go to the library where you won't have to be noticed by anyone. Besides, these men must have had hobbies beyond the crimes they so notoriously committed, and there has to be a public record of it somewhere. By visiting your local library, man-made creatures can learn more about their ethnic backgrounds, religious alignments, and public records, which grants you further insight on how they were used by their previous owners.

Likewise, don't be afraid to pursue education as a way to further refine your identity, since nerds are taking over the rest of the world anyways and it's probably easier not to resist. For most man-made creatures, education isn't considered an option since it directly corresponds with your fear of the unknown, as well as the fact that they don't offer night school for grades K through 12. However, there are many ways to gain education outside of the formal classroom, including basic memory tests, learning puzzles, and watching television for hours on end. And while an education isn't necessary to the development of an identity, there are plenty of benefits in being the smartest man-made creature among the bunch, like being able to outsmart fellow monsters as well as learn how to insult and embarrass more ignorant humans.

Surprisingly enough, you may also be able to develop an identity based on the region in which you're occupying. Considering man-made creatures have been spotted all over the world, you obviously have an understated ability to adapt to various, seemingly uninhabitable climates. However, if this adaptation comes at the cost of hiding yourself away from the world, you may want to rethink your lifestyle choices since there's no reason to read this whole fucking book and then decide, "Oh, you know what? I think I'll stay in the shadows because I'm a pussy punk clown motherfucker. Roar, grumble, grumble, roar."

It also may be beneficial to moderate your time among the members of the community who don't run off immediately in terror, and don't be surprised if you find yourself becoming more accepted in the region. There are always going to be monster bigots, and they should be easy enough to get rid of without too many people asking questions. But if you moderate your public appearances, you'll become much more liked than a desperate man-made monster who shows up everywhere just because they crave attention. This also will help prevent the number of lynch mobs and rabble-rousers from growing in the area, which is often times leads to the relocation of man-made creatures.

Once you've properly stocked up on your mental and physical identity, it's time to turn your attention to your heart, which is an important part of an identity crisis. Considering that your torso is not necessarily yours, it may be hard to accept the feelings coming from your heart. Let us return then to our mantra: "You are more than the sum of your parts." Believe it or not, that mindset applies to every part of you, including the pieces of you that you cannot physically touch and see.

Of course, the first obstacle comes in the form of your issues with your parental issues, or should I say . . . *PATERNAL* issues?! As much as you'd like to deny that those issues exist, and that your beef is with mankind as a whole, there's no bullshitting a bullshitter here, monster man. You were made, ignored, and cast aside by your creator, and that hurts more than any pain you could possibly inflict on others. And even worse, the shadow of this resentment and anger will exist in every rampage that you inflict upon the world, which will serve as a reminder that your dad just wasn't there.

But how do you confront these issues, especially if you and the mad scientist who gave you life are irreparably estranged? While there is absolutely nothing in the whole wide world that will give you your childhood back, you can begin to make peace by first forgiving your father. Even if your father is a real sack of shit, what with his God complex and indifference towards hunchbacks and everything, the best rebellion you could show towards him is to act like his mistakes were your blessings. After all, for a man-made monster, I'm sure you turned out relatively alright in the grand scheme of things, so what's a petty grudge against someone who made you with the best intentions worth anyhow?

But if you can't forgive what your father did, what you can do is move on in a state of independence, proving that you not only survived his absence but rather have flourished. By following the lessons I've told so far in this goddamned book, you've learned to better yourself, seek education, become confident, and even stay the fuck out of jail. Any of those things should be enough to show your creator that he's chopped liver and that you weren't even hungry in the first place, because you're too awesome for food. Also, you're a fucking man-made monster and you've stayed out of jail, which is a fucking miracle and makes you the da Vinci of monsters.

If you can't forgive and you can't move on, then the only way to get over your daddy issues is to forget. After all, the people you're stitched out of all had fathers, and none of them particularly did a great job, or else their son/daughter wouldn't be making up a fucking monster. By accepting that you are a child of coincidence, biology, lightning bolts, and fate, you can bury yourself in denial and realize that your father isn't really your father. If anything, your creator was merely the doctor who brought you to term, and you're a naturally born orphan, just like a certain Jesus Christ people talk about all the time.

And then there's the maternal side of things, whose understandable absence from the equation is also a bit of an issue in your electrified brain. Obviously, the lack of a

female presence in your life has made you a bit of a demanding creep, and your affection-free "childhood" has certainly
helped steer you towards a volatile descent into madness.
But on the bright side, you've lived an entire life without
someone trying to or joke about fucking your mother, and
that's a pretty sweet perk to a pretty heavy existential crisis.

In any case, the lack of parental figures is probably the
most central reason as to why you have become so reliant
on negative philosophies and mindsets. Obviously, many
man-made creatures come from a school of thought that
guides your darker, nihilistic impulses into murder and mass
destruction; obviously, this is not a philosophy that will be
beneficial to your career, even as a game show host. Therefore, you must open a bridge between your heart and mind
that will allow you to feel more empathy, and learn that it's
okay to rely on yourself because other people are unreliable.

Empathy will also give you the chance to understand the
mentality of all the people you killed as well, which isn't the
best feeling in the world. Put yourself in the shoes of those
whose head you just crushed. How would you feel if you
were going about your day and two massive fists cracked
open your skull like a pistachio shell? It's a horrible way to
die, and certainly indicative of poor social skills on part of
the murderer.

Opening your heart is also something that will likely allow
you to explore emotions you have never previously felt. While
you are familiar with depression, you're probably not familiar with sadness as an emotional response instead of a state of
mind. Both are natural reactions the generally awful things
life frequently throws our way, but the latter is much more of
a potent, definable response as opposed to the general aura
of shit that depression encapsulates. Emotions such as joy,
anger, fear, and spunk can be quite overwhelming, and being

overwhelmed is probably one of the reasons you (and, for all intents and purposes, the people you're made out of) made the mistakes of murdering and collateral wrongdoing.

Now I'm going to ask you to do something that you may approach reluctantly, but we cannot go any farther until you do so. Take this opportunity to find a mirror, put this book down, look your reflection in the eyes, and say the following words: "I am beautiful."

Say it again. Now say it again. And again. Every time you say it, believe it more and more. This is your moment of freedom. This is your battle cry. You are beautiful. No one can tell you otherwise. The only opinion that matters is the one you have right now; everyone else's is inconsequential. So if you're out in public and a real loser decides to try to bring you down with words, keep in mind another saying in the Hanley household: "Behind every mirror is a wall."

By accepting your beauty, both internally and, to a degree, externally, you are creating an identity that's vulnerable yet not weak. The vagabonds and killers who make up your exterior died because they were vulnerable *and* weak, slaves to their emotions and to the cruel world around them. However, by standing up to your emotions and knowing exactly what you are, you offer your heart to the world while protecting it from negativity. You'll find an identity that's much more fruitful and forgiving, and soon, you'll be achieving great deeds that men, monsters, and mad scientists could have only dreamed of.

Hopefully by now, you'll have a vague understanding of who you truly are, and we can start putting the final touches on your identity. Now, take a moment to look around you and spot what possessions you have nearby. What do these possessions say about you? Are you living on strings? Are you living on substance? Are you some weird monster-hoarder with trophy skulls and animal furs everywhere?

After thinking about these possessions, realize that your identity cannot be reliant on a compulsive nature, as the resulting anxiety will perpetually prohibit your inner tranquility. Man-made creatures are particularly known for compulsive behavior, which at times can be equally as detrimental to your identity as your emotional impulses are. The best way to combat compulsive behavior is to test your own discipline; if you think you need to do something or steal something, don't do it, because you're not a dick. By abstaining, you'll realize that you're alive and well even without that compulsive trigger in your life, and that step will go a long way towards shaping your identity for the human race.

Once you've constructed an identity that fits you and reflects your heart, mind, and soul, it's time that you put the identity to the test. The first step is to seek out human interaction, and that doesn't mean breaking into someone's home and bringing them to your . . . cave? Abandoned building? Apartment? Wherever man-made monsters common—*basements*! Yes, now I remember; don't bring them to your basement, wherever that may be.

Instead, interact with humans in *their* natural settings, and instead of expecting them to scream and claw at their own eyeballs, give them the benefit of the doubt. With your new look and outlook, the reaction from people may change almost immediately in terms of your looks, but don't be afraid to greet and be polite to people. If you have the confidence to show people your new identity, they'll be much more likely to accept it and treat you as a slightly-below-equal. In their embrace, you'll find gratification and assurance that the crimes of your body parts will be long forgotten in time.

However, the true test comes in seeking out interaction in the man-made creature community. Of course, some of the more bogus creatures embrace the stereotype of "Frankensteins," and may be hesitant or even hostile to the changes you are going through. However, by practicing emotional restraint and showing everyone that you can embrace your monstrosity for positive gain, you will command their respect even if they deny you their admiration. And who knows? There's a good chance that your choices will inspire other creatures to overcome their fears and find their own identity.

Now equipped with your newfound identity and its various internal benefits, you have to remember that building your identity is much like building a man-made creature like yourself. If its individual parts won't work together, your identity will crumble as a whole. Therefore, you'll have to maintain this identity through focus, patience, and the power of will. However, there's nothing wrong with outside assistance as well; even the strongest human needs a shoulder to cry on sometimes because we're just as much trash as the next guy.

So congratulations, man-made monster who paid for this book and has gotten to the end of the chapter. You are not a monster anymore. You are an individual now. You are beautiful. And most importantly, you are more than the sum of your parts. It's okay, you can cry now.

Chapter IV

Unwrapping the Mummy

As a self-help writer and part-time motivational speaker, people often ask me, "Ken, what are you going to do when you're dead?" Of course, the easy answer is that I'm going to rot, or, depending on how dementia works out, be preserved in a giant pickle jar on my front lawn to scare off potential trespassers. But the more complicated answer, and the one I'm most fit to answer, is that I don't know, since I don't have any active religious affiliations and I can't predict how valuable my corpse is going to be in the future. For some, however, "I don't know" is not a good enough answer, as your life after death is akin to your legacy on Earth, and some people are perfectionists.

Of course, many of those perfectionists existed thousands of years ago, and in their primitive brains and short life spans, the afterlife became their main concern. As most perfectionists will do, they also had to add a series of complicated rules to their burial process so as to make sure that they'll be the king of heaven or some shit. To be honest, the history books I read during my "stay" with my father, most of which covered the history of the southernmost region of the United States, which, according to recent maps, is very far from Egypt. So I'm not entirely familiar with the mummification process, but if it's anything like I've seen in the movies, it's super gross, nitpicky, and a little selfish.

Yet for all of my name-calling and veiled envy, something must have worked, seeing as ancient Egyptians outsmarted the Catholics, Mormons, and the Chosen People to be the first to discover eternal life. Although the removal of brains and organs is a bit of a bummer, mummies exist to this day, many of whom feel bound to the curses of their gods in order to keep on keepin' on. However, mummies have earned a bad reputation among mankind, and hence have been labeled as monsters by the mainstream liberal media, who I actually should be thanking considering those mummies probably went out and bought this book.

To this end, I'm not 100 percent sure that the mummies who bought this book know how to read English (a problem that likely will appear time and time again throughout this book), so these words might look like that funny hand-and-bird language that they had. Honestly, I tried to convince myself to take the higher road and learn Egyptian so that my mummy audience would at least be able to read this chapter phonetically. Alas, it was simply a task I didn't feel like doing because I'm not the one who needs help, despite what my therapist and psychoanalyst and accountant tell me. And if I was an eccentric billionaire who had the expendable income, I'd absolutely open mummy learning centers so that they can learn how to read English, do math, fuck properly, and do all the things you learn in regular school but, you know, for mummies.

Now, the one staggering difference between mummies and many of the other afflicted monsters is that people can go to a museum and see a mummy with their own eyes. While most of the more troublesome mummies have made sure any and all spectators never see the light of day again, there are plenty of documented mummies that are dormant and can be proven to exist, which cannot be said about some of their more secretive monster counterparts. Of course, I'm no Jar-Jar Tolkien; I'm not interested in writing a billion-page epic filled with falsities and hocus pocus. These are real monsters with real problems, and for mummies, most of those problems stem from their relationship to expectation.

Now, what do the following have in common: anxiety, agitation, and perturbation? Aside from awesome potential punk rock album titles, these are all words to describe the emotions we feel in the face of expectation. Whether they come from a loved one, your profession, your religion, or even the law who expects you to testify against your loved one, expectations set questionably realistic goals that bring out the internal dread within us and sometimes leave us paralyzed to do anything about it.

While expectations are sometimes necessities in our life and daily routine, it can be very easy to find yourself drowning in anxiety thanks to an abundance of expectations, especially if you're a mummy. By taking on too many responsibilities or surrounding yourself with negative influences, expectation anxiety can control the direction of your afterlife and cripple any attempts at social development. And worst of all, it makes you astronomically more likely to indulge in negative behavior, like unjustified murder or, in the case of cowards, suicide.

But for those afflicted with the mummy's curse, the anxiety of expectations can be taken to what those familiar with Mountain Dew might describe as "extremes." Of course, the gift of everlasting life requires a bit of gratitude, and sure, if I had to kill a few nosy adventurers to make good in exchange for an eternity of not-terrible years, I'd probably find myself doing so without question. But after a certain amount of centuries of killing and sleeping, killing and sleeping, over and over and over, you have to consider your curse paid in full and find something new to do.

However, no mummy's curse is the same, with some of these immortal monsters following a different set of strange, arbitrary rules than the vast majority. Some of these monsters have to kill any and all trespassers, which can take the lives of a lot of accidental land purveyors but does have the upside of making the taxman steer clear. Some of these mummies kill only those who take their treasure, presuming they survive the various traps and viral bacteria that stand in their way. And for a lucky few, there are certain mummies who can kill only those who open their sarcophagus, which is something that many archaeologists can talk themselves out of doing considering how awfully massive those fucking things can be.

But the one thing all mummies do share is their burden of expectation, bestowed upon them by their gods (or worse, shamans), their families, their societies or, in some cases, just their massive wealth. Of course, when setting these expectations, these entities didn't necessarily mean them to have any consequences; when they were set, it was done in an era and environment where honor triumphed above all and good, decent men could appoint their horses to congress. Nevertheless, the gift of foresight was not bestowed upon the ancient Egyptians, leaving countless numbers of mummies with no recourse to their life of post-mortem servitude.

While we're on the subject, I'd also like to address the fact that I'm referring mostly to ancient Egyptian mummies, though mummification has actually been used in cultures all around the world. While my masterful musings and cutting-edge solutions to your problems are applicable to any and all mummies, regardless of location or origin, most of the non-Egyptian mummies aren't afflicted with the same kinds of curses. For the most part, these mummies seem to have a pretty normal life following death, roaming the Earth like a tertiary character in a Warren Zevon song. Meanwhile, Egyptian mummies are basket cases of a more acerbic variety, and hopefully, ones in most need of my brand of enlightenment.

Also, I'd like to address that, due to the nature of mummies, there are far fewer mummies populating the shadows than there are vampires, man-made creatures, or wolfmen. This means that, though I'll be giving 100 percent of my efforts, only a fraction of the proceeds from this book will go to mummies. So if you're a mummy and you get the most out of this book, all I ask is that maybe you track me down and give me some of your riches to make up for the difference. It's not only the right thing to do, it's the fair thing to do and is technically a gift so it's non-taxable income.

Furthermore, considering the wealth that most mummies have, I'm going to be particularly straightforward in this chapter since I'm not the one to waste the time of people who can not only kill me, but will pay others to kill me because they can't leave their tomb. Speaking with complete honesty, there's a good chance that if the mummy community came together and pooled their treasures, they could probably build mech suits made out of encrusted diamonds and conquer the Earth overnight. But considering they don't know what mech suits are, and certainly don't have the tools to build them, I can only assume that the only thing stopping sending mummies down a path of world domination would be my work here in *The I in Evil.*

Is that a threat? I don't think my any legal precedent says anything I might have insinuated as being a direct threat to anyone, and certainly doesn't qualify under the realm of conspiracy to commit treason. However, I would also like to say that if this is being read in a future when mummies have taken over and humans serve as their slaves, I will say that the above paragraph should be enough indication to know that I've been on the right team the whole time, my undead overlords.

But back to the issue at hand: most mummies have to deal first and foremost with the expectations of their gods. Historically speaking, gods can be a judgemental batch, and are prone to some really dickish behavior when provoked by the existence of man. Additionally, gods usually set a bunch of conditions for their blessings, too, whether they be good behavior points that you need to rack up when you finally croak or claiming souls to fulfill their sick, sadistic desires. With mummies, not only are the expectations to deliver good on their curse constantly shoved in your face (after all, they are *literally* written on the walls of your pyramid), but you're also threatened with the fear of your immortality being suddenly taken away.

Yet there is a silver lining to your curse, aside from keeping your endless monies and having life beyond death, and that would be that gods can also be incredibly indifferent. For instance, you can go your entire life doing sickening things to yourself and others, and as long as you pony up and say you're sorry before God pulls your plug, all is forgiven; it's essentially the same rules that the law uses with prostitutes, as long as you kill the prostitute after the fact. So if those rules can apply to your spooky, all-powerful dog-cat-god, you might be able to convince them (it?) to let that whole "having to kill everyone" rule slide.

More importantly, however, is that with a little finesse and the right social skills, you might be able to go beyond the pyramid that confines your mortal soul. Of course, that's not going to come easy, but luckily, this is what I'm here for. I'd like you to treat my advice like the Ferrari in your driveway, or the plastic surgery that makes you look ten years younger, or those pills that make your boner work when you're an octogenarian. I'm here to inspire and give you the confidence to make these possibilities a reality, and if that has to begin with a stern chat with your deity, well then so be it.

So where do you start when it comes to defying your god? Obviously, you're only likely to anger your god if you start testing him/her/it with minor rule breaking and scheming; after all, that seems like an act of blatant disrespect rather than a humble act of disestablishmentarianism. Likely, the best way is to talk to your god one-on-one with all your cards on the table, letting him know you're serious about seizing the day and making the most out of the eternal life that he/she/it gave you. Much like anyone who has ever shot their boss can tell you, thinking about facing authority figures is a small step in making that confrontation a reality.

However, having been exposed to your current state of existence, finding the bravado to step up to your god might be difficult, but it is definitely far from impossible. The good news is that you don't have to change your physical appearance at all, as even though your skeletal frame and dust-ridden wrappings might scare the average human, your god saw you in this state even before you were born, so he's not going to judge you on your fashion sense. On top of that, God also probably knows that this conversation is coming, and has probably made up his mind on the matter before it even came to fruition in your brain. So the question isn't going to be when or why, but rather how, and that's where I can help you the most.

In pleading your case to your god, what is most important is establishing a sense of respect between the two, and as much as it relies on you being respectful to them, it also relies on commanding respect as well. In speaking with your god, a stern-yet-reasonable tone is likely the best way to get the message across without seeming demanding or self-centered, especially if you have your speech memorized rather than bashfully reading it off of your own gauze. Furthermore, posture is key: while you may be naturally inclined to slump and warp into an imposing attack position, a strong physical presence will help sell the illusion of confidence and grandeur to your god. Most importantly, you need resilience in the matter: you've snapped spines, caved in skulls, strangled necks, and bitten off scalps for centuries, and you deserve a bit of a reprieve, all things considered.

But even if your god is willing to let you break beyond the bonds of your curse, that doesn't necessarily mean you are in the clear just yet. After all, you weren't just killing intruders and guarding your gold out of religious tribute, were you? Of course, one wouldn't blame you for catering to the expectations of your family and society, both of whom had a reputation to uphold before and after your passing. With the weight of responsibility that you carried thousands of years ago when you were emptied and wrapped up like a poor person's christmas gift, you might have forgotten that times have changed now and that you might not be the same mummy that you were even a thousand years ago.

On one hand, if your family hasn't become mummies themselves, you don't really have to answer to anyone physically anymore. While your family's expectations and standards may have been crucial to your behavior in the past, they're no longer here to really stake their claim in your life anymore. Besides, you're thousands of years old and you're still living in the pyramid that your parents built for you; if your parents were still alive today, they'd probably be kicking you out of the damn place yourself.

If your family has become mummies, however, and you share a pyramid, then there's only so much advice I can throw your way without recommending a full-force familial uprising. After all, I doubt there are any mummy courts that will grant you any of your estate while they're all undead, so you might have to go forth with a mummy coup. Of course, I don't know how mummies settle their differences; I'd assume they would teach you how to mummy fight shortly before taking out your innards, especially since you would need to rely so much on motor response. Perhaps the best advice I can give you, should you pursue this line of action, is to never accept defeat: either destroy your family with your wretched mummy hands and claim your rightful fortune, or let them put you out of your misery and then maybe you can become just a regular ghost.

In either case, if you're going to leave the nest as well as the shadow of your family, you're going to have to learn to handle the expectations of your namesake and your wealth. Most Ancient Egyptian mummies came from royalty, since back in the day, body disposal for the poor ranged from leaving someone in a river to using their body to build tombs for other people, which is actually super cost-effective in retrospect. So you've proven you can defend your empire and strike fear into the hearts of man, but you can't say that you've built an empire of your own until you break free of your family name while still respecting the legacy they've literally left behind.

However, there might be a viable middle ground for you to honor the expectations of your long-dead family while also doing what is best for you as a person, and that's by honoring your heritage and history. Considering that the walls of your crypt are covered with stories about yourself, your family, and your religion, you might as well use some of the free time in between unwanted disturbances to revisit some of these tales and take them to heart. If you can learn from the success of your family, you can begin to map out your own rise to fortune. Luckily, even the ugliest mummy (and believe me, there are some rough looking mummies out there) can earn respect in the world of finance and also came from historically respectable families. On that point, I'm sure you can probably dig up some of their monstrous deeds from the past, so even your history of horror will become a footnote in the bigger picture of your family history.

But then, any self-respecting mummy has to consider the expectations of the greatest variable of them all: society. For the most part, mummies are more of a cultural fascination than they are accepted into the bigger society structure; even after death, rich people are still more interesting than the lower class. Yet in any case, they're still considered to be monsters, and are expected to act as such as long as they are in the confines of their own property and kept out of the public eye until they're eventually retired into the museum circuit.

Now, in this sense, we have to address a cold, hard fact: mummies look and smell terrible due to thousands of years without proper body maintenance. Hopefully, the outside world will be able to show you the wonders of personal hygiene and personal care. You might want to consider wearing clothing that won't let casual bystanders see your rotting flesh or bony visage. And I also know I'm not one to talk, considering I spent my teen years trying to break the world record for longest time spent without bathing or brushing my teeth, which I can now look back on as a gargantuan mistake. Luckily, your fragile frame will make you more popular than the morbidly obese, so you can at least make yourself somewhat accessible if you're willing to compromise on how you look and how far you should be from people at all times.

For the most part, there's a less tenuous side to the peace between mummies and men, at least compared to the likes of gill-men and vampires who actively kill people. In the eyes of humans, any idiot who feels entitled to someone else's fortune is also subject to their punishments, much like the reasoning in laws that allows people to shoot trespassers at their own discretion. Even better is the fact that mummies do not feel remorse for their murders, and are actually quite sedentary once they've enacted their revenge, allowing you to be a rather low-maintenence monster. And then there are the somewhat ridiculous expectations of mummies, as several humans won't even let mummies into their home out of fear that they will run to the store to presumably get cigarettes and return to find their house bound to the mummy's curse.

Then, there are also the expectations set upon you from your fellow mummies in their small percentage of society. In most cases, the hermit-esque lifestyle of the mummy is considered to be beneficial to all of mummy kind, considering mummies are not covetous or manipulative when left to their own devices. Furthermore, a tomb can only change so much over the course of a few millennia and talking about murder all the time can get kind of morbid after a while. So the mummy populace's expectations of laissez-faire living could certainly become threatened if one bad mummy apple spoils the whole mummy tree.

Now, for a mummy, the system is a bit of a trick to game since, as a whole, humanity treats ugly people worse than war criminals and abortion clinic protestors. After all, there's at least a conceptual evil behind the latter that can be latched onto emotionally and justify our distaste with them, while society wants burn victims and disfigured people just to go away. And even though the wrapping-cloth industry has found ways to make your natural apparel look stunning in the right context, even the most liberal social analysts will realize your dehydrated, malnourished skin is going to be, at the very least, off-putting.

But where there's a will, there's a way, and if you believe in your capacity for intelligence, you can realize that there's plenty of opportunity for social growth if you're the man behind the curtain, figuratively and hopefully literally. As long as you're willing to sacrifice the intimacy of your pyramid setting, you can still work to live up to expectations of both men and your fellow mummies while establishing yourself outside of traditions you've followed for the better part of eternity. But for any of this to happen, you have to take the initiative to make it happen, and that will include the use of . . . whatever weird magic shit resides inside of your brainless skull.

The first step in getting out of the pyramid and into the real world is realizing that the routine maintenance you've so happily indulged in over the years isn't necessarily your responsibility. After all, you didn't build the tomb, you didn't write the curse on the wall, and you certainly didn't ask to be conscious as you've perpetually decayed over hundreds of years. So after what could liberally be described as a grace period, guarding your tomb and your treasure shouldn't fall on your shoulders for the same reasons that a person who was given a faulty flamethrower shouldn't have to treat their own burn wounds. And by refusing the burden of spending more of your time tied to that fucking pyramid, you're showing that you are ready to move forward and leave the past behind.

Now, there is always the option to not leave your pyramid while pursuing a future within a remote lifestyle, considering the modern renaissance men are mostly just multitasking in front of an LED screen for eighteen hours a day. However, if you're going to turn your pyramid into a mummy-cave, you're certainly going to need the help of your riches; there aren't many cell towers in the middle of the desert, and installing Wi-Fi in some of the biggest structures ever created is going to be a costly endeavor. But once you have a way of reaching the modern world from the comfort of your tomb, you'll be able to connect with people from places your ancestors could have only imagined. You can even set up your social media profiles, which is guaranteed to make you realize that you're probably relatively less ghoulish than some of the people on the Internet.

Of course, the Internet is only the first step to catch you up to speed with the twenty-first century, and you can add some fancy flourishes to your pyramid to show your mummy friends as well as your soon-to-be-killed intruders just how fucking boffo a monster can live nowadays. With the kind of mummy money you have, you can add everything from a small-scale skate park to a home theater to hibachi tables to a novelty art installation that looks like a hallway of mirrors but has Bruce Lee from *Enter the Dragon* painted all over it. And after you're done scouring Wikipedia and YouTube to find out just what the hell I'm talking about, you can even incorporate state-of-the-art technology into the traps that guard your treasure so you can add more relaxation time to your lifestyle and kill people with an app. While they say money can't buy happiness, the people who probably said that weren't mummies, so I recommend you go out and you buy happiness and flaunt that happiness like a peacock's big colorful butt.

But outside of the pyramid, a confident mummy has a vast ocean of opportunities waiting at their feet, as long as you commit to the idea that you make your own destiny. You can't rely on others to make those steps for you and make you the richest, most badass mummy in the world; you can't depend on weak arms to lift you to the top. Thankfully, mummies have strong arms, and with a little bit of determination, you can achieve success so fruitful that your ancestors will look like paupers in your wake.

Before we move on to how to better yourself in the hustle-and-bustle world of humanity, I'd like to address a rumor among mankind that mummies have regenerative powers from sucking the lifeforce out of currently existing humans.

Now, I don't know how that works since physics was never my strong suit, and I don't know if that regeneration is somehow permanent, but if you do have this ability, please do so towards the beginning of your exodus into the real world. Now, if regeneration via essence-stealing is something that you can do, but need to do on a regular basis, you should learn to pace yourself, as all it takes is a vigilante with a matchbook to seriously fuck your day sideways.

The most effective way of instilling determination in your mummy brain, outside of actually believing that you can succeed, is to become goal-oriented. Obviously, you are familiar with goals, since any cursed mummy had the goal of ridding their pyramid of unwelcome entities by any means necessary. But now, we shift our focus from killing the living towards something more logical and beneficial, whether that be strangling the life out of Wall Street or putting scarabs underneath the skin of Illuminati members.

Now, don't get me wrong: getting out of the pyramid and immediately betraying your god could be seen as a distasteful move, especially considering the reason you're here is in no small part due to your god. But it's 2015, and as much as your religion was sort of the only thing you knew back in the old, old, old, old days, there are religions everywhere now, from Buddhism to Scientology to Paganism to SPECTRE. Hell, you can even make up your own religion and you can probably find a few hundred people to follow you, and you're just a dirty old mummy who smells like guacamole made out of garbage; guarbamolage, if you will.

An alternate route you can take is to serve your god outside of the pyramid as well, considering your mere existence disproves elements of many of these religions. You would simultaneously be an atheist's best friend and worst nightmare, and would likely pull better recruitment numbers than those fucking nerds who shout on boxes at college campuses. If you're smart, you'll invest in pyramids before you go public and rake in the cash once people know that your God is better than their God. It'd be like investing in whatever shit churches are made out of the week that Jesus comes back to kick our asses.

Once you figure out what it is that you're going to do, you have to figure out ways of doing business and protecting your assets outside of the public eye. Considering the value of your ancient treasures, every fucking lawyer around the world is going to want a piece of your action, and a lawyer will act as a perfect surrogate for building your contemporary empire. Now, there are limits to what a lawyer will do for you, including strangling people or changing your disease-ridden bandages, but a good lawyer will help you make your presence known while keeping your ugly mug from ruining potential business deals.

I know I'm certainly painting a shallow picture of humanity, but as a mummy, you have to understand that your repugnant outer shell carries more implications than sheer shock value. For instance, since you're a decomposed body for the most part, the human race can look at you and see what is coming to them in a matter of centuries, which is not only terrifying but also quite sad. Furthermore, you're up and walking, despite being quite clearly dead, a fact that will upset even more people by giving them hope that by mummifying their own relatives, they might be able to create a family of superhuman monsters that will live forever. But please understand that their grudge is not personal; they would treat any other mummy with the same apprehension and involuntary disgust as well.

However, one of the biggest issues that you will be encountering among modern humans, even your lawyer, is trust. Unfortunately, the byproduct of living alone for so many years is that you may instantly be more lenient and optimistic towards the humans who didn't try to pillage your pyramid, which is something that should be corrected immediately. Mummies, like anyone with money, are always going to be targeted by con men and those looking to take your money and run. And while you can't necessarily kill them, perhaps the best way to instill your driven sense of commitment to your goals is to break into the houses of your business partners and lawyers and watch them as they sleep. Once your moaning has woken them up, they'll know that you're not fucking around, and that they'll never be 100 percent safe when doing business with you, which is the way it should be.

Now, I know that trust is not the strongest suit for a mummy, and that's perfectly understandable. I would probably not trust too many people either if the most recent events in my life were the forcible removal of my organs and then having to kill trespassers who keep trying to steal my shit. But if you think about it, mummies should be prone to trust more than other monsters, considering the side of people they see the most are humans at their most base desires. Whether they're in pursuit of knowledge, treasure, or any reason for you to spare their life, you've seen an honest side of humans that not many other monsters have seen, so you are perhaps more adept at picking up on when humans lie, which is ninety percent of the time.

Personally, I know that my brief experience with mummies during my time with my father certainly showed me that mummies can be trustworthy and compassionate. Sure, I might have been young, and this lady-mummy was wearing far-from-traditional garb, but the rags she did wear complimented her figure. She was very personable and offered me a half-sucked lollipop, a kindness I'll never forget. Unfortunately, my father sent me on a run to go buy garbage bags from the convenience store, and I ended up never seeing that lady-mummy ever again, at least until the photos came out during the trial. Yet knowing my father, he'd never hurt anyone unless they were an evil monster, and a mummy unfit for the world at large is just as dangerous as a spree killer or a cyberbully.

But as a mummy living in this brave new world of texting, porn, and mixed martial-arts, trust is going to be essential to your survival and success. Believe it or not, there are just as many people out there who want to see you make money, find love, and travel the world as there are willing to rob you of everything you have. While the way of your old god may have been fairly black and white in terms of who and who not to kill, things aren't so simple in the new millennium and it all comes down to trust. You might have the riches to literally build an army or make additions to your pyramid, but there are few things as valuable in the business-oriented world as your trust.

Another way you can establish trust is to rely on what you know best: dark magic from the annals of Egyptian history. Hopefully, all the wall reading you did before will pay off as you can change your mummy's curse to a mummy's blessing by practically applying it to your enemies or potential en-emies. Now, of course, mummies like yourself lack the inge-nuity and charisma to come up with a dream scheme outside of "lure them to my pyramid," which this author may wager is a bit obvious. However, from my years learning from my father and, later, as a false therapist, this old dog knows just the trick, entitled "The Sepia Tone Wedding."

As you may have guessed, this patented trick to force people to trust you includes a hoax wedding, which you should schedule just before a company licensing or business deal. Luckily, as mummies, you can throw down millions of dollars on a fake wedding to make sure no one misses it. Likewise, you can hire must-see entertainment to calm your outraged guests once the ruse is up; after all, what helps ease tension better than Ringo Starr and his All-Starr band? And while picking out a bride might be difficult, as even the most desperate gold-digger might be turned off by the foul odor of death, you can always just buy a realistic mannequin (or, for multipurpose use, sex robots) since it won't matter by the end of the day.

Once all the guests have arrived, it's important to make sure that this wedding looks nice and normal, as normal as a wedding for a fucking mummy can be without looking like the monster mash. Then, once you're exchanging vows with your bride, recite the mummy's curse that would compel you to murder any and everyone who intruded on your turf while you were on watch. Once you've completed the curse, motion for that wait staff to pull down the wallpaper off of the chapel to reveal the ancient emoticons that lined your pyramid, and watch those motherfuckers go pale.

How will this make you gain the trust from those who need it the most? Well, that's the most obvious answer of them all: by the word of your God, you have the right to kill every single person at their wedding, including spouses, children, and the elderly. Essentially, you're holding a supernaturally-charged ransom note, and with your deity on your side to carry out each execution. Their lives are in your dehydrated hands. Therefore, if they don't want another nightly visit that won't end in a ruined weekend and a trip to the flower shop, they'll make sure to placate you and won't dare to cross you.

Now, you're probably wondering how any of that behavior can be considered ethical or moral, and the truth is that it's not, but to be a mummy in a world of humans, you have to be above morals and ethics. As seen in great tales such as *Scarface*, *Wall Street*, and *JFK*, history rewards those who operate outside the barriers of what is traditionally right and whose consequences are few and far between. This is a self-help book, goddamnit, and if helping you become successful and powerful doesn't count as self-help, maybe you should go find Tony Robbins' book for monsters. Oh wait, he doesn't have one? Didn't think so.

So, you've got the money, you've got the motivation and you've got a proven track record of following through on your promises. So now you have to find a good place to incubate your nest egg, and the best advice one can give you is to go with what you know. Obviously, the world has changed over the thousands of years since you were a living, breathing human, but that doesn't mean things have changed so much that people have changed their basic needs. So if there are any of our basic human needs that you were particularly fond of during your lifespan that didn't rely on slavery or whoring or public execution, then you should take advantage of it, monetize it, and give it a twist to make it unique to your persona.

The most glaring option would be the food industry, especially since there's never really been an effective Egyptian restaurant chain. Just think of it now: Imho's Egyptian Restaurant and Grill. It corners a market that most people didn't even know existed, and you can even design the restaurants to look like pyramids. It'd be just like eating at home, if you're a mummy and your home for most of your existence was a pyramid. In any case, you could make it the Egyptian equivalent of Applebee's, at least until Applebee's decides they want to do some silly Egyptian bullshit, too.

If food isn't a good thing, then perhaps you can move on to the world of digital development and applications. In the stress-filled and hopeless world where humans wake up to every morning, the slightest of distractions can become a cash cow for anyone willing to string it up by its ankles and cut its throat. And, in a hilarious sense of irony, there are many apps that already exist about raiding the tombs and treasures of mummies like yourself, so perhaps it's about time that an actual mummy adds some authenticity. That's right: add the real, gritty, terrifying experience of going face to face with a mummy, hire a ridiculously expensive game developer to put it into virtual reality, and then it's maybe two to three years until easy street.

Then, there are always the illegal ways of doing things, which I would certainly not condone whatsoever. I would say that you shouldn't take stock of your history in opiate-friendly territories and use the natural drug knowledge to enter the drug trade. I also would add that on top of that, you shouldn't deal drugs man-to-man since you can't be killed via conventional means and that you wouldn't need enforcers because you're a fucking mummy. And beyond that, I would definitely not say that I may have spent some time in Europe soul-searching after my father's execution, and I might know some people who would help move your product for buddy prices. All of those statements would be illegal, and luckily, that's why I so explicitly said not to do it.

Also, I'm just going to put it out there: mummy casino. Think about it.

Now while most of my advice has been financial in merit, I do have a confession to make: all this talk about professional success does contain the ulterior motive of living up to your namesake. OH SHIT. DID YOU SEE THAT COMING? OF COURSE YOU DIDN'T. YOU'RE A MUMMY, DUMMY!

That's right; by inspiring you and giving you a chance to be your own man, you will be making yourself feel better by making your family proud. The fact that your efforts to give people from around the world a reason to remember your name and roots would be enough to bring a tear to your dad's long-since-eroded eye. But what's most important is that in that empty husk you call a body, you may actually feel a sense of emotional fulfillment by doing something for someone else that didn't directly result in a third party dying by your hand.

You see, when you're a monster who is so directly tied to a very specific set of religious beliefs, it makes the most sense that someone like myself might appear as a devil figure and lead you into temptation. But in doing so, I'm also offering you a chance to not only reintroduce yourself to society, but do something in line with those beliefs as well. And besides, the best way you can serve both your god and your family is by serving yourself, which also serves the community and the children and whoever else is in need and is culturally relevant.

By finding that pride and that emotional truth in yourself, you also might be more suited to face some of the shittier obstacles in the way of your success. Unfortunately, there's nothing mummies can do to game the political system; even though there are some people in office that do look as decrepit and simple-minded as yourself, your international status and unmistakable stench is not cut out for politics. Furthermore, sports might be out of the question as well, considering most mummies are frustratingly slow in nature, and your strength might be too far out of your control to be applied in a competitive context. After all, if people are going to shit their pants every time some guy suffers a couple dozen concussions on the football field, just wait until they get wind of all the murders that would happen with your kind as linebackers.

Likewise, with a healthy state of mind, a mummy such as yourself is more likely to give back to the underprivileged mummies in your community. Since your family is dead and your god is at the very least invisible, your mummy neighbors are the closest thing to company that you're going to get, and once you've become successful in the human world, they'll have to let you into their afterlives. By giving back to the mummy community, you will instill a sense of pride into those walking skeletons so that they also can achieve success outside of their pyramid, especially if they read my book. In that sense, you'll become a role model to many mummies around the globe, and if you can't enslave them, you might as well join them, am I right?

So heed my words, my mummy friends: with a goal-oriented mind, a respect for your history, and a sense of trust that you can value, you can literally do great things in the modern age. Sure, there are few substitutes for the pleasure of picking up a six-hundred-pound boulder and smashing it on the head of a brilliant archaeologist, or watching a treasure hunter be ripped to pieces by hungry scarabs in a needlessly complicated trap, but some old habits will have to die (or, at the very least, be disciplined) in order for you to better your afterlife. However, as long as your family and god remain in your . . . soul? . . . they can take the mummy out of the pyramid, but they can never take the pyramid out of the mummy.

Chapter V

The Animal Inside

I've always had a soft spot in my heart for those afflicted with lycanthropy, because at the end of the day, most of them are not even full-time monsters. For twenty-nine days out of each month, a common werewolf can assimilate into society fairly well, perhaps holding a steady job at a sporting goods store or handing out those intriguing pamphlets about the apocalypse in Union Square. Sure, they may be a bit hairier than normal folk, and they might show signs of extreme stress and mental instability in the days leading up to the full moon, but other than that, they're your average everyday asshole. Nevertheless, they do technically classify as monsters, much in the same way that if you just happen to willingly commit a murder, even just once, you're technically a murderer.

Also, to all murderers out there reading this book, there's no judgement coming from this author. People get murdered all the time, and it can be for a variety of justified reasons. Murder is one of the most natural and primal reactions someone can have to chance encounters or petty disagreements, so who is this author to judge?

Now, this is going to be a trickier chapter than the ones before it, because it needs to be divided up for certain readerships. Of course, our main focus will be the monthly lycanthropes whose changeling status is only a concern thirteen nights in a given calendar year. But this chapter is also aimed to help full-time lycanthropes, most of whom really pissed off a wizard, witch, or possibly a major werewolf king of some kind? To be honest, my knowledge of wild werewolf hierarchies are limited to only several days of a full-wilderness immersion, and it wasn't like I could exactly take notes in that scenario. This chapter will also go on to help the families and friends of lycanthropes, as well as lycanthropes who travel or live in packs.

Real quick, let's address what a lycanthrope is, and the difficulties that come with their inherent condition. A lycanthrope, also known as wolfman, werewolf, lycan, and, depending on their age, teen wolf, is a man who, at the sight of a full moon, transforms into a humanoid wolf-beast with the strength and agility of ten men and an insatiable hunger for flesh. Contrary to popular opinion, lycanthropes and vampires do not hate one another; if anything, they're more like ne'er-do-well roommates whose nightly ventures rarely cross paths. While lycanthropes can be killed only by silver, they also lack basic communication skills, cannot speak, and are difficult to reason with.

Just like the amazing Siegfried and Roy can tell you, there's not an animal in the world that is untameable. Additionally, these beasts have a human soul, which leaves them susceptible to all kinds of psychological conditions, including depression, anxiety, fear, self-loathing, and positive ones too, I guess. Lycanthropes are often stereotyped as uncontrollable creatures of relentless rage, and while that may sometimes be the case, the fact is that they're just wayward. If there's anything I've learned in the many years of trying to give therapy to dogs and animals, it's that if you yell at something semi-coherently for long enough, they'll eventually get the picture.

So before we get into this lesson, if you're a werewolf and you've got a human counterpart nearby, please pass this book to them and instruct them to scream every word at your face. Tell them that harsh hand gestures, such as pointing, finger wagging, fist shaking, and general flailing, will help get their point across and help disorient the animalistic instincts inside of you. Furthermore, if you become distracted or disinterested in their screams, recommend that they punctuate that behavior with a firm

"No!" or "Bad!" I know that you might think we're treating you like a dog, but you're a fucking wolf, and if you look at the origin of dogs, they're essentially wolves we downbreeded and domesticated, so whatever, you fucking nitpick.

So, first off, let's talk about deterring your werewolf behavior. Like my father always used to stay, "if you cut off a man's limbs, they can't fight back." That kind of mentality will serve us well here. Not literally, of course, but that's an option too, I guess, albeit an extreme one. On the other hand, that could be an effective solution, seeing as paws can't wrap around a wheelchair and you would probably just howl a lot and look like those dogs on late night commercials that make you sad. I changed my mind: if you're willing to do it, cut off all your limbs and that'll prevent all further lycanthropic problems.

However, if you're a normal person, chopping off your own limbs (or, realistically speaking, paying a stranger you met on the Internet to chop off and cook your limbs) is not an option, so we have to think of other physical deterrents. The first piece of advice is to think with your stomach, and by that I mean that you should deprive yourself of half of your daily dietary intake and then, on the full moon, eat as many calories as wolf-ly possible. Why, you ask? It's simple: Have you ever tried strenuous physical activity with a full stomach? How about any activity at all? Have you ever tried physical activity with an upset stomach as well? Of course you have, and it really fucking hurts.

Additionally, if you're starving yourself on a regular basis, the abrupt change into werewolf may have a debilitating effect on your now-malnourished muscles. A healthy werewolf transformation would normally result in impossibly strong musculature and incredible cell regeneration, whereas a werewolf transformation with muscles unable to support your increased weight and bone frame would create a significantly weaker animal. Your strength would be on par with someone who had just awoken from a coma and pushed them onto a freshly waxed floor.

Also, if this book inspires you to find a coma patient, wait until they regain consciousness, wax their hospital floor, and give 'em a forceful shove to the ground, please don't tell anyone that you heard it from me. I understand that it's a lot of fun, but it's not worth the phone calls I'm going to have to take.

Likewise, if you're a werewolf, and for whatever reason you *have* to go after someone in a last resort scenario, there's no easier prey than a coma patient on a slippery floor, and they'll go down smooth too. But please, if you're a werewolf and you eat a coma patient on a freshly waxed floor, please don't tell anyone that you heard it from me either, and if you hear that some blabbermouth is pushing poor, defenseless coma patients onto slippery floors and is dropping my name willy-nilly, by all means, eat the living shit out of them.

In any case, by using the emaciation-gorging method, you introduce one of two scenarios to the lycanthropy process: "too painful to move" werewolf, or the "vomiting" were-wolf. In the former scenario, just like when the uncle who went for fourths during Thanksgiving (or, as my foster parents called it during my teen years, "Bingemas"), a werewolf that has eaten too much will be reluctant to move from its spot, and will likely groan and make wheezing noises until approximately twelve to seventy-two hours after extreme food consumption. If the werewolf in question does manage to make it to its paws and go on an old-fashioned were-rampage, the good news is that it will at least not eat people, because even the mere thought of consuming human flesh will invoke phantom stomach pain.

In the latter scenario, which is more suited for more stubborn lycanthropes as well as those we in the motivational speaking game have defined as "real pieces of shit," the werewolves in question will push past their full stomachs to rampage at full force, and as a result, vomit all over like a fucking jerk. Streets, subway tunnels, backyards; if a werewolf can destroy it, it will be filled with creamy, delicious vomit. And if the animal instinct to eat the vomit comes up, they'll likely strain your stomach again, and then be the re-vomiting werewolf, and everyone will laugh at them.

Another way to use your own body to curb your werewolf impulses to rage all night long is to become an extreme smoker whose habit goes beyond practical explanation. I'm talking about smoking so many cigarettes, theme park employees will cry upon the mere mention of your name. I'm talking about smoking so much that your parents, assuming they haven't been killed or disowned you on account of your lycanthropy, will be counting the days until you collapse. I'm talking about smoking so much that any good physician will pronounce you legally dead during a routine check-up.

And just why should you smoke so much? Aside from the fact that you will be much more chill and you can stuff that shit with the stickiest, ickiest, dankest herb if you so choose, the fact is that over time, it'll cripple your lung capacity and your motivation for physical activity. In werewolf form, you won't get down two full city blocks at full speed before your lungs give out and you become a wheezing heap of hairy sadness. By the time lung cancer comes to town, running will become a distant memory, and you'll finally be a werewolf tamed by the one thing that created you in the first place: sad, tragic nature.

Now, it's important to remember that, despite what television and weirdo literature would like you to believe, not all werewolves are lean and sexy men with nice composure in their non-werewolf hours. Some of them are big fat slobs, or malnourished basement cretins, or are covered in ugly bullet and burn scars from all the times people tried to kill them. In fact, a sad truth about the werewolf community is that there is a major body image problem in their pre-transformed states, and that most silver bullet suicides are not because of lycanthrope guilt, but rather because they're unhappy with their fleshy, disgusting human form.

However, if you're a werewolf and you struggle with your body image, it's important to remember that at the end of the day, health is just a state of mind. You can be literally a billion pounds overweight and if you feel that you're healthy, then who is to say you're not? If you smoke ten packs of cigarettes a day and drink hard liquor until your eyes turn a brownish-yellow hue, who is to tell you when to stop if you tell yourself that you are indeed healthy? Doctors? Nutritionists? Your family? Listen, if scientologists are too good for health care professionals, then you're better than them too, because I'll be damned if scientologists are better than werewolves.

That leads me to my next point: if health is just a state of mind, then by extension, lycanthropy is a state of mind. Lycanthropy, like health, is not determined by genetics, environment, and available resources; it's determined by your decision to accept it as such. If you say that you're healthy, then you're healthy and the same goes for being a werewolf. Even if your bones grow thrice in size, your hair grows out, and your lust for blood becomes undeniable, you are not a werewolf until you look at your reflection and tell yourself you are a werewolf.

So do yourself a favor: say "no" to the beast within you, and say it out loud. Screaming parents and bystanders

screaming "werewolf" and pointing in your direction? "No."
Small, formidable militia groups garnering up sharp, silver
objects and hunting you down? "No." Waking up naked in a
zoo, genitalia flopping about as you coyly wipe animal blood
of your naked body? "No."

It's something we in the motivational speaking field
attribute to the power of the human will. Some of the most
influential people in the world, whether they be assassins, ter-
rorists, cult leaders, or flight attendants, function on a daily
basis from sheer willpower alone instead of proper food and
sleep. A little willpower can go a long way when coupled
with a complete psychological blockade and a deep-seated
sense of denial. But rather than using said willpower in the
school of "I *can* do this," you can instead focus it on "I am
not a werewolf."

But this book is not called *I Hate Monsters and Want
Them to Die*, no matter what my emails might have initially pitched to Skyhorse. Despite my upbringing, I have no
vested interest in seeing either werewolves, or the family
or friends of werewolves, die or come under scrutiny. Instead, I've made it my job to help you all in whatever form
you might take, so if you're still on the pro-lycanthrope
team, keep reading. Hell, even if you accidentally paid for
the book, you might as well keep reading. Get your fucking
money's worth. Do it.

Now, it's not easy to curb the instinctual behavior of a
werewolf, as it is with anyone, really. But if you really want
to teach an old dog new tricks, you have to work with the
dog, trust the dog, and eventually, condition the dog to do
unnatural things for your childlike amusement. And to teach
a werewolf to be more like its human counterpart, those new
tricks have to be taught in a way that's not only effective,
but in-step with the ways the rest of society acts. By mixing

the human and animal ways of life, a werewolf can convince itself that their new behavior is all a part of its instincts, and can feel more comfortable in its fur.

For instance, one immediate problem that werewolves have is with attire. During the werewolf transformation, various pieces of attire, including shirts, pants, underpants, and mouth guards can be ruined or destroyed completely. If there's anything this writer has learned from regular humans who walk around in public with no shirt or in ripped jeans, it's usually because they're the lowest form of desperate grime humanity has to offer, especially if they're doing it on purpose.

So how does a werewolf spare themselves the embarrassment of running around at night with no clothes on? Well, there's nothing that's more reaffirming and inspiring than taking initiative when it comes to problem solving, and if you believe you can apply that initiative to bettering yourself, then learn how to sew. That's right: find a way to measure yourself in were-form and create clothes that will save you the grief of public nudity, and also reinvigorate your sense of style. You can sew sweaters, T-shirts, robes—hell, you can even don some leather and sell cigarettes, which only the cool werewolves smoke!

You can also sew yourself some wicked spiffy threads and do what everyone else at that hour is doing: dancing. Werewolves have the energy, the flexibility, and stamina to dance for hours, and it'd further instill some much-needed self confidence. Furthermore, dancing werewolves are rather uncommon, despite London-bound lycanthropes having a dance named after them. There's no better way to ingratiate yourself into a crowd than by working that groove, baby. And best of all is that dancing isn't necessarily a group activity: you can dance if you want to and you can leave your friends behind, because your friends don't dance, and if they don't dance, then they're no friends of pro-music, anti-hat activists.

However, if you're terrible at everything, there's no need to fear as there's always a way to take care of the attire problem by using the animalistic aspects of your werewolf personality. The first method is one that should work well for fans of mirrors, particularly because it involves lots of small mirrors. By taking dozens of small, handheld mirrors, tying them together, and creating a suit to fit around your were-frame, you will not only prevent nightcrawlers from casually glancing at your huge, furry reproductive organs (there are message boards for that kind of nonsense), but you will also prevent yourself from rampaging during your were-fits and thus usher you further into society's understanding arms.

How exactly will this mirror-suit be preventative, you may ask? Well, you fucking arrogant idiot, how about these apples: refracted light? That's right: the single piece of kryptonite for the animal kingdom lies in the light that bounces off shiny surfaces. With a mirror suit, the opportunity to distract yourself will be endless, and if it's not the full moon bouncing light with a deeply cosmic irony, it can be streetlights, headlights, flashlights, neon lights, LITE-BRITEs, nightlights lights on kites, and various other lights that can refract and make you relentlessly chase it.

Now, how will the mirror suit help you come to terms with your monstrosity, you may also ask? I might be getting pretty fucking sick of your holier-than-thou questioning of my ideas, but for your information, there can be a lot of emotional satisfaction to be mined from the mirror suit for all kinds of lycanthropes. For starters, you'll definitely become the center of attention in a way that you never have been before, which is guaranteed to eliminate the inherent insecurities in being a monster. Furthermore, a suit entirely made out of mirrors is eccentric as fuck, and you'll probably get into Milan Fashion Week, the MTV Video Music Awards, or, at the very least, the Webbies. That's right: you'll be the first werewolf to stomp the red carpet, and you'll do it while looking fabulous.

Another route to go for both personal satisfaction and social acceptance during lycanthropy is to take a more outrageous route by looking into body modification. A subculture that somehow makes *The Island of Dr. Moreau* seem less creepy in comparison, body modification can be a positive thing for the werewolf kind especially when it is applied to one's were-body. Specifically, the idea of a tail extension, using the same gauging techniques that make punk rock kids look even more punk rock, will yield exceptional results for werewolves, creating lanky tails that your paws will trip over and make you look like a real goof. Also, animals go bananas when they catch wind of their own tail, leading to a bizarrely obsessive game of chase that often results in the animal tasting themselves and realising how dumb they are.

However, the tail extension modification can also be incredibly positive in helping the development of a werewolf into normal society. How so? Well, as said chases become regular, the werewolf will eventually learn strategy and become cognizant of the chase itself, working as a bit of a brain-developing game that will help build the IQ of the werewolf and, likewise, with their human counterparts. After this, you can introduce new games into your full moon freak-outs, and suddenly, you can go from petrifying to proactive; hell, you can even go one step further and start a gaming league for both humans and werewolves to promote integration, and the next thing you know, you can be the next Bobby Fischer, except less anti-semitic and slightly more werewolf.

As for other body modifications, I don't fucking know. You can get your back pierced if you want, or have a beanie sewn into your scalp, or surgically attach your tongue on the tip of your penis. I don't really know enough to care, and at this point, the body mod community seems polite enough to let anyone in, even if they're seven feet tall and look like an extra from Little Red Riding Hood fan fiction. Now that you mention it, if you're a real awkward werewolf, go get some work done and go chill with the body mod people at a milk bar or something; in any case, it's a step in the right direction.

Another way of curbing a werewolf's bad behavior is in the art of misdirection, and for this, you're going to need a little bit of cash. First, I'd like you to wire me $20,000 by any means necessary. After you've sent me the money and filled out the proper taxation forms, spend a bunch more money on some home renovations with a very specific instruction: create and install multiple false doors in your home. Of course, you could attempt to do this by yourself, but I would highly suggest against it: false doors are the number one preferred gateways of ghosts, and once you're haunted, there's nothing I can do to help you.

By installing false doors and renovating your current door to match them (or filling them in altogether), you will be a part of a living maze. Day after day, the nightmare of false doors will ruin your life and destroy your psyche. Reality will become an afterthought in the face of perpetual confusion and failure. If life as a human will be difficult enough with you being unable to remember how to exit your home, just imagine how difficult it will be for your smaller-brained werewolf counterpart. After multiple attempts to slam through a false door, there's a good chance you might just quit to curl up and sleep. This method will be even more effective if you take the extra step to completely remove windows in your home like those 9/11-truthers or the clinically "depressed."

Now, how will the multiple-false-door method help you psychologically become more comfortable with your monsterdom and society? That would be in the form of new beginnings! In the wake of your eventual psychotic break, you'll inevitably face a long road of recovery with your were-self along for the ride. As you patch up your brain little by little, you will be sharing the burden during your monthly visits from Aunt Moon.

The survival of your brain will be equally important to your animal side as well. In that connection, you and your were-self will go back to only one form of schizophrenia, and this time healthier, stronger, and more in tune with your mind than ever before.

Somewhere between the mirror-suit idea and the multiple-false-door method lies the next suggestion, which is ultimately more tacky but extremely effective if you are willing to spend the next day taking responsibility for your actions in a whole different way. If you've got the time and the credit card funds to spend recklessly, your human form can buy multiple tennis ball pitching machines and install them around your property. Next, invest in an automatic timer or a suicidal butler (admittedly, the best kind of butler), and when you go were-crazy, let your animal instincts take over. Fetch those balls! Get 'em! Go get 'em! It's a great alternative to murder and mass destruction!

The tennis-ball-pitching-machine method also provides incentive for werewolf fitness, offering the rare, irresistible sport that both man and manimal can enjoy. Retrieving tennis balls provides cardio-centric exercises that are both frenzied and time-consuming, and will likely shave off those extra pounds from those unfortunate human flesh binges. And if you can't be of sound conscience and mind because of your lycanthropy, you can at least compensate for those emotions with the confidence of someone in peak physical health. If you do end up waking up naked covered in blood after a were-rampage, you can guarantee you'll at least get a couple of ladies' (or mens'—no judgement) phone numbers out of the whole ordeal.

Don't you dare think that the exercise will go unnoticed by your were-self either. Much like in a cartoon or tween fan fiction forum, there are werewolves with six-pack abs, and that's usually a sign indicating that they're the alpha male. Once the cardio does most of the work to remove the extraneous fat, your were-self might decide to start using that gym membership you accidentally bought at the strip mall and take advantage of their twenty-four-hour availability. But be careful: over two percent of werewolves worldwide are killed by changing back to their human forms while bench-pressing upwards of a thousand pounds, so always make sure you have a were-spotter.

Although this next method is more properly associated with the likes of Cat People, there is also a chance that a seabound lycanthrope is more likely to be benign when faced with the alternatives. By getting a job at sea, or if you're one of those rich werewolf families like the Baxleys, a.k.a. the Barksleys, a.k.a. the Buttsleys, that can afford a big ol' boat, you can sail around all the livelong day and put the fear of God in your were-self. The perilous ocean is scarier to mammals than any silver bullet could ever be. So as your monthly destructive urges ebb and flow, the risk of damaging the boat or going overboard is something most werewolves—even in their animalistic state—will recognize as a really awful idea.

With this method, the human alter ego will also likely learn to adapt to discipline and solitude, which are the most important aspects of any personality type. You'll be learning the strength and willpower it takes to survive at sea, while dealing with the fact that you'll have essentially no one to talk to except for the greatest therapists imaginable, Jack Daniels and Jim Beam. When you're at sea, you just can't kill everything in sight; you actually have to learn skills like fishing and crabbing to catch things to eat. That alone takes a tremendous amount of patience and discipline especially if you fucking hate fishing because it's stupid and the TV is at home.

I also should take this moment to emphasize that it's also not a great idea to kill everything in sight in *any* situation. This is probably something that should have been at the beginning of the book, especially considering monsters like yourself are conditioned to murder everyone without regards to consequence and without guilt or remorse. It's generally not cool, and not a good idea; there are cameras everywhere nowadays, and you can't even admit to killing people on camera without getting in trouble with someone. And if you want to integrate into society, the worst way to do so is to come out of the darkness waving your claws around, killing people, and leaving others to clean up your mess.

In fact, if you're a werewolf, one of the best ways to put your powers/curse to good use is by being mindful of your community. After all, you've likely killed many members of families from all across your county, and there's no way better way to reconcile this than by giving back to the community, even if you can't give the community back their dead family members. If you think that your position as a lycanthrope is an excuse to get out of community service, then you haven't met my "lawyer."

Now that you have the *why* locked down, it's time to address *how* you can help your community. The obvious choice would be to help carry the burden of cleaning up our parks, streets, and forests, which are polluted with garbage by a whole different kind of garbage: human beings. And while humans usually rely on animals to eat or at least move our garbage out of eyesight, there are few animals better equipped to clean up community spaces than werewolves, what with their stereotypically big eyes, big ears, and big mouth. Even if you do not plan on killing someone, which I still do not condone unless you sort of have to, make sure that the area around the killing is clean when you leave. Ideally, when the body is eventually discovered, there won't be any candy wrappers or hobo vomit leftover to show how inconsiderate you were during the slaying.

That's not all a good werewolf can provide their community, either. One much-needed project in our parks and recreational areas is to clean up fallen sticks following a hurricane or bad weather. Picking up sticks should come second nature to the werewolf, which you can then properly dispose of in human form. You can also help guard local, state, and national monuments from graffiti artists, who are likely terrified of giant wolf-man hybrids and cannot do their filthy vandalism without their hands. And think of the good you'll be doing as a community watch member: there are few things that deter crime and send criminals cowering back to their families than a near-death experience, which I'm sure is among your skill-set.

However, it's important for werewolves to have a support system in their lives for them to make accomplishments like this, a difficult task considering they're usually the first ones to go when the full moon comes out. The worst part is that this author can't blame you: there have been many times where I've had a roommate who has smelled so good that my first unfiltered impulse was to kill them and consume their flesh. But luckily, I had other roommates there who would have prevented me from doing such terrible things, and they became my inadvertent support systems. And let's face it: people who live alone often kill themselves anyways, because they don't have that special something that makes them interesting enough to be murdered.

But in order to build a house, you first need the bedrock on which the contractor will build it, so if you're currently a single, werewolf loner, you're going to have to recruit a roommate. It can't be just any roommate either: they're going to not only have to accept your physical condition as a werewolf, but also support your endeavors, help protect you against the law, and at times, yourself. It's also not wise to find a roommate in another monster: monster pairings eventually lead to all-out monster mashes, the most dangerous event of them all. Once you've found a roommate with inconsiderate living standards and a "devil-may-care" attitude, you can give him were-bro status and have someone to point you in a better direction than senseless slaughter.

Of course, there will need to be precautionary measures that your were-bro will take so he doesn't become your first course. The first step would be to install standard obstacles: lead doors, human-sized titanium safes, and multiple bear traps should be a decor standard among a dank were-bro. The next would be an abundance of silver bullets and blades, which should be carried openly so as to establish an aura of honesty between a were-man and his mad dank were-bro. And lastly, there's the straight-up decoy method: full body prosthetics filled with raw meat and cow blood, which will satiate your bloodlust while playing the dankest of dank were-bro tricks.

But for a were-bro to truly live up to his were-bro potential, you will need to open yourself up to communication with him/her, with full disclosure about your lycanthropy. Allow yourself, and even your were-self, to become emotionally open and available to your were-bro, and you might find the same emotional vulnerability staring right back at you. Share both the good times and the bad with your were-bro, and allow him to remind you that sometimes, a man has to be a man and a wolf has to be a wolf, and it's okay because at the end of the night, your were-bro will always be your were-bro.

By establishing a stable relationship with your were-bro, a lycanthrope will find a unique sense of resolve and absolution, two emotions integral to joining society if you occasionally turn into a wolf and eat strangers alive. You should keep constant reminders in your personal space reminding yourself that you can't make it alone, thus creating a state of near-constant, anxious fear. Your bones will ache, your stomach will turn and your hair will turn gray just thinking about your were-bro finding another. When that happens, you'll know that this method has worked with flying colors.

In the case that finding a were-bro is out of the question (probably because you kept killing your were-bros) then this "doctor" would recommend the next best thing: family! And for those who might say, "wait a minute, whatever professional classification this hypothetical person uses, doesn't family normally come first?" Well, you could say that, but then you haven't met my father, and if you have, well, then you wouldn't be reading this book. You would end up in the bathtub, just like the rest of the monsters . . .

But let's say that family is an option and were-bros are not, then this author would say to call up any family willing to talk to you and plead your case. Is it embarrassing to move back in with the 'rents after years of being a werewolf? Sure. Did your lycanthropy drive you out into the real world of jobs and responsibilities and perpetual disappointment in the first place? Most likely. But you bought this book for a reason, and it's probably because you're all fucked up in the head and you needed my help, so how about you just go with me here, okay? Okay? Good. Great.

So you've moved in with your parents, or, in the case that you're that rich were-snob Barney Baxley who had his not-dank-at-all parents move in to *his* palatial estate, now what? First things first: you need to catch them up with your condition, if they don't already explicitly know yet; this talk will likely be awkward and polarizing, and all-too-familiar to the proud gay werewolf community. But as with the majority of parents, after the initial confrontation comes understanding, and then they'll be able to weave parental advice and values into your monstrous routines.

Now, if at this point you are living with your family and they are watching after you, I recommend you hand over this book to them. They're much more qualified to be reading the upcoming advice, and furthermore, their minds aren't clouded by the weight of becoming a wolfman once a fucking month. However, if your parents are werewolves themselves, then just keep reading, I suppose. After all, didn't Jesus say help thyself or something?

Okay, so now I should be talking to the parents of the were-afflicted, and to them, I will say that I understand how you feel. One time I found a baby in a box on the street, and for all I know, that baby could be a werewolf right now. In that regards, we are one and the same, and there's not a day goes by that I wish my baby-maybe-werewolf wasn't cursed with lycanthropy so I can stop questioning if I should have put a silver bullet in his soft, soft skull all those years ago.

So how do you first help your son/daughter with being a werewolf? I assume you've had the talk, and that you're taking it as best as you can, so hopefully your support system is established by this point. But right now, we're going to have to take a step back and remove emotion completely from the equation. While emotional availability might work for a were-bro, the same emotion is only going to hurt the werewolf more, and the judging eyes behind every caring statement will cement that hurt in their miniscule were-brain. No, what is instead needed is complete emotional absence in exchange for an abundance of practicality, which will help your were-child become the were-adult they've always wanted to be.

Of course, in the negation of an emotional response, you're allowing your distant, cold responses to be the first sign of acceptance. By taking a strictly pragmatic approach to this new era of the parent-child relationship, you are not necessarily condemning or impeding the behavior in any way, and that should be the focal point of any defense in future arguments. If anything, it's almost like the relationship between a police officer and an effective vigilante: by turning a blind eye, you're not explicitly condoning the behavior, but it's certainly behavior beyond your immediate concern.

Perhaps the next step to take is restriction, and there's no better way to do this than to use what's commonly known in the dog community as a "shock collar." First of all, you'll have to find one with pure silver chains, for the obvious reason of keeping your son/daughter's filthy werewolf paws off the collar and defeating the whole purpose of having one, despite knowing *you're trying so hard*. Second of all, you might want to buy an extra shock collar for yourself and your significant other for moral support; after all, if you do it, he/she will respect the collar and know that you put your money where I assume your mouth might be. And lastly, shock collars fucking hurt like hell. I know this from my days as a motivational speaker for dogs; those shock collars were the only thing that kept me from being killed by all of those dogs, even though I'm pretty sure I would have taken a few of those cute bastards to hell with me.

What follows is an important step as well, and that's the art of overbearance. Much like everyone else in the world, your son or daughter will have natural deep-seated issues with overbearance (or the lack thereof) from their childhood. After years of dealing with that, they likely will have daily moments where they're frozen with inescapable anxiety. The same issues can be applied to lycanthropes as well, and in doing the standard procedure of the overbearing parent, the werewolf in your life will likely find themselves in a such a state of restless frustration that even if they did leave the house, they'd be too anxious to kill anything at all. This can be achieved by questioning the werewolf's every movement, giving him/her numerous unnecessary gifts, and making unforeseen demands at inconvenient times. Remember: remain strong in your resolve, and if an argument begins to get emotional, shut down completely and leave the room without speaking.

And for parents who have a wealth of time at their disposal, you can always make the extra effort to help your lycanthropic child "cheat the moon." That's right, moon-cheating: A popular method of curbing typical aggressive werewolf behavior. This historically-sound approach is dependent on the environmental changes that can re-wire the internal clock of a werewolf. For some, moon-cheating consists of removing windows from the werewolf's living space, programming the wrong time on clocks, limiting access to digital devices, and slightly medicating the human alter-ego in order to extend their regulated sleeping time. For others, the process can go even further to ensure results: some people line aluminum foil inside of the walls of their child's room, install a controlled refrigeration unit in order to generate confusion during the seasonal changes, and even keep extra calendars with different dates to psychologically trick your child into a false understanding of the lunar cycles.

Yet the most crucial aspect for a family to accept a werewolf into their life is through transparency. Do not act like the vicious, wolfen side of your loved one is nonexistent; instead, speak openly about lycanthropy, and do so often. Understand what your child has become and integrate that element of their lifestyle into conversations, expectations, and even your daily routine. There's nothing that breaks up a family like a ravenous, terrifying wolfman in the room, so the more comfortable you all are with your horrifying new family dynamic, the easier it will be to reach that side of your child.

However, some werewolves don't really give a fuck and are pretty hardcore, so sometimes they join a pack of other werewolves and either set up a camp or squat in an abandoned building or something. To be frank, I don't know much about the living habits of werewolf packs; I used to assume that their lifestyle is a mix of biker gangs and standard mountain wolves, but since you can't drive a motorcycle up a mountain, I don't know what to think any more. I mean, maybe they live in the woodland commune, but I assume the human side would get pretty irritated by all the bullshit that comes with living in a forest, like no electricity and fighting to survive on a daily basis. Maybe they live in a motel? A motorhome? On a yacht, off the coast of Tunisia? No clue.

But what these wolf packs lack in clearly defined living situations, they make up for in attitude and aggression as they're more likely to embrace their wolven nature and the animalistic qualities that come with it. Essentially serving the purpose of lycanthropic yes-men, these werewolves have no qualms killing people at the wrong place at the wrong time, and will work as a group to secure their kills. As terrifying as that may be, it's also pretty badass, and if they ever read this book and decided to become a team of reckless yet witty mercenaries, I have a spec script called *The Were-pendables* that might catch their interest. Hell, if I got to make that movie, I wouldn't have to write this book, nor any self-help book, as everybody's lives would be improved by its existence.

In any case, these wolf packs may not be up to society's standards, and may be fueled by their overly emotional response mechanisms, but that doesn't mean they can't be helped. After all, by combining their supernatural powers with a strong impulse control, these wolf packs hold the highest chance of turning around public opinion on lycanthropes as a whole. And above all, these wolf packs also can turn their efforts towards positivity while retaining their pride for their manimalistic instincts.

When dealing with large amounts of lycanthropes in a single area, perhaps the best avenue that a wolf pack can take would be that of event planning and organization. Whether it be a lock-in event at a place with industrial steel doors, like an industrial steel factory for instance, or the time-honored tradition of werewolf orgies, wolf packs know exactly how best to tend to their needs as both human and wolfman, making guests both lycanthropic and normal tended to appropriately. Furthermore, having the extra man-wolf-power to organize and set up any event will lend to a less stressful environment that will surely lead to a quicker descent into the earthly pleasures the dark lord graciously allows us to consume. In organizing these get-togethers, there's a good chance that wolf packs will meet new, local werewolves that could potentially become more active in the pack.

However, for those who do go down this path, I cannot stress enough the importance of purchasing standard-issue Werewolf Insurance. As you know, werewolves can be catastrophically destructive and not even be aware of it. Irreparable scratch marks, hard-to-remove blood stains, quantities of shed fur and, in the case of were-orgies, spooky wolfman jism, are all things you don't want to be held liable for. Most insurance companies won't carry Werewolf Insurance (and if they don't, please feel free to send emails to your insurance company demanding they do so), but in case you're desperate for Werewolf Insurance, I offer it through my Monster Insurance company, Monster Shield, Inc.

"Now, wait a goddamn second," you're probably saying to yourself, "is it ethical to write a self-help book for monsters while also running your own Monster Insurance company?" And to that, I respond that I don't see the correlation between your points. If you're accusing me of writing this entire book as a way to draw out monsters into the public eye so that they destroy things and force people to buy my Monster Insurance, I think you should better check your sources. Furthermore, you should check yourself, especially before you wreck yourself.

However, organizing remote events pales in comparison to an even more ambitious option for packs of werewolves to become productive while boosting their self-esteem: sports. As stated before, your increased size, strength, and agility will automatically make you better than humans at sports. Any human that gets in your way will be deserving of whatever fate they encounter. There is documented evidence that one werewolf is all that it takes to bolster a basketball team; now imagine the results of a full court of werewolves. Sorry, LeBron James: werewolves play basketball now. Deal with it. And if your wolf pack is more inclined towards winter sports, this author is more than confident in saying that you and your fellow wolves will have a leg up in this year's Iditarod race.

Just think of the opportunities: werewolf boxing, werewolf BMX, even werewolf paintball. And don't even get me started about how a pack of trained werewolves could change the Olympic Games. Get your country back on top of their respective games and be the first werewolf to take home an Olympic medal in every single event, with the exception of water sports, as even werewolf can't legitimize doggy paddling.

Now, of course, there will be figurative hurdles to jump before you can jump over literal hurdles in the Olympics. In fact, there are probably firm rules in most sporting organization to keep animals (and by extension, werewolves) from participating in their events. You cannot let your were-self be discouraged. You must fight your way into the games by any means necessary, even if that includes going back to college and getting into law. Little does the political system of the US know that all-nighters are a werewolf's best friend, or that a pack of werewolves can slash, claw, and debate their way into congress to push through anti-werewolf discrimination laws to enforce your participation in professional sporting events.

However, that shouldn't be a werewolf's only goal while in office, as one day, I dream of someone else's grandchildren seeing our first were-president in the oval office. If we need a president to take action and ensure a safe and prosperous future for America, I want that president to be a werewolf. I don't care if it's a werewolf who isn't a naturally born American, or even if it's a woman: it just needs to be a president who turns into a demonic beast wolf at the sight of the full moon.

And as for settling the emotional impulses and psychological conditioning that go hand-in-hand with wolf packs, this author recommends a simple approach called "co-dependency." By denying the essential physical and emotional needs to your fellow were-brethren and ensuring you are the only one who can tend to these needs, your wolf pack will learn to respect you via complete desperation and the fear of abandonment. Whether it be threatening to leave them at even the slightest sense of subversion, or by going as literally as bloodletting your fellow wolves every night until they're weak and crippled, co-dependency is a sure-fire way to make sure loyalty is not only the best policy, but the only policy.

But this author would be real stupid if I happened to forget a whole subsection of the werewolf community: the full-time lycans. Untethered to the full-moon and abominations in the eyes of God, Satan, and every weird dude in between, full-time lycans are werewolves that show off their affliction 24/7. While they still retain the communication skills and thought processes of a human, their exterior still looks like a giant, upright wolf-person. They are subject to the same powers that regular werewolves carry without being able to turn back into their human visage. And, as expected, they've got some serious fucking problems, too.

Full-time lycans' mental issues run from delusions of grandeur to bipolar disorders to just the complications of being a wolf with a human brain. And while those kinds of solutions are often best in the hands of "real" "doctors," there's no "doctor" more "real" than the "doctor" writing this "book," which is real. So, much like in the cases of the other lycans, the name of the game is centering a full-time wolf-dude's emotions and grounding them into something positive. And much like my father used to say shortly before the law caught up with him, there's darkness within all of us, and it's how you use it that counts in this life.

For instance, if you're a full-time lycanthrope, you can use your curse proactively by registering as a service animal. With your wolf-like senses and your status as a monster (which leaves anti-slavery and labor laws in a delicate gray area), you can help the blind and handicapped be more active while also developing a tolerance for compassion and responsibility. And beyond that, you'll be earning respect from the humans who see you in action as a service werewolf. "Oh, what a nice, young werewolf," they'll probably say.

Another opportunity would be to use your wolf-man frame to your advantage by taking up the popular yet befuddling art of cosplay as the Egyptian god Anubis. Whether it be greeting duties at some weird religious theme park, or harassing tourists on the Hollywood strip, or maybe even appearing on television, you'll be the most authentic Anubis in the industry. Not only that, but you'll have a stunning were-resume down the line, and you might even be in line to win a Nickelodeon Kids' Choice Award for Best Animal Performer.

As for the deeper-seeded emotional baggage of full-time lycans, and werewolves in general, the secret cure to the weight brought on from monthly bouts of destruction and murder lies in compartmentalizing the truth. Who is to say you should feel guilty over mauling a stranger in a subway station? They might have been on their way to jump in front of a train anyways! Who is to that say the animals you slaughtered at the zoo weren't going to get sick and unleash some kind of devastating pox upon the world? The truth is what you make it, my friend, and by adjusting the truth with hypothetical scenarios, it's easy to live with a clean conscience.

At the end of the day, isn't that what we all want? Whether you are a man, a wolf-man, a full-time lycanthrope, or a robot programmed to feel depression, we all want to wake up after a night of being our worst selves with a clean conscience. And since any day that you're living and breathing is a good day, then you should be able to paint your past to look as bright and exciting as your future. So as long as you're using family interactions or nighttime activities to try your best to not kill people, you should be able to not only forgive yourself for your monstrous transgressions but also forget them altogether. After all, it's the human thing to do.

Chapter VI

The Other Drinking Problem

What do you give to someone who has it all? Now what do you give to someone who not only has it all, but can also fly, turn into animals, and fuck women while levitating? While some people may say that time or love or some other hippie bullshit is the key to happiness, this author is a realist, and when it comes to writing self-help for monsters, honesty is the best policy. And for someone who has it all (plus supernatural enhancements), the one thing that you can give them is the one thing they've probably wanted all along: normalcy.

If you think about it, there are absolutely reasonable and normal desires in the cold, lifeless heart of a vampire. Feeding off humans to satiate their eternal, ferocious bloodlust? Vamp's gotta eat. Killing their way to London in order to seduce the doppelganger of their ex-wife? Vamp's gotta love. Stealing an amulet with the blood of Christ in order to fulfill an apocalyptic prophecy and bring forth an era ruled by vampires? Vamp's gotta party.

Now, I know that when most people think of vampires, the first thing that comes to mind is the elegant, unorthodox lifestyles in which they inhabit. People think of imposing, enormous castles, perpetually surrounded by a thick fog, populated by myriad bats, wolves, and potentially large spiders. People think of sprawling silk capes, refined tastes in fashion, poetic self-presentation, and the courtesy of mutual respect between the hunter and hunted. Some people think these misunderstood creatures are driven to do monstrous deeds by a cruel fate, tragedy, and darkness (which, coincidentally, was also my father's legal defense) and believe vampires to be more deserving of our sympathy than our ire.

Other people find vampires to be something far more sinister altogether, seeing past their melodramatic visage to see the creatures from Hell that they arguably are. These people think of sharp fangs sinking into screaming women as their blood is drained from one vessel to another. These people think of animals with glowing eyes, moving around undetected among the living as they find their nightly prey. They see the indescribable beast that vampires turn into when dry of blood and desperate enough that they'll rip a newborn from the clutches of its mother. They mentally paint the picture of the monstrous side of vampires, which, while not entirely untrue, is at least exaggerated for an effect.

Meanwhile, some people see vampires in a much more modern light, showing them as one of the few creatures on earth who has adapted to every environment. These people think of the artist mentality of vampires, mingling among secret societies with other vampires and their familiars like creepy, billion-year-old Andy Warhols. Others see them as chameleons, able to blend into the shadows of any town or village with no regards to their looks or living situation, as long as there is an access to their food source. And then others see them as sexually-driven perverts, fucking and sucking away at their endless orgies while offering their own flesh to further desecrate the bodies of those around them.

However, as you may know, the reality of vampires is much simpler, and way less exciting and arousing than fiction might have you believe. At the end of the day, vampires are still people at heart, and if you want to see what vampires are really like, take a look at the weirdos who you see hanging around the 7/11 parking lot every night. In fact, the evolution of nightlife in this country, from cocaine discos to Denny's, has driven most vampires towards a domesticated living, where they simulate normalcy but without the fulfillment they so earnestly desire. Meanwhile, the vampires who remain in the country and even metropolitan areas have found their lives watered down as the digital age has robbed perversion of its intimacy, and finding victims has become much more of a task than ever before.

While vampires are often vain and mystical creatures by nature, the eccentricities of the vampire have become quite a burden over the years. There are countless vampires in the world who stay up all night, buying hundreds of products from late night infomercials as they deduce that this puts them ahead of their prey by giving them a better, affordable way of conveniently cooking eggs or compressing four workouts into a single machine. Then there are vampires who have found the grind of meeting people who want to fuck vampires a chore, often resorting to late night vampire-centric phone sex lines like *FangFone* or *VampStamp*. And then there are the many who turn into animals to stalk prey and wind up bagged and tagged at the animal shelter, who luckily have vampire protocols nowadays to get you home before sunrise.

Of course, this isn't even considering the vampires who still carry the ambition of conquering the world and bringing incomprehensible darkness into the world of man. However, their actions have become a series of frustrating events, considering most public record offices and religious associations close before nightfall, and reading legibly at night is difficult even for vampires. Furthermore, the aesthetics of doing an occult ritual in a brownstone as opposed to a castle, chamber, or dark chapel are plainly disappointing. If I was a dark lord who saw that I was summoned into a two-bedroom, one-bathroom, new-age loft in SoHo, I know I'd certainly reconsider taking over the world, that's for goddamn sure.

And don't even get me started on familiars, considering the quality of vampire assistance in the past few years has taken a dive compared to the golden days of Count Dracula and Renfield. Most familiars nowadays resort to working nine-to-five jobs in order to secure the freedom to help vampires in their off-time, but considering their commutes, personal responsibilities, and sleep schedule, familiars have really become the salt of the Earth. Familiars have been found sleep deprived, weak, confused, and malnourished. They don't have the same resolve as the days in which familiars were proud to eat insects and lure people of power into compromising positions for their vampire overlords. In fact, the only familiars among vampires that have been noticeably effective are those weird goth kids who listen to *The Lost Boys* soundtrack all day and don't wear shirts, and not even vampires want to be around them.

Even though there is an alluring aspect to still living by the old code of the vampire, I'm sure there are very few vampires who are satisfied with that existence anymore. If you're the kind of vampire that went out to actively buy this book, then I might be right to assume that you're taking the steps to become a conscientious, passably normal member of society, even despite your supernatural affliction. Fortunately, while contemporary society has left the way of the vampire in its dust, they're more than willing to accept vampires who want to be regular humans. Unfortunately, that does mean that we're going to have to rewire your priorities to think of others besides yourself, and that means compromise and sacrifice on your part to better yourself as both man and vampire.

Now, the first thing you're going to have to do on your path to normalcy is cut out the things that will be immediately off-putting to humans. This includes human sacrifice altars, obsessively lavish tributaries to your dead lovers from thousands of years ago, and any human-sized cages you may have laying around the house. Likewise, any large painting of yourself where the eyes seem to travel along with the guest is probably not going to work in your favor during parties and social gatherings. You can't have houseguests fear for their lives and your sanity if you want to be Johnny Vampire America, so you're better off finding self-storage or perhaps just buying another property where you can conduct your killing altogether.

However, while human society may be tough on your vampire aesthetics, we are also very fair. For instance, this author would never suggest that you rid yourself of your coffin, which is admittedly close enough to a bed that it could be seemingly kosher, especially in 2015 now that beds can even look like race cars and rocket ships. Likewise, any furniture or trophies that you've made from the skeletal remains of your victims should be just kitschy enough to be acceptable in modern society. You don't need to travel to another country to justify the reason for owning it like most awful white people. Furthermore, any ominous, large organs in your home should be fine as well, as there are Iron Butterfly cover bands from around the country who play their organs all the time without question or hassle.

I would like to take this opportunity to address a common misconception among both humans and vampires, and that is to formally apologize to any and all non-caucasian vampires who feel their cultural needs are underserved by my ramblings so far. While I mean not to offend the Blaculas, Blades, and myriad other ethnic vampires, I took upon this chapter as a colorblind writer, speaking to the needs of the vampire whole instead of skin by skin. However, I understand where the confusion might stem from, and I'm hoping that my advice will transcend the barriers of race so that vampires can sit together at the table of brotherhood, feeding from victims based on the content on their character. After all, blood is always red on the inside, and that's what counts at the end of the day since blood is what vampires drink.

Unfortunately, the world of the urban vampire has changed greatly over the years thanks to stupid fucking gentrification. The world of proud African American vampires shown in Wes Craven's groundbreaking 1995 documentary *Vampire in Brooklyn* is all but gone as property values rise and potential meals grow skinnier and frailer in appearance due to the influx of kale-eating hipsters. Even worse is how bad you *want* to kill these holier-than-thou miscreants, but they're literally not worth the trouble since a strictly Brooklynite diet will lead to protein deficiencies, which is not good for creatures whose sole source of fuel is blood.

On your journey to normalcy, you're also going to need to be more thoughtful of how others see your vampiric elements. For instance, before inviting guests over, make sure that you have enough time to clean up blood from the hard-to-get corners of the house. I would also consider installing some kind of an aqueduct system in your floors to help clean up and preserve the blood of your victims much more efficiently, especially if you invest in an effective floor wax that will leave staining to a minimum. Furthermore, you can always use the assorted items that your victims were carrying when they met their untimely deaths for nice gift bags after parties. This is not only the nice thing to do, but also follows the Native American tradition of using every part of your kill, so you'll be showing how cultured you are as well.

Another sacrifice you're going to have to make in attempt to be a normal, conscientious human is to cut out suburban behavior that, as a vampire, you might not have noticed may be problematic. After all, what might be considered standard operating procedure among the vampire community could be considered as genuinely maddening to humans unfamiliar with your kind. Perhaps the foremost of which would be the late night yardwork, consisting of sending your familiar to mow your lawn and powerwash your home at two a.m. on a weekly basis is likely not a great way to solidify your reputation as a neighbor. Likewise, you have to realize that your behavior is more transparent than you might think; your neighbors definitely know you weren't checking your tire pressure when you abruptly leave social gatherings and return literally doused in blood. And then there's just the examples of goofy vampire bullshit that you pull in your neighborhood, including scratching the neighbors windows at night or dragging screaming people into your home as people are getting up for work.

In general, an integration into normalcy and mankind starts at the community level, and if you can't reach out and become a part of your community, then you're never going to find the acceptance you so crave. While this means making the compromises listed above as well as generally not hunting those in your immediate vicinity, this also means reaching out to improve your dynamic with your neighbors as a whole. This could be doing something as small as buying thicker drapes to hide your terrifying activities from the neighborhood children or as personal as inviting your neighbors to your undead orgies. In any case, the consideration will be noticed, and soon, you'll be invited to all sorts of nighttime activities in the community.

Believe it or not, shaping the public's perception of you is not only a necessary measure in becoming normal, but it's also beneficial to your vampire lifestyle as well. Considering vampires have moved into the suburbs, vampire hunters have been sure to follow and will be taking notice of people's behavior. And while the right circumstances might lead them to take down a pedophile or adulterer to buy you some time, any apparently vampiric behavior will lead them right to your doorstep, and you certainly don't have the dangerous edge that you had back in your vaguely Eastern European days.

Of course, perhaps the biggest obstacle in your path to normalcy is the fact that you feed off living humans, which is something most, if not all, of your neighbors do not do. However, turning a blind eye to murder is not a new trait to the human race, and as long as you can find ways to not be graphic or explicit about your murders, no one has to lose sleep over the whole ordeal. And lucky for you, you have me on your side to help walk you through streamlining the process and making murder easy and convenient.

Now, according to the laws of the great United States of America, I've never been convicted of committing murder, a fact that not many citizens can admit. However, as described in my opening chapter, I've certainly killed people in the past, although my reasoning was sound: it was either self-defense, or they had it coming. But the one thing that anyone will tell you about me is that when I talk about my experiences with killing, and surprisingly there have been many, I don't speak with an ounce of regret or dissatisfaction in my actions. That's likely because I learned from the best, as my monster-hunting father instilled in me the basic tenets of the craft: make it quick, make it quiet and, at the end of the day, killing is killing, so leave your emotions at the door.

I've carried that knowledge through every endeavor that I've ever had, whether it was in my days as a traveling pit fighter in my teens, to my years of alleged fraud, to motivational speaking in a room full of riled-up dogs in a situation that was bound to get out of hand. While I don't have many tokens from my time with my father since most of it was bagged as crime scene evidence, I still pay tribute to him whenever I can, whether it's writing his teachings in a self-help book for monsters or writing his teachings in a self-help book for monsters. For full disclosure's sake, this book can't be considered exploiting my father's crimes, so it's not subject to wage garnishing "victim's families," if that's who you really are.

But as a vampire, you have plenty of ways to make your kills quick, quiet, and emotionless by keeping your feeding out of the neighborhood's eye. Of course, the most important aspect is the quiet part, and perhaps the easiest fix to that problem is to start any attack by instantly ripping out your prey's tongue (fact: dead people don't need tongues), thus taking care of the "crying for help" element fairly quickly. Then there's the "Thumber's Crack" method, where you can use your claw-like thumbnail to penetrate their larynx and silence any potential scream. If you're particular about the freshness of your meal, then you might want to research which vertebrae to snap that will allow you to drag them back to your home without protest.

The quick part is a bit trickier, considering draining the blood out of someone's neck isn't necessarily an instantaneous death. Sure, compared to cancer and Zelda's disease from *Pet Sematary*, human blood consumption is a quick death, but it doesn't hold a candle to execution-style shooting, snapped neck, or death-by-explosion. But in order to speed up the process, you can sling your victim over your shoulder, draining them of blood as it runs to their gravitationally disadvantaged brain.

Furthermore, a quick death for your victims will be important to your neighbors, since it will provide you with the aura of empathy that's not there when you decide to chase down and taunt your victims like a real jackass. You see, much like vampires, humans have their own problems to deal with, and they certainly don't need their lives punctuated by a prolonged, insulting death, so if you can stop fucking with your food, that'd be great. To that point, your neighbors will see that you consider your human victims to be on an equal level if you make their deaths impersonal, even if we both know how you really feel, you vain fuck.

Actually, it's fitting that vanity should arise right as we are about to cover keeping emotions out of your human-hunting in a very organic way that no one orchestrated whatsoever. Obviously, vampires have been synonymous with "superiority complex," and I suppose I can't blame them since they do hunt and kill human beings on a regular basis. Unfortunately, vanity can be a double-edged sword when it comes to kills, since your natural response to killing humans is joy whereas humanity might respond with with sadness and reluctance. However, there is a middle ground that not only plays to your vanity and their expectations, but also to you being the fucking boss: indifference. Having to drain the blood out of someone should be no big deal to you, and after it's done, you can move on with you life because it was totally whatever.

Vanity, in general, is a tough tightrope to walk considering it's a key trait of humanity, but too much of it can put you firmly in monster territory. And while that may work out if your long-term goal includes getting on reality shows and begging websites to show your nude pictures, it's abysmal if you truly want to ground yourself in normalcy. However, to tell a vampire to get rid of their vanity would be equal to castrating them, and that's a sacrifice you shouldn't be willing to make. However, you're going to need to balance vanity and humility very carefully, and that means looking in the mirror and taking a good look at who you are.

Actually, not a mirror; I forget that your kind can't be seen in mirrors. Can you see your reflection on a digital camera? Does the invisibility on apply to film stock and reflections? If you're a vampire and you have a digital camera, please take a picture of yourself and mail it to me. In fact, send me the digital camera, too. I need it for more, uh, vampire research. Yeah, that's right. Wait a second, why did I type "uh"? That makes me sound *extremely* guilty of lying. Oh well!

Anyways, one of the most vain elements of vampirism that you have to tone down is reminding everyone that you are immortal. For starters, you might want to stop starting sentences with, "Well, I am a vampire, and I am immortal," and you also might want to stop using phrases such as, "Machiavelli called; he wants his joke back!" Those are actually incredibly on-the-nose statements that will remind everyone that you're a vampire, and will get tiring to everyone. Likewise, you shouldn't go around showing everyone photographs of yourself from over a century ago looking exactly as you do now; not only is it creepy and not normal, but that photograph should definitely be preserved in a museum or something. Besides, just because you live forever doesn't mean you have to rub it in everyone's fucking face, okay?

Then, there's the smaller elements of vampire vanity that leak through your behavior and your rapport with the human race that should be changed. Perhaps one important trait to change is your compulsion to laugh when people inform you of their loved ones' deaths; even though you may find the fragility of the human body to be a laugh riot, humans generally will react negatively to that kind of behavior. Also, you might want to learn proper room-leaving etiquette so that the last thing people remember from your interactions isn't you rapidly floating backwards with your cape over your face, somehow slamming the door on your way out. Then there's the tendency to change into an animal as a party trick; while entertaining when your guests are drunk, it's a show of desperation and would be akin to a porn star coming over your house and whipping out their meaty dong next to the artichoke dip.

Of course, then there's the louder and colorful depictions of your vanity, of which there are likely many. Some of the more extravagant pieces of your fashion sensibilities should perhaps take a rest until they're back in vogue, including any gemstone walking canes, capes, and decorative red-tinted glasses, which would make vision harder even to vampires. Other things that might have to go the way of the dinosaur include large gates featuring your family's crest, statues of yourself posed in victory from a battle that took place centuries ago, and the hearse that your familiar drives you around in during the day. Meanwhile, you might be allowed to have kitsch on your side, so you may be able to keep your amulets, jewelry, and vanity plates that spell out K1NGVAMP, which is a triumph nonetheless.

In order to get closer to normalcy, you're also going to have to make some changes in how you handle your familiars, especially considering it's dangerously close to slavery and, if you haven't noticed, most humans have moved on from slavery, and the ones who haven't had at least the courtesy to call them "indentured servants" or live outside of America. This, of course, means that either you have to start creating work boundaries for your familiars, or, preferably, pay them to be your full-time assistants. These familiars live to serve you, and to treat them like anything less than an employee is going to not go over well with the rest of the community.

Likewise, you can also find positive uses for your familiars as well, including having them do your bidding in a constructive manner that will ultimately reflect better on you. For example, even though stepping into a church would set you ablaze where you stood, you could technically send your familiar in your place, which would make you a religious man in the eyes of your community. Furthermore, your familiar can stand in your stead for anything during the daytime, including doing favors for neighbors, recording live events you have to miss since they're in the sunlight, and even doing the majority of your shopping and errands. Hell, your familiar can even stand in for you for parties and events with your significant other, and know with certainty that he won't make a move on them as it would cost him everything he holds dear.

Now, in building a sense of normalcy with your human neighbors, there's going to be extra scrutiny towards the beginning in regards to your behavior because you're going to have more to prove. With this in mind, you have to be careful of your vices and behavior beyond the simple standards of maybe not committing murder in public. Among this also includes not being seen as a buffoon. This can be avoided by making sure that you don't drain too many alcoholics. During this cautious period, you need to make sure that you're not getting blood drunk, as alcoholic neighbors are almost always a goddamned headache in the long run, and are especially unpredictable if they're vampires.

As a vampire, you're also going to have to make yourself presentable to the world at large, and, unfortunately, traditional Transylvanian garb will make you look like the neighborhood weirdo. That doesn't mean you can't wear what you want to wear in the privacy of your own home, but a vampire such as yourself in all of your vanity should take a lesson from Jerry Dandrige's playbook and dress to impress. Furthermore, hair upkeep should be somewhat prioritized as well; unless you can make Rasputin-chic en vogue, you're going to have to shave and cut your hair to look like all the normal people on TV, or at the very least, like Bono.

For optimum normalcy, I would suggest that vampires present themselves in a fashion that would land them on the cover of *Deathquire Magazine*. That includes sharp suits, brawny haircuts, clean jaw lines, and the allure of mystery, all played against deathly-pale skin surrounding black, entrancing eyes. Not only will it make vampires even more inexplicably sexy, but it will present a sense of sensibility to your community, instilling you as their tastemaker. Of course, being a community tastemaker is a huge step to being accepted as one of their own; in Al Qaeda terms, it's like going from an outsider to the guy who tells Bin Laden what to wear in those videos where he takes responsibility for terrible things.

While I've never considered myself to be a Casanova, and I've never seen *Casablanca*, and I've never gone to a Mexican restaurant and ordered the *Casa Especial*, I do know that love (or at the very least, predatory sensuality) is a large motivation for vampires to find destiny in normalcy. Obviously, a life of vampirism is no place for a husband or bride, except for a vampire husband or bride, and it's certainly not a place for families. To many humans and monsters, family is the cornerstone of a normalcy in the United States, no matter what our divorce and infant mortality statistics might tell us. And while I don't have a family of my own and the thought of spawning my own children gives me physical pain, I have watched enough *Divorce Court* and Lifetime Original movies to know what kind of matriarch/patriarch/husband/wife a vampire should be.

For you men vampires, all of your decisions depend on who you're going to take as your wife, or for some vampires who don't conform to hetero-normative vampire condition, husband. Knowing vampires, you probably have several brides already who are naked all the time and eat babies, which is kind of not cool in general. In that case, you're going to have to decide what these women mean to you, since bigamy is only a facet of normalcy in Utah, and no vampire wants to go to Utah. Hell, their fucking basketball team is the Jazz! WHAT DOES JAZZ HAVE TO DO WITH SPORTS AND BEING GOOD AT SPORTS?! IT'S THE MOST CHAOTIC AND RANDOM OF ALL MUSICAL GENRES!

Back on the subject of your vampire brides, you have a few options to choose from, none of which are easy unless these women were just toys for you to play with, you sick misogynist pig. The first option is to declare your love for the bride you love the most, and either send your other brides on their own way or bury them alive (undead? Dead alive?) in stone coffins until the vampire they're meant to be with comes along and saves them. The second option is to make your vampire brides compete for your affection through a series of challenges and games, which you can televise yourself and provide as the monster alternative to other reality programs I won't mention here for legal reasons. The third is to file for vampire divorce on all three of them, which is a desperate move but at least one that is acceptable behavior in your neighbors' eyes.

Should you choose to stay with a vampire bride, the good news is that you can work together in your combined quest for normalcy since you'll be able to set up a check and balance system for each other's bullshit. Of course, you both will have to keep up appearances as the community's new vam-power couple, and that means working on your dialogue with one another and treating each other as equals. It's important that in the middle of Tad's annual Fourth of July barbeque that you refrain from hissing at one another like animals. You both will have to learn the art of passive aggression, just like every other couple in the neighborhood. Besides, with everything that happened with Tad's son over the past year, the last thing he needs is two vampires scratching at each other like dogs over a delicious bag of beef jerky.

Furthermore, vampire marriages are destined to last longer than monster-human marriages, and not just because both partners are immortal and will last on Earth longer than humans; the shared experience of vampirism will naturally bond a husband and wife. By treating your vampire bride or husband like an equal, you can show your community just how well you compliment one another. You can work together to take down prey in an orderly manner and you can even help protect one another from the sneakier monster hunters around town. The only downside is that, with a vampire bride, you'll be unable to have vampire children, as even the most powerful resurrection ceremony isn't able to get that barren womb working again.

As for all the single lady vampires, what's going on girl-*fang*? Oh Jesus, what just happened? Oh no. That was awful. How did I fuck that up so quickly? Okay, wait, let me start over.

As for all the single lady vampires, don't think I've forgotten about you one bit. I am just as dedicated to making sure that you get the same, if not better, advice as your male counterparts. Therefore, I'd highly suggest you check out our ninth chapter, which explicitly focuses on monster brides.

For vampires who decide on pursuing same-sex marriages in this day and age, congratulations! It's 2015, and the fact that there aren't more same sex vampire unions is a little bit disheartening. You're on the forefront of fundamental changes in the vampire community, and both humans and vampires should be proud at your bravery in pursuing this way of life. In fact, there's not much advice I can give you; if anything, you're much more prone to happiness and contentment than heterosexual vampire couples, so I'm surprised that you even bought this book, although I am still willing to take your money.

However, for vampires who want the whole nine yards of normalcy in their life, then the answer lies in seeking a human bride. Of course, this is not a new concept by any means; after all, ninety percent of fucking vampire novels are all about how a vampire wants to fuck some human girl but it's going to take three novels for it to happen because they're tormented or something. But there are advantages for a vampire in marrying a human that might be not be found elsewhere. Furthermore, if book sales are any indication, all many human women want to do is fuck vampires, whereas most vampire women seem just content putting their meals before their creepy sex impulses.

Of course, a marriage between a monster and a human, as opposed to a monster and a monster, normally is accepted well by their community, even despite reservations from the more conservative bigots in town. But for a lot of humans in these neighborhoods, a human in a relationship with a vampire will help "tame the beast" so to speak, and make you more of a fitting breed for society as a whole. That's not to say that you had nothing to do with getting closer to normalcy and the embrace of your surroundings, but a human bride will certainly make the transition more digestible to outsiders; in human terms, she's the bacon to your cheeseburger.

But it's not always going to be sunrises and sunsets with a human bride either; as with any marriage, there will be a fair share of trials and tribulations thanks to your respective culture clash. First of all, and most importantly, you're going to have to find a way to accommodate one another's eating habits, and this may mean eating "prepared" meals for the rest of your life. For vampires who had never had a "prepared" meal, it usually means opting out of the traditional

146

neck-drain technique and instead killing your victim before you feast upon them. Then you can prepare the blood as if it was a traditional meal or tomato soup. While not as fresh or as invigorating as the old way of eating, it will give you essential quality time with your bride that can be used for conversations, anecdotes, and other boring, arbitrary ways of developing relationships.

Then, there's the sex question. Yes, it's true that vampires have super sex. There you go. Have your bride take the same precautions she would in a destruction derby and you'll be A-OK.

Another big hurdle with having a human bride is in establishing a proper communication between one another, especially since neither of you come from the same backgrounds. You have to be upfront with your human-wife about your habits, the people who dedicate their lives to hunting you, as well as your turn-ons and turn-offs, each of which might not apply to her since she's not a vampire. Likewise, you've lived for so long that you probably don't even know the lingo of human women, what with their LOLs and their Tinders and their evil secret feminist websites dedicated to the downfall of the phallus. You're going to need to develop a shorthand with this woman if you ever expect her to love you back and have your children, so by learning her language (and, by extension, her body language), you can go from steady vampire boyfriend to *fang*-ancé. OH GOD, I DID IT AGAIN.

Now, one of the few things I was able to learn about relationships through my father's endless rhetoric about women being evil-incarnate and his need to bathe the soil of our earth in their blood was that sometimes, women can turn the tables on you by using what they know about you. Rest assured, this is fairly common in most relationships, and usually won't result in a stake in your heart. However, what it could lead to is some cold-hearted gender wars, most of which could have been resolved with a simple talk amongst adults but instead turns into a mental battle of extreme pettiness.

How so? Well, after a fight with a vampire bride, you don't have to worry about waking up and finding every door in the house lined with garlic aioli, which wouldn't be a walk in the park. Or perhaps you'll find that someone inconveniently left a wooden cross on top of your favorite pair of shoes, forcing you to wear one of your less favorite shoes instead. And then there's always the chance that she'll reset your clock so that you "accidentally" wake up at eight a.m. instead of eight p.m.

As for retaliation, all is fair in love and war, but whatever you do, DO NOT EAT HER. DO NOT EAT HER. DO NOT EAT HER. EATING YOUR WIFE IS NOT COOL, AND EVERYONE WILL KNOW IT. JUST GO HIDE HER BRA IN A TREE OR SOMETHING, AS LONG AS YOU DO NOT EAT HER.

But even beyond communication, compromises are the key to handling fights with a human bride. There have to be some ground rules as well considering that this woman is somewhat at your mercy since you're a creature of the night. The chief point would likely be "no hypnotism": while the chance to fuck with others now and again is too fun to pass up, messing with your wife via hypnotism is generally not cool and can be borderline rape-y, you sick misogynist pig. Probably also important is to not eat her family. We've all heard of sisters being werewolves, zombies eating our neighbors, but vampires draining our parents? Get the fuck out of here. And then there's generally treating her as only a vessel for your children, and if that's the case, you might as well install Sharia law up in your vampire crib.

Now, let's move on to the most important element of them all, and the guarantee to your spot as a normal, accepted member of the community, is becoming a family vamp. In a cruel twist of fate, vampires can still produce semen, or at least whatever the Devil's equivalent of semen is, and with a human host, they can have a half-vampire child. I swear to God that I knew this before *Twilight* was written, and frankly, they got it all wrong. In fact, if I was a member of the half-vampire community, I would make sure a decidedly grumpy letter made its way to Stephenie Meyer to let her know, "Sorry, lady. You fucked up. I'm a half vampire, and here's a letter with my opinion on it!"

I cannot stress enough just how important it is that you are educated and prepared before making the leap to have a child with your human bride. Luckily, the last part of this chapter of this book is all the preparation you need, and if anyone tries giving you another book about child rearing, burn it immediately, and then send them a link to buy my book and give it to you. Being a father is not going to be easy, and being a vampire makes it even tougher as it makes *everything* tougher. But it's definitely not some impossible feat, and with my know-how, you'll earn that "World's Best Vamp Dad" mug in no time.

The first thing you need to know about being a Vamp Dad is that you're going to have to be ready for a huge schedule change. Your half-vampire baby is primarily going to need blood to survive, and you don't want your child accidentally draining your wife's blood through her boobs, even though it would be a sight to see. No, Vamp Dad has to go out of his way to make sure there are blood bottles refrigerated at all times, and hopefully in reasonable distance from the child coffin where the child will rest. Of course, the first few years of raising the child will be a delicate balance between making sure your baby is safe and educated while making sure it doesn't kill other babies and feast on them, but with the power of improvisation, you should be able to handle everything nice and easy.

Also, one of the best early lessons to teach your child is how to turn into an animal. Otherwise, the little shit is going to be transforming all over the place, doing awful things to miserable people, and you're going to have to clean up a much more complicated mess than just feeding on nighttime joggers in the park. But once you've taught your child how to control their power and be responsible for their actions, then the only shit you'll have to clean up is the blood-filled shit in your child's diapers.

Then there's adolescence, and that's a where things can get a bit complicated considering the social politics that get involved between children and parents. I'm assuming the birds-and-bees talk is slightly different considering the non-existent moral standards of vampires, so make sure to be delicate and find ways to talk about blood orgies and not drain the life out of sexual partners in terms that preteens can understand. And then there's, of course, conditioning your kid to live at night; as a half vampire, sunlight won't exactly kill them, but it is certainly going to burn their skin something fierce, so a quick and steady introduction to night life could be exactly what they need.

Perhaps the most valuable lesson you can learn as a father is keeping restraint of your own powers in matters that concern your child. For instance, you just can't go around hypnotizing anyone trying to date your daughter and then convince them to commit suicide. Eventually, people are going to notice a pattern, and that might be the turning point where the community decides to burn down your house and decapitate your whole fucking family. Ditto goes for dealing with your child's bullies, since you can't just dangle them as you fly hundreds of feet in the air to intimidate them; in fact, it's those battles that your child must fight on their own to learn that they are a vampire, and they can fuck people up when they want to, as long as they know not to turn them into vampires themselves.

Then, we move on to the teenage years, and now, we're dealing with raging hormones, manipulative cognizance, and the need for rebellion against their parents, one of whom is a vampire. For these lessons, I would suggest you hand them this book, as I'm sure all they want to be seen as normal too. But there also needs to be a sense of relaxation and patience with your teenage vampire, since all sports that don't take place at night will be out of the question and they might consider pursuing a career in the arts. Of course, we both know how those artsy types may be, and instead of spending your nights spying on them and betraying their trust, let them get into some mischief. Hell, you can even help teach them to start murdering their meals on their own, which they will surely thank you for when they get to college.

All things considered, a half-vampire teenager might be a handful in their own right, considering how heightened their emotions will likely be as compared to the human experience, which I'm assuming you had before you were turned into a vampire. Your teenage child will likely face a fierce depression, probably because it's half-vampire. That same child will also feel intense anger and self-hatred, probably because it's half-vampire. In fact, that child might even feel blessed and happy all the time, probably because it's half-vampire.

Also, raising the child will not be entirely your sole endeavor, considering that you will always have this book by your side. Is the child out of your control? Hand over the book. Your wife trying to raise the child? Nope, the book already did it, sorry. From now on, this book is going to be that cool uncle that lets your child watch porn and listen to The Ramones, and one day, when your child is fully grown up, he'll pass this book on to your quarter-vampire grandchild, and they'll learn to worship my words as if I were a god. Actually, you know what? I am God, and because I said it, I believe it and you should, too.

In any case, the establishment of a vampire family unit as consisting of a vampire father, human mother, and hybrid child is a sure way to not only be accepted by the community, but also feeling fulfilled while doing so. Of course, being fulfilled might be a foreign concept to you since, at this point, you've been feeding an insatiable hunger for hundreds of years, but take my word for it, it's going to feel good and probably a bit confusing.At the end of the day, you'll have someone who looks up to you outside your familiar for the first time in years, and that should be a win for any monster, let alone one who pretends to be spooky all the time and drinks blood out of a wine glass.

At the end of the day, you still need to remember that you're still a vampire. As much as my words and, to a smaller extent, your actions have made you a better, less selfish (yet somehow more self-serving) being, you still are someone who has to kill people to live, and you'll be killing people more than ever now that you have a family to support. Despite the probably sadistic actions of your past, present, and likely future, it's all going to be worth it when you look into your child's eyes and see that darkness staring right back at you. That, my friend, is love, and that's something even Van Helsing can't eradicate, no matter how many sharp wooden stakes he has.

Chapter VII

Act Like a Lady, Think Like a Gill-Man

Despite holding the promise of the most terrifying death imaginable, the ocean can often be a beautiful place. It is largely a figure in many of our wildest dreams: flowing blue waves, cooling waters, and an entire ecosystem of creatures that live among us and yet will rarely meet humans face to face. In that way, the ocean is much like the shadows in that there's an inherent beauty in the nature and depth of each world, and yet, there's also an equal amount of horror. After all, no one books a deep sea diving trip after watching *Jaws*, *Deep Blue Sea,* or *Creature from the Black Lagoon.*

While they only have had limited on-screen depictions over the course of their existence, gill-men are among the most appreciated monsters on Earth, at least in comparison to vampires and wolfmen. In fact, because they're so limited to the ocean, gill-men could almost be considered the first "out" monster, one of which we're not incredibly fearful of due to their limited environment. Because of this, humans would most likely be comfortable with gill-man co-exist-ence. After all, there are legitimately scarier things in the ocean than gill-men, like giant fish with teeth, smaller fish with deadly stingers, and scariest of them all, dolphin rape gangs.

Hell, there's even things out at sea that are of human or-igin and *still* are scarier than most gill-men. Pirates are a rough sort nowadays, making up for the cowardly man-ba-bies who sit behind their computer stealing intellectual prop-erty. These actual pirates are carrying automatic weapons and carve body parts off people when they don't need them. Then there are just genuinely creepy assholes with yachts who like to use the "international waters" excuse to "legally" do things like watch people fight to the death, host Russian roulette tournaments, eat endangered species, or hunt other humans on the high sea like some fucked-up twenty-first-century Teddy Roosevelt.

Now my first exposure to gill-men as a whole was one most people can relate to: I was shooting the music video for my neo-new wave band, Dream Secrets' debut single, "The Flight of the Jellyfish," when one of our many unpaid interns happened to go missing. Immediately, I presumed that she had fallen victim to the briny deep, and that any evidence of her existence should be destroyed or, at the very least, altered significantly as to remove myself from liability. When the crew began to show significant concern for the missing intern, I briefly considered taking command of the ship, forcing everyone overboard and leaving them to die in the ocean while I began life anew in France, teaching dogs how to play new wave music.

However, it wasn't long before we heard her concerned screams, and despite my protests (we had a day to finish, and the lateness of the jellyfish already cost us an hour of daylight), we set off to find her. There wasn't really a land-mass in immediate sight, and the screaming didn't seem to be coming from the direction in which we came, but rather from what appeared to be a formation of large, protrusive rocks nearly a half mile away. And when we tracked her screams to a cavern nestled in these rocks, we were shocked to find her in the grips of something that was not human, yet not fish either.

Considering there were six of us and only one of the gill-men, we were eventually able to free the intern and return to shore, where I fired her for costing us a day of valuable film-ing with her bullshit. Yet the gill-man was not one to give her up without a fight, using its natural strength, sleek scaly exterior, and our legitimate lack of knowledge about its ex-istence to send us running for our lives. In fact, I'll never forget when it wrapped its webbed fingers around my skull, and I knew just from its basic grip that it could squash my brain as easily as a human could a head-sized peanut.

But in that gill-man's black, lifeless, animal eyes, this author detected a raw, emotional vulnerability, and even a bit of shame. Clearly, this gill-man went out of its way to kidnap this woman, and from the looks of its cavern, it likely had not been around a lady in a very long time. While, in our eyes, this gill-man had kidnapped our friend to presumably kill her and then eat her corpse or something, there was a better chance that he wanted to break the ice with her, and we were cockblocking this creature with our rescue attempt. It probably even felt bad about the kidnapping part; I'm sure if it was better at communicating, it would have come onto the set and at least tried drawing our intern away on her own recognizance.

So when I decided that I would lend my valuable time, talents and efforts to helping monsters fulfill their monster potential, this experience stood clearly out in my mind. After all, gill-men have a notoriously terrible track record with women, which one would assume is fueled by their human desire for lust and their animal instinct to reproduce. If gill-men put nookie at the top of their priority list, I would assume that they've got most of their life pretty much figured out, so we might as well figure out how to turn these lady killers into ladykillers.

To be completely honest, I don't know how you gill-men are going to read this book, since even if you do miraculously known how to speak English, you would have to do so in an environment where the book will not be completely submerged in water. In fact, I'm not even sure how you were able to even buy this book in the first place, since you can't just give Amazon.com a latitude and longitude and expect UPS to drive out on a speedboat like a cocaine dealer and tie my book to a buoy. And I don't think gill-men have currency, unless they have a ton of hoarded treasure from all the boats they've sank over the years.

I mean, it's probably best to assume that you have befriended a crusty old seaperson over the course of your life, and maybe they have bought the book for you and are communicating my lessons to you. If that's the case, I say, "Hello, crusty seaperson! Please write to me to let me know about the facts of gill-men, and how I can better understand gillmen communication for the audiobook version of this chapter. Should I just make whale sounds and hope for the best?"

Now, why exactly are you and your kind so terrible at meeting and making whoopie with human women (and I am talking to the gill-men now, not you, crusty old seaperson)? Well aside from the obvious language barrier and geographical issues, the most obvious reason would be that you are two different species, and to be honest, a majority of women don't date outside of their species. Despite a small percentage of the human population who do date interspecies, most of them do so for money in creepy, tourist-drawing live sex events in other countries, or do so in secret while indulging anyone who will listen on bestiality message boards. As for the women that gill-men are most often attracted to (read: huge tits, tiny waist, gleeful disposition), there is enough competition among humans that even considering dating outside of their species becomes a drama-inducing chore unto itself.

Unfortunately, that's not even factoring in the cultural division between human women and gill-men, starting with the basic connective tissue between one another. Gill-men have never had the experience of going to school (unless it's a school of fish, get it?), don't watch television or movies, and generally have lived on uncharted islands or systems of caverns for the better part of their lives. They've never driven a car or had a job. Likewise, gill-men have little to no social media presence, since you cannot have a computer out in the middle of the ocean with no power source, and there is no cell phone service since there are also no cell towers in the middle of the ocean. Most human women have not spent their entire life at sea, and will probably find your experiences examining rocks and kidnapping people not very accessible or interesting.

Then there are the inherent difficulties that your kind brings to the relationship that many human women have instilled in them through repetitive cultural hypnosis and a worrisome internal clock. After all, when most women move in with their boyfriend, they hope to have a living situation that doesn't include rock floors and a fear of the high tide. Then, there's the question of marriage: even though you look like and have the mannerisms of a man, can a woman legally marry a gill-man anywhere in the world? And when it comes to family, you will likely have to resort to adoption, which is like getting tickets to arena football because the NFL season pass didn't pan out for you.

And if you're a homosexual gill-man, then I say good for you, because finding a suitor will probably be easier and less of a fucking headache. Pretty much find any man that likes to fuck fish, find some common ground in your particular needs and voila! Next stop: St. Croix honeymoon!

But, for monsters like yourself, not all is lost as there is a silver lining to your situation as a gill-man. First of all, you do have the appeal of being an exotic man, coming from an indeterminable foreign origin and having an air of mystery and appeal of a distant culture. Second of all, some women might find the whole "looking like a fish" thing sexy to a degree; after all, many people in the body modification community have healthy, active sex lives, and many women still find Mickey Rourke sexy for some inconceivable reason. You also exude this aura of danger; you carry the natural instinct to kill on your sleeve, and women will find that not only attractive, but comforting in knowing that you'll protect them. Don't even get me started on the Furry community, to which gill-men would help to fill the needs of a very underserved portion of that subculture.

So with those elements in your corner, how do we expand upon that hope and turn it into a reality? Well, to get in the right mindset, you're going to need what I call "the three Cs": Confidence, patienCe, and tempered expeCtations. That's right, these three qualities each have the letter "C" in them, and once you've learned them, mastered them, and made them your bitch, then finding a respectful woman with a brilliant mind, versatile sense of humor, and proportionate cans will be as simple as 1-2-C. And I will tell you what my father used to tell me, "The easiest way to get a woman is not to be who you are, but who you want to be, and then God will do the rest."

Of course, the first thing you need is confidence, and you might think that you have confidence as evidenced by your record of kidnappings. This author thinks you might be confusing confidence with determined self-approval much akin to dictators and corrupt police officers. You see, while you have the motivation to go on out there and lurk around a foxy lady, the complete and total absence of swagger indicates that your intentions are less romantic and likely closer to complete fucking maniac territory. Furthermore, a real sense of confidence will distract your dates and they will focus on your communication skills instead of your monstrous exterior or the possibility of you strangling/drowning them.

One way to instill confidence in yourself is to talk to yourself using a different language, as after all, you are only as personable to others as you are to yourself. For instance, when you're approaching an attractive woman, don't say to yourself, "PRETTY LADY. MUST TAKE." Instead, say to yourself, "That beautiful woman looks like a strong, interesting individual, and is probably an outgoing woman who appreciates a night in just watching Netflix. I'm sure that she'd be perfect for a gill-man, and vice versa." That way, not only are you centering your mentality firmly in the realm of positive self-esteem and confidence, but you're painting a reasonable picture of your potential date in case anything goes wrong.

Another way to gain confidence in yourself is to become more comfortable within your scales. In fact, you should realize that you and your potential partner have many of the same basic needs: you both breathe oxygen, eat food in order to survive, and also probably need to poo because of that food you ate. And speaking of pooing, you also should realize that no one on Earth is perfect; in fact, over twenty percent of the world's entire population is afflicted with being caucasian. With those kind of numbers, you should feel more than fine to look at your own green scales and fish-man hybrid body and feel like a diamond in the rough rather than the runt of the litter.

The next step in making yourself into a ladies' gill-man is by becoming well-versed in the art of patience, especially since relationships that begin at the beach rarely result in cave-sex an hour later. In your courtship, you're going to have to realize that you're going to have to take things slowly, and you can use that waiting time to your advantage. Besides, I assume the crusty seaperson who is reading this to you probably takes a while to boat out to your location, and I'm sure your friendship didn't have the luxury of igniting at a local pottery class with a "Oh, how do you do, Mr. Ocean Person?"

The best way to learn patience is to look at your past relationships, and looking how rushing things didn't work out. For instance, every time you've kidnapped a woman instead of trying to break the ice, did she ever give you her number afterwards? Was the woman screaming the entire time, indicating that she's not only uncomfortable but also completely afraid of you? Well that whole rigamarole and the issues that follow could have been easily avoided had you simply gotten the woman's number first, gone on a series of dates to get to know each other better, and then become physically and romantically intimate. Believe it or not, that stuff rarely happens overnight, and when it does, it certainly doesn't happen to gill-men, so the more time you're willing to wait for your partner, the better chance you have at fulfilling that sad, cold-blooded heart of yours.

However, considering the ADHD world that humans live in nowadays, you can use your newfound patience and your organic living situation to your advantage. For instance, let's say you hit it off with a woman, and she gives you a number; you can now use a little thing called "the waiting game." Firstly, you do not text her, because you do not have a phone. Then, you do not call her either, because you do not have a phone. You don't reach out to her on an instant messenger service, social media, or even Snapchat, because you do not have a phone. When she finally comes back to the beach/ocean, she'll be so fired up from your complete and total negligence that she'll want your body more than she wants her parents to get back together.

Then there's the final concept that has the letter C in it, which is tempering expeCtations; in short, lowering your standards so that you can find a woman who loves and cares for you, and isn't slowly accepting that her death is imminent. Remember this: you're a fucking boss, and as a fucking boss, your shit is nothing to fuck with nor is your fuck to be shit upon or around. But you're also a gill-man, and on a scale from one to ten, even the sexiest gill-man is going to be a mere six, and that's if you are the Joseph Gordon-Levitt of monsters. So with that in mind, you can't keep fishing for a megalodon if all you've got is a fairly up-to-code crab trawler, and those are terms I hope you understand since you're part fish.

When looking for a potential mate, this author recommends that you start exploring your options more carefully while realizing that the more supermodel-looking types either have a "loving," convenient boyfriend or will only be wasting the time you now value so much. So it's important that you keep an eye out for anything that would indicate a potential partner who is more in line with your unique look, whether it be missing limbs, a form of blindness, bulbous tumors, red hair, a terrible fashion sense, a few extra hundred pounds, or burn scars along sixty percent of their body or more. That's not saying that there is anything wrong with those qualities at all; in fact, beauty is in the eye of the beholder, and they may be absolutely beautiful as they are. But in this case, the beholder's eye is a half-man, half-fish creature with a homicidal temperament, so you have to can't be aiming for a Heidi Klum when there's a perfectly good Heidi Montag acting much more desperately on the same beach.

You also are going to have to temper your expectations for the relationship as well; after all, the dating game is a tricky one, and it's even trickier when you're a gill-man whose existence may defy the entire known universe of any potential mate. In your opinion, what do you think is going to happen when you bring your date to your place for the first time, which is, for lack of a better term, a dark, murky cave? Or what do you think will happen when you take her out to a seafood restaurant and you incidentally see a neighboring table eating relatives of your lifelong underwater friends? Relationships are a tricky tightrope to walk, and the balance can be lost at the slightest shift, so realizing that neither you nor she will be able to craft the perfect relationship will make dealing with the hard times much easier.

Now that you are ready to jump into the dating scene once again, let's briefly talk about the environmental factors that come into the dating game. Of course, geographical location is a big part of any relationship, as anyone who has been in a long distance relationship can tell you. Whether you reside near a tourist trap or are in straight-up *Cast Away* territory, you're going to need to know what works for and against you when it comes to your location and the women who may frequent it. After all, even once they've had Black Lagoon, that doesn't necessarily mean they won't go back . . . lagoon . . . you get the picture.

Speaking of, while most humans are familiar with the Black Lagoon, that doesn't mean that you won't have a chance at other lagoons around the world, especially if you're a bachelor gill-man trying to live the fast-paced, high-risk life of a single monster. Of course, there have been many sightings of era-appropriate sexiness at the Blue Lagoon, even though it's been awhile since a solid accredited babe sighting has explicitly happened there. Let us also not to forget the Red Lagoon, the Yellow Lagoon, the Purple Lagoon (located off of Prince's private island), the Brown Lagoon, the Aqua Green Lagoon and the Butterscotch Lagoon, each of which has their regular frequenters but often becomes a fishstick party with the amount of desperate gill-men showing up every weekend.

So how do we find you the best place to find a lovely, loving lover willing to give a good gill-man a fighting chance?

Obviously the Lagoons of varied colors will certainly yield disappointing results, if any results at all, and popular vacation spots will only lead to a long distance relationship that cannot last because you do not have a phone.

Perhaps the best spot for your dating needs would be a seaside town with as many residents as it has tourists, especially if the area is low-income and would keep the richer, more travel-friendly folk out of the area. These areas can normally be spotted thanks to the quality of nearby beach houses, as well as the regularity of large boats and yachts as opposed to sailboats or smaller speedboats, and the odds of you finding a relatively normal-looking girl are more likely to appreciate your exotic brand of interspecies sexuality will be much better than, say, at Club Med or in Rio de Janeiro. Besides, these areas will also work wonderfully when it eventually becomes time to take your relationship onto dry land for good, but that's for a different section of this chapter entirely.

Another factor to consider before we go forward is your competition, which is all the more reason for you to take "the three Cs" seriously. Obviously, you have competition from other gill-men if you're searching for love outside of your comfort zone, but as long as they haven't bought my book, you will at least have an edge on those fucks. Then, when you're going home with a woman who isn't screaming and kicking while slung over your shoulder, you can make sure to namedrop my book and tell them where someone bought it for you. However, gill-men won't be the only competition you have out there for stealing babes at the beach, and for your human competition, you need to know how to exploit their weaknesses to make yourself seem more desirable, as well as send them running home with a bathing suit filled with their own shit.

The most serious competition you'll find out there for seaside romance is a category of human being we call "the bro." These hyper-aggressive, outwardly masculine types are driven by testosterone and are constantly on the prowl for women who are dumb and shallow enough for them. Luckily, if these women are dumb enough to give these jack-holes the time of day, they should be dumb enough to give a human fish a chance as well, which means—if given the opportunity—you could potentially steal these dames from a handsy, excuse-laden "bro." However, to do that, you're going to have to shame "the bro," which could be tricky since "bros" often travel in packs, like a pack of hungry wolves with paws full of rohypnol and Hawaiian shirts.

The best way to eliminate "the bros" from the competition is to show them up at their own game, and that is to out-masculine them. Since "bros" are often more likely to engage in competition, they're also likely to underestimate you, which means you can challenge them to an arm-wrestling competition (see: *The Fly*) or a game of beach football (see: *Point Break*) with results almost unanimously ending in your favor. And should the "bros" turn physical against you after you've robbed them of their potential booty bounty, remember: you're a gill-man, and you can rip each of them in half like a phone book made of meat. In fact, a standard beat down of their crew should not only give them a fair warning but show your gal that you're pretty badass.

Then, the second most likely type of human competition you will find on the seashore are the surfers, who put their prowl for ladies second to their search for thrills. These humans are usually laid back and physically fit, but have traded in delusional macho-man bullshit for obnoxious stoner philosophy, which makes their moves harder to predict. The surfers are likely the most versatile threat that you have in the world of romance, considering they can be as equally attractive to the punk rock surfer girl as they can be to the innocent Christian girls.

While there's always the temptation to knock them off their board at sea and use your strength to snap their legs like twigs, that approach may actually work in their favor, as a potential mate is much more likely to find their determination to get back on the board more attractive in the long run. Rather, your best approach to do away with the surfer-types is to merely ignore them, as they're bound to go away sooner or later as long as you're able to keep your potential mate distracted and focused elsewhere. And if that doesn't work, you can always prey upon their natural curiosity to send them on a wild goose chase for drugs while you whisk away your date to an actual location of beauty, like a phosphorescent cave system, to seal the deal.

Then, there's the most annoying breed of your competition: the sensitive type. While they're not as common around beach areas, they certainly do find their way there from time to time with an acoustic guitar in hand, laying in wait for the next bonfire to show off their piss-poor excuse for lyrical poetry. While these men lack the physical appeal of their "bro" or surfer counterpart, they play music and can write generic, heartstring-pulling music that can work just as effectively on potential mates. And they are also experts in the art of patience, and can steal away a woman from your clutches gradually rather than take the aggressively immediate path.

For these men, the solution is actually one that you might be relieved to hear: just be a ruthless, unabashed bully. That's right: break their guitar and throw it in the fire, challenge their physical status, and pants them if they dare to go into the ocean. By establishing yourself as king of the beach, other beachgoers—including your date—will find the humiliation of the sensitive type to be hilarious, and you will only look awesome by comparison. If the sensitive type decides to step up and prove himself as a man, one punch caught in your webbed grasp can turn into a mush of irreparably mangled fingers, and then you won't have to worry about them playing guitar at your beach ever again.

Then, there are the wildcards: the rugged seabound hero, the cheating husband on vacation, the single dad who uses his son to lure women into assured death. But these particular types of human suitors are so rare that their potential to ruin your love life is negligible. Besides, should they ever appear and start encroaching on your territory, keep in mind you're a fucking gill-man so you can just chase them off and threaten them with your nightmarish visage. After all, there are always other fish in the sea for those humans, while you are literally a fish in the sea and need all the help you can get.

Now that you're aware of your surroundings and your competition, the next move is the all important first move. When it comes to women, a bad first impression could always become your last impression, so it is vital that you come out of the gate strongly. And since you're a hulking mass of scales and muscles who arguably has the anatomy to communicate with human women, you're going to need a tried-and-true game plan. Luckily, if there's anything this author is good at, it's convincing people to do things that they probably shouldn't do and how to get away with doing those things without repercussions.

Of course, the best approach to winning over a potential date would be to break the ice with a conversation, so if there's any way that you can learn English (or, realistically, Spanish and Chinese), you can start from there. While it's true that you may lack the common ground in one another's cultures, you are both at sea at the same time, so why not talk about your immediate environment? Not only will it give you credibility as a "local," but it will prove that you're educated and adapted to your surroundings, which will look even more impressive to your potential mate. But more importantly, it will give you a chance to listen to her speak, and for a creature who has adapted to survive the terrain of the ocean, rolling with the punches should be as easy as pie, even though you likely don't know what pie is.

In fact, you probably don't know any of these references I've made so far. If your crusty seaperson is still reading this to you, please instruct them to go back to the text and explain everything that hasn't made sense so far. And if you're the crusty seaperson reading this, please chastise your gill-man friend for not speaking up earlier and wasting all of our fucking time.

Now, the best conversation icebreakers in your situation can range from the overt, such as "Nice weather we're having today"; to the inconspicuous, such as, "Hey, have you heard about all those kidnappings in this area lately?"; to the smarmy, such as, "I ought to throw you back in the ocean because you're one hell of a catch." Once the conversation has started, you should take the time to listen to her, but don't be afraid to lead in the conversation, especially if the subject matter turns to weird things that have existed for centuries in the ocean. And also don't be afraid to get flirtatious, especially if you can make allusions to how frequently you can sink down below, because that will make them think you're good at cunnilingus even though you are a fish person. Also, don't be shy about talking about your monsterdom; in fact, women might be more comfortable hearing about your past as a monster than you talking about your exes or your parents.

Another way to make sure you make a good impression is to manipulate your surroundings so as to naturally lean your first meeting into your favor. For example, by leaving pearls and crystals along the beach side, you can create a natural interest in these things among your desired women. Then you can you break the ice with a story about these crystals, and then lead these women to a place where they can find more of them, thus making you seem like a fucking environmental genius. Or you could always beach a porpoise, sea turtle, or orca whale, which will gain their sympathy and attention as you "miraculously" show up and bring them back to sea, making you seem like a hero *and* an animal lover, which are bonus points with the opposite sex. Or if there is a beautiful woman on a boat, you can always sink the boat and drown her potential lover in the ensuing chaos, which will allow you to rescue her and bring her to your place while she "overcomes her grief." The mix between the "gratitude" for saving her life and her *Beauty and the Beast* complex will turn the odds in your favor, probably.

If you'd like to make a more extravagant first impression, you could always put on a show for your potential mate and win over her affections via flair and your natural physique. Of course, one option is to put on a one-man show, using the natural appeal that dolphins so often take advantage of to jump out of the water and do fancy tricks, which will turn any potential mate's trip to the sea into a surrogate SeaWorld trip but without all that discouraging animal abuse. Another option is to dig up some of that treasure you're probably guarding and hiring a full-on stunt team to put on a water show, complete with jet skis, a ring of fire, exploding barrels, and fireworks, which will not only make you seem like a rich, eccentric entrepreneur, but might also convince women that you're a seasoned stuntman in a costume, which will likely buy you more time among those not used to interspecies dating.

Now, once you've made a first impression, you're going to have to play cultural catch-up in order to groom this developing romance for a full-fledged relationship. Luckily, you can have your crusty seaperson buy you a tablet with a waterproof cover as well as a fuel-powered generator so you can charge it; getting fuel should be easy considering how many boats you can sink from which you can pilfer the gasoline. So once you've gotten the tablet and purchased the ebook version of *The I in Evil*, you can start setting up your public persona via the power of the Internet. While you can use search engines to find out more about human life and educate yourself on how your personal needs can be adapted for landlocked life, you can establish yourself and connect with your potential mate on the only platform that matters in the twenty-first century: social media.

Of course, the first thing to do is to set up your Facebook profile so that you can "fairly" "represent" yourself on the Internet in a way that lets people know that it's 2015 and if a gill-man wants to connect and network with humans, then goddamnit, he's going to do it. As for your mate, it's important that you appear to have a lot of friends, as popularity is always going to make you seem more attractive; this author suggests that outside of arbitrarily trying to friend anyone who is suggested to you, friending monster sympathizer groups and old mariner's clubs is the best way to up your friend count. From there, it's all about painting a picture about how you want to be seen, whether it's a cool dude in touch with ocean life or the tortured artist who is finally coming out of the dark after a rough upbringing. In any case, your mate will judge you very carefully on your movements on Facebook, so don't go around liking pictures and statuses willy nilly.

Then there is Twitter, which is a much more public social media platform, and ultimately more important to how your mate will perceive you. Usernames such as "@black-lagoonbuddy," "@gillsforreals," and "@therealgiill-man" will confirm that you are really who you say you are, and that aside from being a monster, you have a sense of humor about yourself. From there, taking pictures of yourself, your whereabouts, and your meals will help to not only show your mate that you're not skimping around with a girl on the side, but that you trust anyone to look into your life intimately, which will do wonders for your sense of trust. In terms of popularity, you will likely become an Internet sensation just from the fact that you'd be the first verified monster on Twitter and you'll bring in followers who inherently (and understandably) thought you were a parody account.

And should your relationship go sour or if you realize that you courted the wrong woman, the Internet may help you out so you don't have to resort to kidnapping and murder again. Social media applications like Tinder will help you find other people with black hearts and monstrous dispositions who have trouble normally meeting people. It may seem like an inane and morally reprehensible sense of social darwinism, but Tinder will help bring those interested in an interspecies relationship directly to you. This will significantly cut down on your efforts of finding a mate. Alternatively, dating sites such as *OKSatan* and *GillPeopleMeet* will help you find other monsters to date in case you have closed the book on finding a human bride.

Since you're entering the dating world for the first time, you should also look into readying yourself for on-land life as well as transporting yourself. Don't be ashamed if you have to buy an astronaut suit and fill it with water or if you're forced to carry around a man-purse filled with bottled water all day. While looks and perception will always matter to a degree on a date, your potential partners should be willing to accept these stipulations if they are literally a matter of life and death.

Now that you've broken the ice and nurtured a relationship into first date territory, the question is no longer "what should I do?," since you've obviously gotten that part under control; the question is now "what should I *not* do?" After all, you've established a solid connection with your counterpart and home plate is just around the corner, and as long as you don't fuck this up, you should be in the clear. Unfortunately, there are opportunities to fuck this up *everywhere*, so it's better to know what could potentially go wrong and prevent it than to walk in completely blind.

The first rule of the first date is no more showboating; it's important to keep the real you on display rather than going around trying to challenge complete strangers to arm wrestling competitions or jumping around in water fountains. Establish an intimate shorthand between you and your mate by being honest and, if possible, kind. Make sure she knows you're serious and that this romantic rendezvous won't be just another notch in your scaly, wet belt. In fact, you shouldn't be afraid of being a monster if a unpleasant situation occurs; in the case of a rude waiter or a catcaller, don't be afraid to excuse yourself from your date's presence and rip their jaw off their hinges with a ungodly swipe of your claw.

Another thing to avoid on the first date is anxiety; after all, your date is under the same amount of pressure as you, and if she's not sweating it, neither should you. Besides, the oils that seep out from a sweating, nervous gill-man smell unbearably potent, so much so that anxious gill-men might want to go somewhere near a beach-side shower in case of emergency. But if you're able to remember "the three Cs" that got you where you are and realize that the hard part is already over, then your natural instincts should take over. And don't get wound up over a faux pas or misstep either. Accidents will happen, and to screech into the sky in futility over an accident on a date just shows an unattractive weakness in your character, and if that's the case, you might as well cut your fish-cock off and sell it off to Red Lobster.

The one thing you have to keep in mind is that there are plenty of things women *won't* wear on their sleeves either, and those factors could impact your date either way. For instance, women are highly suggestive to the words and insights of their friends, who will undoubtedly snoop all over your social media page and make their own assumptions about you as a suitor. It's very important that you win over your potential mate's friends, but since you're a genuine freak of nature, a sit-down conversation to clear the air and let yourself be known might be out of the question.

So perhaps you should do what you do best: find these friends and break their doors down, scare them into submitting to your demands, and force them to rescind any negative statements they might have said about you. By letting them know they're never safe and that human laws don't apply to you, you're guaranteeing yourself a future of fear-driven goodwill for yourself and your relationship.

Another thing a woman might not be entirely open about is how you stack up against her ex, and that's a whole different ball game. The good news is that their ex is almost undoubtedly a human, which will make your experiences together unique and rarely comparable to her previous relationships. The bad news is that her ex could have easily had the same levels of confidence, patience, and tempered expectations as you have. The smallest sign of similarities between you two could plant the seed of doubt that will grow in your relationship until its vines strangle you both.

The best, and possibly only, way to counteract this dynamic is to be completely open about your past relationships as well, even if it means lying about every experience you've ever had in your life. By doing so, you will inject that same fear into your significant other, and she will likely return the favor by squashing her own emotional anchors. Furthermore, this openness will earn you more of her trust, which is essential considering she probably doesn't know how you were created or what a future with you would even look like.

Now, let's move on to the big question at hand: how do you approach the question of sex? Well . . . I don't know. Frankly, I'd assume that since you're part fish, you're likely accustomed to external breeding, which would mean you'd have foreplay with your human mate and then just release your seed everywhere and patiently await her to do her thing. But you're also part human, so there's also the chance that underneath those scales is a wet, crustacean set of genitals. And also, considering your sharp teeth and claws, I'm not sure how well anything other sex acts are going to play into the equation. But then again, I've never seen gill-men reproduce, so I'm going to let you figure that out, and if you keep kidnapping these ladies, I'm sure you can do *something* in that department, you creep.

After date one (and presumably, nasty sex fuck time), it's time to think about where to go from there as well as the eventualities of your long-term relationship. Obviously, moving back to your place isn't really possible; the cave you're living in can barely fit you and the assorted skeletons you so ominously leave around, and I'm pretty sure U-Haul doesn't have a wealth of seafaring helicopters either. So after a few more dates, you might want to turn your attention to a life on land, and what that might mean for you as a monster.

Obviously, life on land is scary for any monster, but for gill-men, it could be even more scary considering the constant threat of dehydration or being sold into the world of exotic black-market seafood. But with all of your cards on the table, it's certainly manageable; in fact, chances are you can walk through Times Square on any given day and find some weirdos who are scarier and more desperate than a human-sized fish person in a water-filled astronaut suit. With your other half by your side, you should be able to have the same confidence and patience in adapting to life on land as you did to the dating world.

Of course, perhaps the first step is to take all that treasure and rare minerals you've been protecting and finally cashing them in. With your new riches, you can skip the house-haggling and apartment-searching that most couples go through, and go straight into building a home that will suit both of your needs. While you can provide her with a living space that reminds her of home and provides her a first-class standard of living, you can also cater to your living needs. You can install a pool system that goes through every room of the house with mold-proof tiles so as to not make your future a financial nightmare. By custom-making your home to be both practical and eccentric, you're not only winning over the in-laws and the neighbors, but you're prioritizing your relationship, which can be an issue in such a hustle-and-bustle world we live in today.

However, as with any relationship, you will always have to condition yourself to be ready for the worst, and as a monster, hopefully you're intimately familiar with the worst. Of course, there will always be rejection, which I must implore that you don't immediately respond by breaking necks or kidnapping or eating eyeballs out of their sockets. If a woman doesn't want to date a gill-man, your best bet is to move on and try again another time, unless she starts shacking up with another gill-man in which case, all bets are off.

Then there's always the chance for divorce, which I'm sure will no doubt be complicated by the fact that you're a gill-man. Custody hearings (if it comes to that) and division of assets will usually go in the favor of the person who isn't a monster, though considering how much money you likely reaped from your treasure, you can hire a team of divorce attorney all-stars to tear at your ex-wife's credibility from the inside out. It would depend on how amicable your split was, as well as if you had gone off and fish-fucked another woman, you sick misogynist pig.

Lastly, there is one last issue you would have to worry about: death. While heartbreak is a familiar part of a gill-man's life, the natural death of a spouse following a life of love could be devastating; especially considering you'll be living with that on your mind for at least a few more centuries. It's important not to let that built-up love go to waste and to consider what your wife would want for you: I'm sure she wouldn't want you to walk into a Joe's Crab Shack and slit your throat at the counter. I'm sure she wouldn't want you preying on people in the streets every night until your eventual suicide-by-cop. She would want you to be happy, even if that means moving on to a new woman or going back to your cave to wallow in your own sadness.

"Why would you ever help me find love if all it's going to lead to is endless depression and emotional devastation?" you may ask. Well, at the end of the day, you bought this book for self-help because you needed to rebuild your life for the better. And for gill-men, love is life, like it or not, and therefore, if I can steer you towards a life of love, then you will learn to love life and the love within your life. Because if you can't love life, how can you learn to love love in a life without love?

Exactly.

Chapter VIII

Second Chances

In today's society, men are what they make of themselves, and what they make of themselves depends on whatever obsession consumes them. Some men choose to focus their lives on cars: building cars, racing cars, or even just saving up for the car of their dreams can be enough to make the grind of a laborious day job bearable. Some men choose to focus their lives on their work: by becoming the best at what they do, they become very proud of their work as well as the results and rewards that follow. Some men choose to focus their lives on their family: by saving their money and rejecting the vices that so often take control of our impulses, these men spend their time paying tribute to the family that raised them while passing along those lessons to their own progeny.

But somewhere in between those men are the men who focus their lives on the advancement of knowledge: in their search to solve the universe's many unknowns, they are willing to create and destroy at a moment's notice, all the while keeping in mind the answers their work may behold. Often times, it's this focus on knowledge that helps forge the path of a mad scientist, many of whom are blind to the world around them by their need to discover the secrets of life and existence. Sometimes, that means obsessively building and innovating new technology that can do everything from open portals to new worlds, or even destroy the old world with the mere push of a button. Other times, the madmen create new life from scratch, whether it be from a subservient robot or a brain-dead corpse who somehow walks again.

In any case, the world of mad science wears many masks, and is rationally not far from many of the scientific experiments being conducted around the world today, only without the burden of ethics and righteousness weighing down upon the scientists themselves. In fact, mad scientists are like the punk rockers of the science world; they don't give a fuck about what you think, they march to their own beat, and they don't care what mess they create as long as it benefits the craft. But above else, mad scientists love to play God, whether it's to just have a taste of God's power or to mock the Almighty with illogical and potentially evil expansions of his/her creations.

Now, this writer has had his fair share of unethical practices in the past; in fact, one might say my entire life has been built around defying ethics. I could talk endlessly about the independently-run orphanage I ran in Munich in my early twenties that conveniently happened to burn down when I was on the verge of bankruptcy. I could talk endlessly about the Internet identity protection program I created shortly before Y2K that I may have used to sell information to credit lending houses when I was on the verge of bankruptcy. I could talk about the self-help book for monsters that I'm writing which I can always sell to monster hunting mercenaries in case I fall onto the verge of bankruptcy again. But at the end of the day, I've always had the smarts to know my limits, and I never tried to play God in order to continue these unethical practices until they dragged me down to Hell with them.

But this author understands why one would want to play God, and in a way, this book allows me to do so in some ways. After all, the power to influence and manipulate men is a power very few have outside of the most influential and rich in the world. Of course, who wouldn't want to have endless power at their fingertips in order to bring the world closer to their preferred vision? Hell, the need to play God has even been proven to shape history: had the Nazis not spent so much time investigating the occult, who knows if they would have been able to obtain the power of the atom before America could during World War II? Where mad scientists and normal control freaks differ is the ambition to play God: while normal people are satiated with some kind of definitive end result, there is no quantifying the power of God for mad scientists, which makes their endeavors a perpetual search for more. Trying to contain and deconstruct the human soul? Not enough. Trying to find the limits of our universe and break through those barriers? Not enough. Disproving the finality of death in order to create an entirely new race of human entities altogether? Not *nearly* enough.

In any "playing God" scenario, there cannot be an action without a consequence, and when you're dealing with life, existence, and eternal knowledge, you know that the cosmic blowback is going to be massive. As one might presume, God must really not like being mocked or fucked around with, and knowing God, the bizarre sadistic punishments he lays upon his own worshipers become almost a non-issue when compared to the karmic smackdown he's going to lay on his opponents. God is way too petty to be insulted without at least watching you fall too. While you might be able to put up a good fight, he will rob you of everything you've ever loved, including your work and your life.

Then there's the issue of your discoveries themselves: most of these people and forces were not asking to be found, and to be brought into our world could incite their worst behavior. While most mad scientists, such as yourself, are particularly known for your sense of apathy towards others, these discoveries are willing to come after you directly and will do just about anything to hurt you for disturbing them.

Knowing exactly how mad scientists operate, you are much more inclined to unleash these beasts and their lust for blood onto our world as long as it buys you time, you fucking asshole. Whether you're obsessed with the search for God-like status on Earth, or with your betterment of mankind via vast new scientific intelligence, such ambition and its consequences must certainly leave a hole in your heart, which is likely the reason you are reading this book today. As you may have been told by your colleagues Igor and/or Fritz, there is nothing wrong with asking for help in a time of need, especially from someone whose brilliance rivals yours in every single capacity. But in order for me to help you, we must understand what it's going to take to help you and how to find an emotional satisfaction within your redemption.

Now let's start off by talking about how you've gotten here, and what you can tell other scientists in the future in order to keep them from suffering the same restless fate as a result of their mistakes. After all, the first step to redemption is to take responsibility for your actions, no matter how great your intentions were. In order to take that responsibility and use it in a practical way, we must discuss exactly what you did and how we can prevent it from happening in the future.

If you're a mad scientist who has been looking for the secrets of the human soul, you have likely gotten into your current situation by giving life to a man-made creature who was likely not too happy about your horror and anguish regarding its existence. I can't blame you too much; after all, there's only so much a parent and/or God could do to rear a child-like creature to be a functioning, intelligent version of its old self. But you also need to not be a crybaby just because your experiment didn't work out the way you wanted it to, and rather than giving the world a fucking orphan with the powers of the Hulk, you should maybe grow some balls and do the right thing. While you're at it, you might as well give the rest of the scientific community a heads-up.

Now, if you're a mad scientist and you're dead-set on constructing a man-made creature, you have to make sure that you are prepared to do so and that you're willing to rid yourself of the doubt that plagues many new parents. With that in mind, it's important to dress your laboratory to look like a child's bedroom before the experiment itself, as a calm, welcoming environment will do wonders to soothe and distract the terrified monster on your slab. From there, you have to make sure that you have the proper tools and teachers necessary to help your newly alive creation understand its situation and develop its brain to a more emotionally steady state. And also, you need to make sure that you are communicating with your monster directly in measured doses, as all the caretakers and tutors in the world can't properly replicate the familial bond between father and son.

If you're a mad scientist who tried to erase the line between life and death, chances are that you've probably found an "effective" method of re-animating the dead. You also probably found out that the re-animated are very persistent in trying to escape your clutches and eat your brains. While the concept of eternal life is a . . . fascinating . . . idea, it is much more complicated and terrifying in practice. I can't blame you for treating your warped creation as a "back to the chalkboard" situation by throwing your undead out into the world like it was your wastebasket. But as I'm sure anyone who has been attacked and turned into one of the undead could tell you, perhaps you could have disposed of your work in a more permanent fashion instead of risking the entire world's population. And yes, it does matter even to those living in a castle atop a treacherous mountain, you fucking jerk; you can't keep your drawbridge up forever!

Now, as a real quick aside, if this book is being read in a world that exists after the undead have taken over and humans are being farmed as a food source for the new world order, I'd like to say that whoever first created the undead wasn't a fucking jerk but was really a brilliant person. Also, as brilliant as they are, I am equally brilliant, and I would have no problem working as a bloodhound to sniff out pockets of a human resistance in exchange for sparing my life. And I've never tasted brain before, but I'm sure it's delicious from what I've seen in *Temple of Doom* and I would be more than willing to try under the circumstances.

But if you're a mad scientist and you're in the midst of trying to properly revive the undead, then the best advice one can give you is that practice makes perfect. Invest in buying a lot of weapons before you conduct any experiments, and make sure any and all potential test subjects are locked down tightly while wearing a muzzle. This way, should any of the undead come back and decide to eat people, you can quickly and safely send them back to Hell where they belong. However, as with any scientist, there's no reason to call it quits after one failure; try and try again, and eventually, you'll find one undead subject who might act relatively normal. You might not be able to do much about the brain-centric diet, but they'll at least be eating it off of a plate with a fork and knife, like a well-mannered individual.

Now, if you're a mad scientist who decided it was somehow a great idea to start exploring doorways to other dimensions and, to no one's surprise, it didn't work out great, I'm inclined to say that you shouldn't have done that in the first place. I mean, holy shit, what is wrong with you? What? Was black magic not cutting it for you? Not enough to just fuck with the spiritual planes that already exist? Are you fucking kidding me? Do you even know what you brought back? We're fucked! We're all fucked and it's your fault!

And if you're a mad scientist who is thinking about exploring other dimensions, DIDN'T YOU JUST READ THE OTHER PARAGRAPH? DON'T DO IT! NOTHING GOOD CAN COME OF IT! IT WILL LEAD TO THE DEATH OF US ALL, YOU FUCKING MORON! DESTROY YOUR LIFE'S WORK AND KILL YOURSELF, FOR THE SAKE OF OUR UNIVERSE!

In any case, whether you've been exploring this mortal coil or, god forbid, tampering with worlds that you have no business investigating, the art of mad science will naturally take a toll on your humanity. Essentially the cost of doing business with God and the Devil is losing pieces of yourself, whether it's the ability to love others or simply to empathize with those in pain and suffering. Much like all of those exorcists who have to murder children to keep demons from walking among us, it takes a cold, numb hand to do the work that the rest of the humanity cannot. But there is no person who does not feel that loss in every moment of their being, and if the purchase of this book is the first step to reclaiming your humanity, I applaud you for making the right choice.

Now, the first step to recovering what is left of your soul is to retain whatever sense of hope you have left. It is important that you have something to focus on during the darkest hours of what is to come. I'm not talking about *A New Hope*, or *Hope Floats,* or even *Hope & Glory*; I'm talking about standard-edition bronze-and-brass hope, which will serve as the bedrock for your self-improvement. After all, people commit the most despicable crimes imaginable on a daily basis only with the hope that someone, whether it's God or next of kin or future generations, will forgive and understand them. So with hope on your mind, you don't have to look at self-help as the end of an era where you did a lot of terrible things to a lot of good people and unleashed an unspeakable evil unto the world, but rather a new beginning in which you can learn from the mistakes of the past.

To be honest, you probably will be reminded of the mistakes of your past every day, and there's pretty much no getting around that. You probably will be looking down from your castletop, gazing at the destroyed homes in neighboring villages and the spiteful townsfolk who are depositing their dead at your doorstep, and you'll have to ask yourself if it was all worth it. A weaker man might say no before sobbing incessantly and throwing their hands into an open fireplace, but you're no weak man. You look at those bodies and that destruction and you realize it was necessary, because now you're trying to be a better person and fuck everyone else who is trying to make you feel bad.

In fact, by addressing the carnage that you have directly caused via your experiments and creations, you are incidentally on the second step in your redemption by taking responsibility for your actions. Obviously, responsibility is an afterthought in the world of a mad scientist, considering the mentality of "do now, justify later" so commonly fuels your work and subsequent discoveries. But once the blood starts to flow, and eventually it will, you have to take responsibility for what you created and for what it did. Yet by accepting the responsibility for your poor parenting skills, you do not have to admit that your scientific experiments were anything short of brilliant and groundbreaking.

Hell, you can even take responsibility for your monster's actions and not feel shame or regret, but rather pride. After all, even the unparalleled destruction of life and home is still *unparalleled*. By creating something that is the absolute best at a very specific thing, whether it's killing people or knocking down schoolhouses in a single blow, you nonetheless broke the mold, guaranteeing that your work will never be forgotten. Of course, you can still feel bad because it was unleashed upon your fellow man. You likely didn't buy this book if you were throwing up confetti at the prospect of your monster stepping on children's heads like grapes under concrete. But that doesn't mean you should not insist that the world give credit where credit is due, even if the results were unintentional.

Speaking of those unintentional results, the next step towards your redemption comes in the form of acceptance; particularly, accepting the gravity of your situation and the possible effects if the results are not amended properly. While the repercussions of your actions may bounce off of you because "shit happens," the fact is that you've angered a lot of people both philosophically and personally with your experiments, and if you don't start thinking of rectification, they're probably going to come after you. While your imposing residence may make it difficult for them to come for you, you might be underestimating the suicidal determination of those whose friends and family experienced terrible deaths at the hands of your surrogate child.

And then there are the repercussions on a very personal level: what does your creation feel about what you've done, and how you've reacted so far? Chances are that you haven't reached out to your man-made creature to support him/her/it in their time of need, and you probably haven't even shown up to prevent their potential destruction. If the creature has returned to personally threaten you and your family, did you attempt to counter that discord with love and care? These creatures need a father figure in their lives, now more than ever, and for you to keep denying them the right to a fair life is almost as criminal as setting a furious monster on an unsuspecting populace. That's still illegal, right?

Now, I would assume you've long since guessed where this conversation was heading, and allow me to make it clear: if it is redemption you seek, you will need to step up as the father of your creation. There's almost no outcome that will end in your redemption if the lingering darkness of child abandonment weighs on your shoulders, and you need to take advantage of this second chance while the opportunity remains. It's the only way to guarantee that the monster will not rampage again without your direct supervision, and it's the only fair outcome for your monstrous creation, who could clearly use the endless knowledge and wisdom that you could bestow.

If reconnecting with your creation is a dealbreaker, then the only self-help advice I have for you is to kill yourself, you dumb son-of-a-bitch. With a scorned creature determined to kill your whole family, you might as well do yourself a favor and make a quick introduction with a grave plot since there will be no one who will miss you. And while you're shamefully dictating your will to whatever poor sack of shit is stuck with your worthless lightning machines and wheely-turnies, make sure you will this book to your creation so that someone of value can read my words and learn from them.

But if you're choosing to do the right thing and make good for all of your countless fuck-ups, then let's talk about how you can reconnect with your creation. If it hasn't yet returned to your castle to kill you and/or your entire family, then you're going to have to track it down, which shouldn't be too difficult considering it's a giant, insane monster who causes people to run in fear upon first sight. But once you find it, you should speak with it man-to-creation with not just a respectful vernacular, but an apologetic tone. List your myriad mistakes to it to show that you're as vulnerable emotionally as you are physically. By stripping away the presumptions the monster had of you as an uncaring absentee father, the monster will at least be somewhat shocked and caught off-guard, which may be just enough for it to trust you and return back to your abode.

Once they return to your castle, it's important to make sure that you have physical proof that you want to reconcile with your creature, whether it be giving it your room for the night instead of ushering it to a dungeon, or offering it a delicious "Welcome Back" cake covered with blood-infused chocolate. Of course, earning back your creature's trust is going to be a costly, time-consuming process, and will likely drive you mad because it will probably keep you from being scientifically productive. But being a father is going to keep you away from work on plenty of occasions for plenty of reasons, and it's important that you get used to it now instead of when your creature is about to impale you on a massive antennae.

Earning your monster's trust can come in many ways, shapes, and forms, and it's never necessarily a predictable endeavor either. Sometimes, building trust could be as trivial as sitting together for every meal or teaching your monster about the very basics of chemistry so that you have some-thing outside of consciousness to bond over. Other times, it can be very demanding and challenging, such as potentially building a second monster for which your creature can call its bride. Sometimes, it's something that you *aren't* doing, like feeding your monster heavy sedatives or building es-cape protocols around your castle, which would help estab-lish your dynamic of trust as a two-way street.

Following the building of trust between father-man and son-monster, the next step is to prove to your creature that you not only care *for* them, but care *about* them. By reach-ing out to them to talk about their emotions, you can provide these man-made creatures with an outlet that they have only otherwise found through their fists, feet, and teeth. Furthermore, by starting up a shorthand with your creation, you will find someone that you can bounce your ideas off, which will help you get an outsider's perspective on any and all future experiments and make your creation feel more valuable. When your monster trusts you unconditionally, then it will not look at you as just its God, but also as a member of its family, and it may actually feel whatever the closest thing monsters have for love towards you.

Either that or it will kill you; that seems to be the status quo for whenever a monster loves something. Maybe you should attempt to be a little more blunt with your communication to your monster to make sure it doesn't kill you. After all, you have invented machines that have defied God and physics alike, so I'm sure you can whip up a screen-printed T-shirt that says "I am not trying to kill you. I am your father." That message seems clear enough that even a big, undead dummy could get the picture.

Now, the last thing you need to do in order to reconnect with that fucking mound of flesh and occasionally hair is to accept it into your heart as if it was your own son, especially since it will likely be the closest thing to a son you'll ever have. To do that, you should do what any loving parent does for their children: remind everyone around you that you love your child. In the same tactic that secretly closeted Republican congressmen and Mets fans have used so dearly for years, by repeating the same thing over and over incessantly and obviously, you're guaranteed to make people believe you and never once question your authenticity.

How do you show your love for your new monster-son and let it know it's a part of you now, whether it likes it or not? Easy: buy a bunch of customized T-shirts, coffee mugs, hats, basketball jerseys, rings, and wristwatches with images of your son's hideous face, just to remind it and every living thing in your life that your monster is your new priority and you love it very much. Likewise, you should change all of the passwords to your accounts, whether it be for your bank accounts or your home security system, to the name and birthdate of your monster, as it will always remind you of how great you are as a parent. Lastly, and this should be a no-brainer, is that you should get a tattoo of your creation's name on your body somewhere, preferably on your neck or your lower back, where people will see it the most.

Do these measures seem intense and extreme to you? They should, but if redemption is what you are seeking, this is only the beginning of a rigorous and exhausting parenting process, which has to be bold and incredibly obvious if you're going to gain any traction. After all, you're not raising little Victor Frankenstein Jr.; you're raising a nameless creature who preferred being dead as opposed to being alive. But by the time you're done with all this insane bullshit, you'll be the one reaping the rewards; after all, what greater redemption and solace is there than receiving a "World's Greatest Scientist" mug from the thing you birthed in a lightning storm?

So what are the essentials of being a father figure, especially one that has the tools and resources that you have? Well, for starters, you're going to have to act as a source of guidance for your monster so that it learns that your word is law, and also that the law is law. Once the grace period is up for your monster to trust you, you should immediately start conditioning it as your son using your newly crafted goodwill to push your monster in the right direction. Thankfully, you have everything it takes to get that guidance through its thick skull, and as per your nature, you should not use anything sparingly.

For instance, for your monster to learn to take direction, you should awaken it every day to the sound of blaring emergency sirens and a gallery of blinking lights, forcing it to follow big red arrows on the floor to escape the cacophony. However, rather than getting furious at you, it will be met at the end of the path by a welcoming breakfast table, with eggs and pancakes and maybe even some bacon made of human flesh for your special little monster. After several dozen weeks of these exercises, your monster will not even need ear-piercing noises and confusing strobe effects to get to the breakfast table, and your instructions will be trusted from then on out.

However, the big test will be in public. After all, it's easy to get to the breakfast table when there's all these lights and sounds to get you there. Once you feel comfortable going outside with your monster, you can start assigning it simple tasks, such as buying batteries on its own accord in exchange for treats, such as large quantities of alcohol. Even though your monster has the brain of a four-year-old, it certainly has a body built to drink a whole lot, and the sudden wave of happiness that alcohol will bring to its monster body will train it faster than you can say, "fostering a booze dependency." And once it knows about its reward and the fact that it is helping out its father, the monster will actually look forward to behaving in public, and you'll reap the benefit of seeing your dumb monster smiling in public without people running it off with a fucking pitchfork.

The next essential quality of being a father to your monster is to be able to accommodate their many needs, which is actually going to benefit you because it'll make you more productive than ever. However, instead of building your wacky fucking machines for your own dastardly purposes, you'll actually be building new inventions to help your monster-son in their time of need. Comparatively, it would be like buying a regular child medicine or buying a pre-teen girl a training bra, but instead, you have the power of God at your hands just to make your sick kid well or to zap some fully-formed breasts onto your daughter with the hit of a button.

One example is that, with the exception of select man-made creatures, most of these creations are dummies, and in lieu of a formal education, you can always build a machine that will neurologically transmit an entire text-book into their brain. Therefore, not only do you have the inspiration to build something new and groundbreaking, but it will save you hours upon hours of homeschooling that you can instead spend cooking or taking a shower or something. It's relatively painless for your creation, whose monstrous hide can take hundreds of thousands of volts multiple times without batting an eye, which you should also be proud of.

Furthermore, you can make sure that every step of your dumb creature's development phase is accommodated through your scientific expertise and seemingly unlimited funding. When your monster finally comes of driving age, you can build it a monster-proof car that will fit your creation's massive frame while helping it read road signs and not kill pedestrians; God can only imagine the wrath of a man-made creature with road rage. Furthermore, when your monster comes up to you and discusses the birds and the bees, you can invent a pill or treatment that will bring your creation's sex life back from the dead, considering your monster's cock has already been stricken with rigor mortis and hasn't had the proper rejuvenation yet. Besides, any father in the world would be proud to give their son a firm erection; wouldn't you?

Another essential quality to being a father is making sure to defend your child against even the smallest transgressions, and in turn, learning when to hold 'em, fold 'em, walk away, and especially when to run. By teaching your child when to defend themselves and when to step away and let you take care of the bad guys, you're teaching them the value of restraint and discipline, which is something you obviously never learned yourself considering you live in a castle and build evil gadgets for a living.

If you'll indulge me, I would like to tell you a personal story where learning the balance between action and inaction paid off in a valuable way. When I was a child, inadvertently helping my father in his monster-hunting trip, there was one night where one of the monsters my father found, who I believe was a were-lady, turned out to be an undercover cop. After my father eradicated the evil within her in a motel room tub, there was a knock at the door: it was the police, and the room was surrounded.

In a panic, my father handed me a loaded six-shooter revolver, a gun so heavy that my childlike arms and hands could barely carry it. My father told me to aim it at the door, and that anyone who came in would not be the police, but was instead pure evil. But once the police kicked down the door, I knew that they were not evil, and that they were human; suddenly, I threw the gun aside and ran screaming out of the motel room. It wasn't long before they left with my father in cuffs, bringing his monster-hunting campaign—and later on, his life—to an end.

But had I fired that gun at those police officers, there's a good chance I wouldn't be writing to you right now, helping you get over whatever problem it was that you had again.

I would either be in jail (or, best case scenario, freshly out of juvenile hall) or, even worse, I'd be dead, shot down in a blaze of glory and giving at least one police officer the most harrowing session of paperwork they would have in their entire career. Luckily, I knew that inaction was smarter than action in that situation, and I thank my father for showing me that in the most backwards, accidental way possible.

So how do you teach these valuable lessons to your monster-son without having to put them in the line of police gunfire? Perhaps the best way to do this is to roleplay with your monster and simulate conversations with possible trigger subjects. By doing this, not only will your surrogate child refrain from ripping apart its bullies at the slightest provocation, but the exercise will give you the peace of mind to rest easy when your monster eventually leaves the house on its own.

Now, the best method is to associate the most basic questions regarding any sensitive subjects with a peaceful resolution, as those are the ones that will come up largely during small talk with curious parties. These subjects, which could include the location/existence of your creation's mother, what religion the monster associates with, the monster's skin inflection and accent, or the monster's likely virginity, should be treated with the utmost care and respect. A surefire way to drive the point home is to have the monster ask you the very same question. This way, it will learn about its father while learning from your reaction to not get angry or upset at the mere asking of the questions.

Meanwhile, you can also simulate conversations with your monster-son where violence may be the best answer, including threatening statements, monster hate speech, and street solicitations for charities that supposedly require your credit card number for some vague reason. By clearly differentiating the inflections and intention between, "Hey, are you a monster?" and "Fuck you, you Frankenstein-looking childkiller," your monster will learn that violence is not only a last resort measure, but also one that clearly will be provoked in a very specific way. That way, in case you're at home building a machine that will allow mice to travel through time and you get a phone call from your lawyer, you will know that the issue was undoubtedly provoked and justified. In any situation, however, you should always outfit your monster with a portable camera and a T-shirt that says "I am recording everything," since monsters don't normally get the benefit of the doubt.

So, you've properly raised your creation, you've learned the skills that come with being a single father, and you've invented plenty of helpful machines along the way, giving you the out-and-out redemption and mental peace that you deserve. Now what?

Well, obviously, you have to prioritize your happiness, even if pursuing mad science is out of the question, and this is assuming you never broke the dimensional barriers between worlds and doomed mankind to a death by surreal, undefinable entities. Obviously, you like inventing things from your time before becoming a father, so why not continue doing that? Perhaps over time you will find ways to even retrofit your old inventions to be benign instead of outwardly malicious; that way, you can start selling them on your own accord and not directly cause harm anymore.

The quickest way to post-fatherhood happiness is to find companionship as soon as possible. By not being alone, you definitely won't want to kill yourself as often, and you will also be able to communicate with someone even if they don't know how to speak back to you. If you create them in the confines of your own lab, you'll appease the control freak in you by molding these companions to your liking. After all, what good is a self-help book if you don't take the initiative to literally help yourself?

Now, I know what you may be thinking: "Hey Ken, if I am a super genius who can build anything I want, why do I even need your self-help book? Why don't I print a self-help book with my own advice and read that instead?"

While you bring up a valid point, I'd like to remind you that you have already purchased *The I in Evil*, and there's not a single machine in your entire imagination that will be able to get your money back. And since that's true, go for it: print your own fucking self-help book and suck your own dick until you die. I don't care, but you probably won't learn anything, and anything your artificial intelligence comes up with will probably be more applicable to a computer than yourself. What are you going to do when your self-help book tells you to swallow a bunch of microchips or install Windows Vista in your brain? THAT'S WHAT I FUCKING THOUGHT.

Of course, the first companion that comes to mind would be a wife, which would likely need to be a cybernetic organism equipped with fully functioning artificial intelligence. While *The Terminator*, *Ex Machina*, *Westworld,* and to an extent, *Weird Science* have taught us about the dangers of playing around with machinery and technology we don't understand, none of the scientists in those movies had previously had to deal with a Frankenstein monster, and therefore preparing for betrayal or an escape would be a contingency well planned for. Furthermore, you can screenprint multiple T-shirts for your robot wife that outright say, "I am a robot. Please do not have sex with me. Please turn me off," and have her wear one for every day of the week, which should do the trick.

If it's at all simpler, you can always program your love companion to be a standard issue fuckbot 4000, which will fulfill your primal instincts of sexual satisfaction while eliminating all the boring shit like conversations and emotions. By completely leaving out all attraction outside of the fuckbot 4000's basic physical visage, not only are you decreasing the chance of rebellion but you also create enough distance to pride yourself on the robotics side of things alone. After all, if you can't be proud of the groundbreaking scientific work in building an advanced fuckbot 4000, then what can you be proud of?

But if you decide to opt out of building yourself a wife, an absolutely gangbusters way to construct your own happiness is to build yourself a robotic pet, and I'm talking something much more impressive than those blocky Japanese robot dogs. I'm talking body-accurate 3D printing, state-of-the-arts hydraulics system, refurbished animal teeth, and a fully functional intestinal track that will guarantee the most authentic pet experience possible, whether it be a dog, cat, ferret, snake, or even hedgehog. And thanks to the nearly-impossible number of videos featuring these animals on the Internet, you can perfectly code an animal to be as authentic and realistic as possible, but without the heartbreaking shelf-life that comes with these beautiful animals.

In fact, by having an dogborg on hand, you can have a faithful animal-esque friend with a low chance of revolt, and also program it to help you save more time to relax and enjoy. Need to pick up groceries at the store? Program your robot dog to do it by teaching it basic math and how to balance its weight on its hind legs. Don't want to get the mail? Program the dog to lower the drawbridge, open the mailbox, grab the mail, and wind the drawbridge back up using only its snout and teeth. Want to amuse yourself for hours on end? Program your dog to re-enact the entire series of *Everybody Loves Raymond* and let the show go on.

The same can go for any animal you might be willing to build, but let's be honest: if you can make a dogborg, you're going to make a dogborg. Catborgs will find a way to fuck things up and be selfish, even if science stands in its way, and snakeborg will just constantly remind you that it exists and is, at its heart, a waste of time and energy. But hey man, to each their own; if you want to build a whole petting zoo of robots for your surreal amusement, go for it.

Should you want a companion that is less mechanical and more reflective of your time as a father, then you can always attempt to build your monster a sibling. Of course, you will want to have a talk with your firstborn about pursuing that option, especially if they're still waiting on a bride that you have not found the time to build. Yet at the end of the day, it's ultimately your choice to make, and if you want to be a father for a second time, there's nothing stopping you besides the horrible memories of what initially happened when you last brought a monster back from the dead. However, this time around, you can learn from the mistakes you made with your last monster and build a monster that will be born out of acceptance rather than scorn.

By repeating the parental process as before, you can help shelter your latest creation from the hatred of the masses and give them a clean start. Should you go for another son, you know what to do: new merchandise for its face, new boner pills, etc. The only real difference in its upbringing will be the occasional visit from its older brother, which I'm sure will be handled admirably. In fact, the older monster may be actually relieved that you built it a sibling, considering it's now off-the-hook for taking care of you on your death bed, which is the saddest fact to celebrate. And the younger monster will also be much less prone to a monster's temperamental nature, which will make it easier to handle by the time it finally reaches the outside world; in fact, I'd wager that windmills don't even exist anymore, leaving your second-born already more privileged that its predecessor.

However, for a bigger and ultimately more rewarding parental challenge, you can go for a daughter and start from scratch. In doing so, not only will your daughter-monster learn how to socialize and behave from a great scientific mind, but you will also learn things *from* your daughter-monster considering its reactions will reflect a perspective that you know little-to-nothing about. After all, if there's anything all the fucking nerds on the Internet will tell you over and over again, it's that you can't learn how to interact with women from science, no matter how many websites you visit. Nevertheless, creating and raising a daughter-monster will be a more comprehensive and exciting experience as a whole, and for mad scientists who want to stay busy, that's your best bet.

Now, I know what you're thinking, "I bought this book for self-help, but instead, I spent the last years of my short mad scientist life helping others. What gives?"

Logically speaking, you likely began this chapter looking for redemption, considering how much horror was let loose on the world as a result of your goddamn curiosity. And outside of walking to the town courthouse and demanding a public execution, there were only so many ways of righting the wrongs that your creations had caused. So by helping others, you *were* helping yourself, and to be honest, there would have been no chance for salvation if you took in your monster only to suffocate it with a pillow as it slept. As much as the world likes to humanize killers, they like to humanize monsters more, and you'd be left without any chance for forgiveness, redemption, or absolution by yourself, God, society, or otherwise.

But in following my instructions, you have not only bettered yourself as a scientist and as a man, but as a father as well. Sure, you're probably left with dozens upon dozens of useless items featuring your monster-children's faces on them, and you probably will accidentally wake yourself up with glaring lights and blaring horns. You shouldn't look at these as inconveniences, but rather as constant reminders of a job well done, as even the most incredible inventions in the world can't make a great father out of nothing. And so you can look back at the past with no regrets, at the present with a fond stability, and at the future with an optimism knowing you've achieved most of what you wanted to do in this life, and it's all thanks to me.

However, if you're at the end of your life and all this reminiscing makes you feel as if you've got nothing to lose, DO NOT EXPLORE THE BARRIERS BETWEEN DIMENSIONS. THE WORLD BEGS YOU, AND THE DEATH YOU WILL EXPERIENCE WILL MAKE YOU WISH YOU HAD GONE BY THE HANDS OF THE DEVIL. DON'T FUCKING DO IT. I'M SERIOUS.

Chapter IX

The Broken Matches

There's a brilliant old saying among humans that hopefully my readership may remember from their past lives: "A man is only as good as the woman beside him." And while this saying may not entirely be accurate anymore considering the progressive modern society we live in today where you can have sex with and date all kinds of people, the saying is equally applicable to the monster community. However, in the case of these monsters, good would mean bad, because monsters are naturally evil and good would be bad for them.

Regardless of how you use the saying, the gist of it is that men drool and ladies rule, and in the monster community, it is very much the same. Whether you're a bride of Frankenstein, bride of Dracula, a gill-woman, a were-lady (regardless of affiliation with the SS) or a mummy mama, a monster by himself may be strong, but with you by his side, he is infinitely stronger. Monsters with brides find themselves to be much more confident and devoted to their particular calling in their afterlife, whether it be killing the human race or killing the human race. Unlike their male counterparts, there's almost a universal sexiness about monster brides even beyond death, which is guaranteed to make mortal men feel creepy and weird and need to talk to someone professionally.

But even though we know how a monster bride fits into the bigger picture of monsterdom, do humans really know the story of monster brides? As far as this author can tell, most monster brides treat their relationships akin to that of an arranged marriage, but an arranged marriage built on pure, unadulterated terror. Actually, scratch that: it's *exactly* like an arranged marriage.

As you know, one doesn't necessarily really live their life with the goal of one day marrying a member of the undead; it's more or less making the best of a bad situation.

Of course, much like how there are women who write dirty letters to spree killers in jail, there will always be exceptions to the rule, but most women don't have fucking a man-made creature on their bucket list. And the worst part is that, as you know, being a monster bride could have been prevented with the proper knowledge and preparation, whether it be with garlic-laced pepper spray or carrying a knife to fight off any murderous assistants of a mad scientist.

Luckily, there are benefits to being a monster bride, whether it be immortality for vampire, mummy, and man-made creature brides or the enhanced natural instincts of a were-lady or gill-woman. Vampire brides have the power to walk on walls and ceilings, which I'm sure is a benefit to women for some reason or another. She-creatures, meanwhile, have the strength and agility of an entire Olympic team, which will come in handy if you ever have to . . . uh . . . challenge an Olympic team. Also, there's the safety and security of being in a committed relationship, right? Ladies?

Okay, so being a monster bride is pretty terrible. If you're a vampire bride, you normally have to do everything with other vampire brides, whether it's participate in exhausting weekday orgies or feast from the same dirty stolen baby that your husband brings home every night. Would it kill for him to just wash the baby once? Who knows where that baby has been?!

For she-creatures, you really got the short end of the stick, considering you pretty much met your husband on the day you were born, which is some creepy, fucked-up *Twilight* shit. Your normal course of action after being addressed or talked to is a frightening hiss, which is the only fitting response when men start to paint sick, misogynist-pig stereotypes of she-creatures as real b-i-t-c-h-e-s. And furthermore, you're kind of born with one hairstyle, and any change to switch into something more modern is often met with criticism by your husband and creator/dad.

For gill-women, the biggest issue towards your kind is just feeling desirable; after all, most gill-men want buxom blondes in bikinis while your kind is met with rolled eyes and afterthought marriages to the gill-men who couldn't shack up with a human woman. But the fact is there's nothing that those women can offer the gill-men that you can't; in fact, you're more suited to their anatomical needs, including perpetual water consumption and external breeding, if that's how they breed (see Chapter Seven). And the worst part is you can't even resort to being a crazy cat lady if things don't go well; you'd have to instead be the crazy cat*fish* lady, and that's a pun that even this author had difficulty writing.

For were-ladies, the issue is proper grooming and maintenance; if you thought cat women were catty, think again. Rumors that a specific were-lady is carrying fleas can be devastating in the were-community, and can even pit were-families against one another. The were-drama is real, and with the B-word flying around like no were-body's business, there are only so many ways a female werewolf can avoid it. With werewolves eyeing up every fire hydrant on the block, the were-lady community just never can find the respect that they deserve, especially considering how feisty they can be when their pack is challenged.

As for mummy mamas . . . eh, I guess the biggest problem is that you're a mummy. You're pretty much set everywhere else, and the fact that black magic might possibly restore you to your former glory is something that a lot of these women don't necessarily get. But still, being a mummy kind of sucks, and you're probably the only group among monster brides that will still smell like pungent death no matter how many showers you take.

Then there's the factor of human women who marry monsters, many of whom probably did so thanks to the top-notch self-help advice I was able to give to their horrific husbands. While there is no judgement from this author, the monster bride community might have a case against these relationships, not out of hate, but simply out of quantity, as there aren't many monsters to go around between both potential human and monster brides. Though I'm sure there are more than enough human men out there who have a thing for monster brides such as yourself, you will rarely find human men who will be willing to put a ring on your undead finger.

Ever since Kenny Rogers sang the immortal, Lionel Richie-penned words in the smash crossover single, "Lady," there has been a stigma that women need a knight in shining armor who loves them, which may be noble in concept but understandably demeaning to some, especially monster brides. But rather than be the dependent, parasitic creatures depicted on screen over the years, monster brides like yourself have the power to transcend your situation to be truly independent women. With the help I can provide in this chapter, you will be able to stand toe-to-toe with your male counterparts and tell them that anyone they can kill, you can kill better.

Luckily, there are plenty of songs that also talk about being an independent woman as well as the many benefits that status holds. However, what is unique about these songs is that they come from all walks of life: country music encourages you to embrace the tomboy mentality with "Man I Feel Like A Woman," R&B expresses the capability of strong-minded ladies with "Independent Women," pop gives women a wake-up call with "Miss Independent," and rock and roll proudly creates a battle cry for the transgender community with "Dude (Looks Like A Lady)." But in any case, the collection of these cultures center around a single issue—independent women who defy expectations and buy their own stuff—should indicate that if there's ever a human cause willing to accept outsiders (such as monsters), it would be this one.

The first step in becoming an independent woman in the monster community is to recognize what kind of relationship you are in, and whether or not it is healthy even by monsters standards. As you may know, the idea of "my one and only" isn't necessarily a philosophy subscribed by the monster community, especially when eternity is involved as well as the various unforeseen elements (read: monster hunters) that can cause an abrupt split. So while there may always be philosophical differences between a monster and his monsterous bride, sometime it is worth taking a closer look at each partner's behavior to know if something wrong is happening.

Now, here's the tricky part: if through reading from this chapter, it dawns on you that you are in a relationship that is not only unfair, but also abusive, you need to find the strength in yourself to break it off and seek help. It may be difficult at first, especially when you've been with a monster for so long and, in the case of vampires, they just look so damn good in a cape, but it's a necessary step that has to be taken lest you find yourself damned to an endless life of steady, harrowing abuse. Do not be afraid to sneak off to the Monster Wellness Centers mentioned back in Chapter Two, and you even might be surprised just how effective the support system is within certain circles of monster women.

Now, let us start by determining if your relationship is fair and based on the standards that you had when you entered the relationship. For instance, if you're a vampiress, do you get to sleep in a coffin alongside your husband or are you instead banished to an iron maiden with the symbol of the cross etched between the spikes? If it's the latter, you're likely in an unfair relationship, which even a terrifying monster such as yourself should not be enduring. Signs of an unfair relationship come in all shapes and sizes, whether it be keeping you in a cage during your free time or trying to destroy a castle with you and your friends in it, and if you treat it with indifference, you're guaranteed to remain in a grip of terror forever.

So with that in mind, there is only one recourse is to take action and start becoming a strong, independent monster bride who doesn't need a monster man in her life. Starting now, the night does not only belong to the monsters with a member; in fact, there are more opportunities in this day-and-age for monster women to excel in a male-dominated world than ever before. And even though you'll be taking advice from a man to find that inner strength and break free of your social/physical binds, this author wants you to look at him not as a man but as a *hu*man, which would be the equivalent of getting relationship advice from your dog.

The first step to living as a free woman is to fight for the equality that you deserve, as a level playing field between husband and wife is crucial if you're looking to salvage this relationship. For vampire brides, it is about finding what exactly is being deprived in your life and making it work in your favor. By turning disadvantages into advantages, you're taking the power from your husband and making it your own. For instance, the next time your husband comes to deliver your filthy-infant dinner to share with your fellow brides, say "No!" and demand that you get a full-sized man to drink from, just as he does. By accepting a baby instead of an adult man, you're perpetuating the stereotype that you deserve less than your vampire husband, which is not kosher.

Likewise, vampire brides should find small rebellions in their power plays whenever possible; after all, what can your husband do to you? Kill you again? There's nothing he can do to you that won't hurt him as well, so if you're in the mood to go for a night on the town with your familiar against your husband's wishes, then what's stopping you? Furthermore, you should have the right to wear what you want when you want, so if you want to trade out that flowing white nightgown for the Vampirella one-piece, just do it and don't think twice.

Meanwhile, if you're a she-creature (not to be confused with the crustacean she-creature), perhaps your rebellion should come through your habits, many of which can turn off the notoriously particular man-made creatures. For instance, taking up a habit of smoking cigarettes will not only give you some time to wind down for a demanding relationship, but will also scare your husband away any time he sees the glow of the embers. Likewise, you can also teach him your value in the relationship by not immediately being his arm candy, forcing him to come up with a reason why you are absent during monster mashes.

As for were-ladies, hunting at night on your own is a great way to show your were-man that you can do just fine on your own, and will garner some jealousy from the attention you'll be grabbing from nearby wolf-packs. Likewise, gill-women can spend some time turning heads at the beach, while mummy mamas can look the other way and let an adventurer or two take a little bit of treasure while on her watch. While these moves won't be enough to throw the relationship into full-on monster divorce, these actions will be the first sign of a marital revolution, and let them know that you're not going to take it anymore.

The next step is to stand your ground, which is important since these monsters are going to pull every dirty trick in the book to break you down to subserviency. They'll come at you with name-calling, will suggest that you're ungrateful (or possibly unfaithful), and will definitely threaten you with banishment or worse. But if you're being pushed, push right back: if you're so disposable, why is he keeping you around? The answer is simple: he needs you more than you need him, and the fear of losing you will put him on the edge, which is the best place to gain another inch against his fascist regime of man-monster bullshit.

Redefining the way you communicate is one way to stand your ground in an effective way that solidifies your role in the relationship while challenging his. In the past, most monster men have often talked down to their brides as if they were insolent children instead of their partners, either because they don't know how to convey their feelings, or their environments have propagated such an attitude over the years. However, one doesn't need to be a relationship doctor to understand that would lead to an unhealthy relationship, and rather than let yourself cower back in shame and fear, perhaps it is time to switch up your approach altogether.

For vampiresses, your biggest ally is also your husband's most defining quality: his vanity. By intimately understanding his vanity, you can use it against him in a way that will not only knock him down a peg or two, but you will also earn his respect as a force to be reckoned with. If your man is going to talk to you about how he knows best, you should ask him why he needed a self-help book to realize that wearing a cape in 2015 was behind the times. Don't be afraid to take cheap shots either; if you want to remind him that sex with him is like having sex with a cold, dead corpse, you're in the right to say so since you are not 100 percent wrong.

For she-creatures, you should take an approach that focuses on defeating your opposite sex in mind games, a battle you should easily win even if you're as confused as your counterpart. You should go through the dictionary (or for monster brides who are less of a fucking nerd, the Internet) and try to memorize as many long words as possible, shoehorning them into conversations whenever possible, or maybe you should just write them down on your walls, floors, and windows to remind your significant other just how dumb they are. Furthermore, simple shifts in your conversational dynamic will make the biggest difference in your relationship; for instance, answering every question he has with another question will likely overwhelm his primitive brain, resulting in a perpetual state of madness and allowing you to get the upper hand in the relationship.

In the case of were-ladies, you should make sure you are loud and clear with your dissatisfaction with both his human and wolfen forms by making him look like a fool during fights and arguments. For instance, if he's ever being controlling or manipulative with his masculinity, don't think twice about shaving off all body hair completely in his human state, which will make him look completely ridiculous in either state. In fact, making a werewolf seem too effeminate or bizarre is a surefire way to not only have their role challenged within their pack, but on a more intimate level as well. Therefore, all warfare should be fair game, whether it be painting their nails hot pink as they sleep, strapping them with an industrial-sized muzzle, or fitting the doors with a solid silver framing to keep them inside and make their pack think he's one of those werewolf shut-ins.

As for gill-women, perhaps the best approach is to predict your man's moves beforehand and then make sure you have the upperhand when it comes to communication when they're caught in the act. The next time your husband is going to "go pick up oysters for dinner," maybe you should make sure you get to the local beach or yacht party first so that when he goes on the prowl, the first thing he'll see is your grinning fish face. Of course, not only will your husband be on the defensive with his hilariously inept social skills, but all the nearby women will know that he's a married man and therefore off-limits, lest they suffer a "coincidental" underwater mauling.

And with mummy mamas, mummies are used to being able to strongarm their way out of situations, or during their human times, buying their way out of bad situations, so rather than allow him to influence you at all, you might be better off giving him the complete silent treatment. Walk around your pyramid without acknowledging your man whatsoever, maintaining a dead, empty glare akin to that of a war criminal while refusing to speak. Do not write or communicate in any way, shape or form. Once the fear of living for eternity alone again sinks into your monster husband's head, he'll practically be shining your wrapped feet with his dried, dusty tongue to win you back into his affections.

In standing your ground, you're going to need to exude femininity as much as possible while being careful not to come off as too desperate or spiteful; after all, should your monster husband get the upper hand, he won't think twice to use it against you. Things like changing the interior design of your manor/castle/pyramid/cave and changing the color scheme from dreary, foreboding blacks to bright, optimistic pink and yellow will let him know that he has no control over your feelings and that no matter how much black paint he has, you'll always be pink and yellow on the inside. And furthermore, don't be afraid of spilling blood in places where it will compliment the room, thus building an aesthetic that is simultaneously monstrous and accessible.

Then, there's always the option of breaking all of your vows and just fucking everything. That's right: just run around town night after night, giving the crazy monster fuck eyes to any Drac, Frank, and Imhotep willing to indulge your darkest carnal desires. You don't even need to be subtle about it; by coming home reeking of monster sex, the most foul stench of all, you can let your monster husband know that he will be a cuckold if he's not going to do right by you. If that's going to be the case, you need to be careful: sometimes, your husband will attempt to disguise himself as another man in order to lure you back into his bedroom, and if that's the place where your relationship is at the moment, that's scarier than anything either of you could do to one another.

However, rebellion isn't the only way to declare yourself an independent monster woman, as there are plenty of places outside of your domicile where you can let your freak flag fly. Proud monster feminism can be embraced in various situations and events, whether it's through beat poetry night at the local graveyard, or aerial yoga at the mortuary. Through these activities, you can feel less alone as you will become a part of a greater community of monster women. You can also reach out to other monster women in need, as there simply will never be enough blogs in the world that can reaffirm the same exact sociopolitical messages ad nauseum.

Another way to show your monster-man who really is boss is by living up to your reputation as a monster and giving your local townsfolk a rampage that they will never forget. Men, women, and children won't be safe from your reign of terror, bringing entire bloodlines to an end while striking traumatic fear into any person who does manage to escape your clutches. A vampiress can paint the skyline crimson with the blood of her victims; she-creatures can leave a path of splattered skulls and broken bones in their wake; were-ladies can litter entire neighborhoods with disgusting, disturbing human viscera; gill-women can cover the streets with a monsoon of blood, and mummy mamas will make the air thick with the aura of death. It can be monster-born carnage of which the world has never seen, and it will be because of a *woman*, not a *man*.

However, if murder and genocide aren't ladylike enough for you, there's always the opportunity to be productive outside of the castle and outside of the control of your monster husband. After all, the workforce is growing and changing every day, and as it becomes a more tangible place for women to rise on a corporate level, it also becomes more accepting of monsters. The increasing presence of late-night shifts have been working wonders for vampiresses and she-creatures, while positions allowing you to work from home have helped accommodate mummy mamas, gill-women, and were-ladies alike.

Once you've found an outlet and a support system, then you can ask yourself an important question: is my relationship worth saving? After all, most monster husbands are just ignorant of what they're doing to you because they come from ridiculous caste systems with a focus on Darwinian social skills instead of tender loving and caring. However, with your help, there's a good chance that not only will they become a better man because of it, but they will also respect you more for not giving up on them. With all relationships, the prospect of a new beginning can hold wonders for both monster and his bride alike.

The first major step in saving your unholy marriage is to find common ground on which to rebuild your relationship, as the prior dynamic of your relationship likely marred any previous connections between the two. After all, what is a relationship besides sharing yourself and your experiences with someone you love? Though love is inherently absent in any relationship by two evil entities who hate one another as well as the world at large, that doesn't mean marriage has to be a living hell (unless that's your intention).

In the case of vampiresses, perhaps the most solid ground that you share with your vampire husband is the need to feed off human blood on a regular basis, an act that—up to this point—has been mutually exclusive between the two of you. However, considering there is more than one major artery in the human body, there's no reason that the both of you can't share meals together like normal, rational monsters. Of course, there's nothing better to reignite the spark in your monster love life than investing in coffin sex swings, which I'm sure someone will build if you're willing to pay.

For she-creatures, there are always ways to use this re-connection as a way to revitalize your humanitarian efforts, despite the fact that humanity will likely want nothing to do with you and may actually come at you with torches if you're out for too long. Of course, this can range from a variety of options, whether it be in providing swimming lessons for underprivileged children or lending your time and energy to help the blind, all of which are viable options. And should the human race make it very clear that you're both unwel-come, why not use both of your talents to scare and torment any potential rabble-rousers who get in your way? After all, they might act tough around one man-made creature, but *two* man-made creatures? I'd like to see them fucking *try*.

As for were-ladies, rebuilding your relationship depends on how exactly you and your husband view your lyncan-thropic affliction. If you both are the sort to embrace the beast within you, then it's best to make your monthly freak-outs into a couple's night out, hunting and chasing in tandem with one another as opposed to spreading your rampage elsewhere or fighting for scraps. However, if you are the kind who wants to stop your rampages (as I suggest any owner of this book should), you can support one another in that endeavor, whether it is by chomping at each other's necks on the kitchen floor or by just keeping your wild side in the bedroom.

With gill-women, this second chance should be used as a way to give you and your husband the honeymoon that you never had, with opportunities to explore both your human urge as well as your monster impulses. Perhaps swimming in seas outside of your comfort zone will be a chance to find nautical treasures you had never seen before while knowing that even the most adept deep sea monster hunter will have no chance against one of you with the other watching your back. While you're out and about on new beaches, rivers, and reefs, you can take the time to give humans the frightening photo opportunity that they never knew they could have, which would be a much needed boost to both of your self-esteems.

As for mummy mamas, your reborn relationship should give you a chance to learn something new about one another and apply that to something relevant in your lives. For you, while your husband has seen the strong and exotic sides of you before, has he ever seen you as an intelligent partner? Perhaps with a lesson in your unseen knowledge, you both can work on making new additions to the traps and puzzles between the entrance and your tombs. As for him, perhaps the chance to see his sensitive side will give you an opportunity to encourage his killings in the future and help him gain more confidence as man. In any case, these new qualities can be a chance to fall in love all over again, and find that the things that drove you apart might just be what brings you back together again.

However, for all this talk about finding common ground, one must not forget the flip side of the same coin, which is making sacrifices and changes to their old behavior to show that they really care about you. While monsters will rarely be able to achieve "Mr. Right" status, and nor should they, considering they're cut from the same cloth as pure evil, that shouldn't mean that they can't make this marriage worthwhile and make some necessary changes that will benefit the both of you. Considering how many years you've used your seductive charms to lure in unsuspecting victims for them, the least they could do is show a little gratitude to the opposite sex.

As for vampiresses, the most practical request would be to ask them to use their dire vanity in a much more practical way. Perhaps the best example of this would be to request that your husband start taking pride in who he eats, as well as his frequency of eating. Though it might be easier to target late-night joggers and the hot, horny teenagers on lovers lane, those are targets that don't necessarily deserve a death such as having the entirety of their blood sucked out from their jugular vein. Instead, he should aim for much more worthwhile prey, and those who would actually be beneficial to subtract from humanity, such as pedophiles, narcotics peddlers, and narcissistic clubgoers. Not only will they be bettering society as a result, but the hunt will keep your husband on a regular diet so that they don't gain a worse fate than vampirism: "blood gut."

In the case of she-creatures, you should request that your man make some more permanent changes, considering he's not very much the kind to be cheating on or leaving you in your current condition. But still, even the smallest change to his look would mean a world of difference to your confidence as a wife, whether it be having your name stitched into his skin (only applicable if you actually *have* a name) or even giving you a piece of himself as a romantic gesture, like a hulking, evil Vincent van Gogh. And not only are these acts relatively short and to-the-point, but they're genuine expressions of affection, which is the closest thing to real emotions either of your dead bodies may get.

Now, for all you were-ladies, change is going to be a familiar experience for you and your husband (*get it?*), but perhaps the best sacrifice you can make for one another comes in the form of your physical possessions, considering that destroying things around the house is an unfortunate byproduct of your transformations. This a not only a natural concept but a very fruitful one: no one enjoys anything more than receiving a surprise gift, especially if it's for something you recently lost or accidentally destroyed. By making every post-werewolf morning a sick, twisted version of Monster Christmas, you're guaranteed to make your relationship stronger than ever while feeling better about yourself as a charitable person.

As for gill-women, you might have to ask your husband for the biggest sacrifice imaginable: his bachelordom. That's right: if there's any chance for saving your marriage, it's in giving up your swinging lifestyle and settling down to become parents to a pool of gill-children. While he may be sad to no longer go to the beach and kidnap people, the fact that you'll both be the most sexually active as you've been since being gill-teens should more than make up for the lack of excitement. The gift of parenthood might be what you both need, as even animals can be great parents under the right circumstances, unless they're the kind who eat their own kids because they don't give a *fuck*.

In the case of mummy mamas, there's always the opportunity for him to hold up his end of the deal by tidying up the pyramid in case of unexpected guests; after all, you're monsters, not slobs. Whether it is arduously dusting the hieroglyphics to make them more legible or merely scrubbing out decade-old blood stains from stone columns in your traps, he should take any chance to let you feel appreciated in your tomb. This shows a greater sense of responsibility as well as physical evidence that he wants to make this relationship work. Even though he might have once been a Pharaoh doesn't mean he's excluded from a little general maintenance work from time to time.

By pursuing these lifestyle changes and general attitude adjustments, you can show your monster husband that you are not only your own person, but that if push comes to shove, you will be fine on your own. Of course, this is mostly in worst-case-scenario situations; if trying to save your marriage isn't in the cards, or if he's not taking the hints, then splitting is the best thing for both of you. However, you really need to be careful about threatening a break-up if things aren't at their absolute worst; there are many dangers to life as a single monster, and there will always be better odds of surviving in pairs.

However, there should never be any shame in looking out for what's best for you, and whether God or your husband are responsible for your current situation of unhappiness should be irrelevant to the conversation at hand. No matter how many people you've killed or maimed, or how many people find you to be repulsive on a fundamental level, you have the right to be happy and you should have the means to facilitate that happiness readily available. While love may be important to monster brides, as well as women as a whole, it doesn't necessarily go hand-in-hand with happiness, nor

nor is it a bare necessity for you to continue on in your eerie endeavors. What is important is that you figure out you, because forever is a long time for an immortal to live in someone else's chains.

Now, before we wrap up this chapter of *The I in Evil*, there is something I need to address and get off my chest, because if I don't, it will eat away at my soul for the rest of my life. If you've been reading the whole book, you may have picked up on some facts about myself, especially some things about my childhood. So whether you're a vampiress, a she-creature, a gill-woman, a mummy mama, or a werelady, I would like to formally apologize for the disgraceful, inhumane hunting that my father did to your kind when I was young.

It is now, after all these years that I understand that you were not harming anyone in your actions, and that my father's actions were primarily caused by wrongful, paranoid delusions. You were all within your rights to work at night at those backwoods motels, where you caused no threat to man or monster alike, and the deaths inflicted upon you by my father were not in the least deserved. His actions were sick, twisted, and deplorable; in fact, they were so sadistic that I wouldn't even wish them upon the most inhumane human women on the planet, including reality television stars.

And trust me, I am on your side in this matter; even when the law kept referring to your lost kin as humans, I defended your kind. When the media would corner me on the way to the courthouse, I would sing the gospel of your kind's hardships, and yet it would fall on dead, sometimes mocking ears. When psychiatrist after psychiatrist would tell me over and over that I was repressing the truth, I raised my fists in protest and never forgot the debt I owed your kind. Even when the prosecutor took me to identify . . .

Wait a second . . .

Did I go with the prosecutor to identify my father's victims? I . . . don't remember. It's all very hazy, but it feels so . . . familiar. I remember being picked up that morning to be taken to the city morgue . . . and I remember boarding an airplane and being told my father was executed for his crimes . . . but everything else is unclear. Surely, I testified against my father, despite my love for him and the myriad valuable lessons he bestowed upon me. And surely, I was the only other one to see the bodies before they went into those haunting black garbage bags. . . .

Oh, God. The garbage bags. Oh my God. It's all coming back to me now. Jesus Christ. Their faces . . . my God . . . THEIR FACES. . . .

They weren't monster faces . . . they were people faces. But why? Why did I think they were monster faces? WHY DID I THINK THEY WERE MONSTER FACES???

It's all . . . so clear to me now. The affection. The screams. Everything was so . . . human. They didn't even put up the fight like a monster would. . . .

But . . . monsters still exist, right? I mean, just because all of those women he killed were human doesn't mean monsters don't exist. There are shadows everywhere, and I've lived among them and have studied them . . . at least I think I have. In any case, I'm doing right by them, even if I can never do right by those women . . . those poor women. . . .

Chapter X

So You're Dead; Now What?

For lack of a better term, death is for chumps. Even though there's the commonly accepted belief that sooner or later, everyone will die and our souls will move on to another plane of existence. And while that might suit the losers out there who believe in things like "destiny" and "logic" and "physics," this author has bigger and better plans for his soul. Once the singularity comes storming through town, I'll be first in line to get my consciousness uploaded onto a hard drive, paying for my digital immortality with sweet, sweet *The I in Evil* money.

But for all the z-grade zilches out there who have accepted their fate at the bottom of God's asshole, you're going to have to come face-to-face with the life you lived. If you were a good person, making an honest go of your existence with every lemon life threw your way, and assuming you did the little dance to get past the pearly gates, you'll likely spend the rest of eternity hanging in heaven with all the other nice people and playing board games, I guess? If you were really cool and you liked to actually live your life, chances are you are headed downstairs, where the devil has a burning hot VIP room waiting for you where you can chill out with Joey Ramone and J. Robert Oppenheimer. Or maybe one of those other wacky religions are true instead, and you are either re-incarnated, or drifting into space, or you were in heaven the whole time or something; to be honest, it doesn't really make a difference since you're not really alive anymore anyways.

However, as with any set of options, there is always a loophole that can fuck up the whole system, and in the case of life and death, that loophole is ghosts. For any of the adults out there who can buy a book but somehow didn't know what ghosts were their whole life, ghosts are transparent representations of our lifeforce that exist beyond our corporeal form, usually because they have unfinished business to attend to.

Were you murdered? If so, you're probably a ghost. Did someone steal the treasure you gave up your life to attain? You are also probably a ghost. Did someone kill your baby and never saw justice? You are probably a ghost, too, and your baby is most likely a ghost.

But unlike vampires or gill-men, there are actually many different kinds of ghosts out there, each with their own set of powers and restraints. However, there are unifying qualities among all ghosts, and if you're a ghost reading this, you probably know what I'm talking about. Almost every type of ghost is incredibly territorial, and you will rarely find more than one specific kind of ghost within a shared space. Yet there is a good chance that, in cases of mass killings or just generally evil areas, you can find multiple ghosts of the same kind in an area; almost like a frat house of horror, if you will. And ghosts, for the most part, will move on to the next life once they've found peace in their current state, which means if they kill a human who trespasses on their property, they're probably not going to be satiated and, if anything, they likely added a new roommate.

The first kind of ghost in the world is the standard-issue specter, the ones that are usually on the front of those haunted attraction sound effects CDs. These ghosts usually resemble the physical frame in which they died, minus legs and plus a weird glowing aura. Since there are so many specters, they are relatively unpredictable in nature. While these spirits are the easiest to remove from a house or property, they do find strength in numbers, and can be nearly impossible to get rid of in areas of particularly negative vibes. If you're a ghost and your forte is creaking floors, slamming doors and making the walls bleed, you're likely a standard-issue specter.

The next kind of ghost is the ever-famous poltergeist, and these ghosts are among the most outwardly aggressive and "bro"-like on the spectral plane. Poltergeists are, for the most part, not only transparent but 100 percent invisible, and usually have the power to manipulate your surroundings on a stronger level than a typical specter. Poltergeists are among the most difficult to remove, and are often striving to find vessels to inhabit to extend their earthly presence. If you're a ghost, you're really good at assembling things, and you really think you'd enjoy living as an adolescent girl, you're definitely a poltergeist.

Our third kind of ghost is not as common as the specter or the poltergeist, and also not necessarily one to worry about: the benign spirit. Often victims of a very specific act of heinousness, these spirits don't necessarily have the power to hurt people but will often show up in parts of your room with their head down to point at something. These ghosts have been called "messengers" and "harbingers" over the years, and are likely doing what they can to find peace while staying indifferent to the lives of the people around them. If you're a ghost and you stopped caring a while ago, you're likely a benign spirit.

The penultimate kind of ghosts are known as "goofs," and you can most likely guess why: because they're fucking goofy. Coiners of the term "boo" and poster boys for *Casper the Friendly Ghost*, goofs are the single most harmless of ghostkind, and are mostly in it for their own amusement. To be honest, I don't know exactly how goof spirits are made and I don't necessarily know how to make them go away; in fact, they don't seem interested whatsoever in moving onto greener pastures. If you're a ghost and your top priority when a family moves in is to see how many bananas are on the counter, you're a goof.

And then, we come to our last type of ghost, which is the rarest ghost of all: the Wendigo. Usually paired with Native American mythology, the Wendigo is a spirit in search of a host in whose flesh it can consume and, therefore, live forever in a mortal body. Wendigos are the most dangerous of ghostkind, but also are the most picky in terms of their vessels because they need something that they will be happy with for the long run. Also, the ease of ridding the world of a Wendigo all depends on how you find them, as their physical flesh will be killable but their spiritual form is much more difficult to remove. If you're a ghost and you have read every word of this book so far wondering how the author tastes in a stew, you are a Wendigo.

As ghosts may appreciate the sentiment, I might as well use this opportunity to explain that demonic presences do not technically count as ghosts. Demons may want to think that they are a ghost so that you become vulnerable. They're much more interested in destroying the earth and all of mankind than any ghost ever could. Demons also are not territorial, but rather travel with a potential host, which is also not a ghost's M.O. The best way to separate the two is via the "GB/EP" memory game; by associating the letters GB with ghosts and EP with demons, you'll help yourself remember that ghosts' greatest enemies are the ghostbusters while demons' greatest threat is an exorcising priest.

Now, if you picked up this book, you likely have questions about your place in the afterlife as well as where you go from here now that you're a ghost. And while you do have a cool set of new supernatural powers, ghosts have plenty of problems to deal with, especially considering you have been so used to existing in your human identity. Let's take this chapter slow and, hopefully, we will help you become more accustomed to existence as a ghost and maybe even get you a little closer to that shining white light.

Have you been particularly disappointed by your experiences in the afterlife so far? Do you long for individuality in your preferred territory of haunting? Do you miss who you used to be in the physical realm? Or do you long to change from who you were during your life? If so, you are likely suffering from a condition I made up called "Ghost Identity Syndrome," in which a spirit is having trouble establishing their identity thanks to the various complications from being a ghost. And while the condition afflicts hundreds of new ghosts every day, I assume, it also gives ghosts a second chance at finding satisfaction in their identity.

Firstly, as a ghost, you'll have a little bit of control over what you look like and how you want to present yourself to both humans and ghosts. For instance, while you may have been a boy, girl, or transgendered in your previous life, most ghosts are androgynous blobs, giving a certain amount of freedom from the expectations and boundaries that gender establishes. Furthermore, if you want to still associate with those gender choices, you're more than welcome to, especially considering ghosts are going to be a lot more relaxed towards your gender identity. Haunting victims, on the other hand, might still be uncomfortable, but to be fair, they're probably more uncomfortable with the fact that you're a ghost.

The same rules go for ethnicities, as ghosts do not carry very much about their ethnic background into the afterlife outside of their original language and rough outline of their physical visage. After all, there are not many ways to celebrate your ethnicity since you can't eat your traditional food, you can rarely take time for holiday celebrations, and finding multiple ghosts of the same ethnicity in the same territory is very rare. However, incorporating elements of your ethnicity into your ghostly existence could be beneficial to help you stand out in a crowd; messages written to your victims in your native tongue will be sure to make you a ghost to remember.

However, one of the best things a ghost can do in the wake of Ghost Identity Syndrome is begin exploring new options and avenues that you might not have been able to pursue as a human. For instance, as a ghost, you'll finally be able to haunt people, in case that was your desire when you were a human. You also are able to explore parts of your house quicker than you used to, and don't have to worry about sleep or picking up after yourself. I mean, sure, it pales in comparison to the powers of a wolfman, or vampire, or man-made creature, but c'mon, you're going to live forever until you're at rest, so what more could you ask for?

Another thing you have to consider is that ghosts have different rights than human beings, especially considering humans can be assaulted and harassed on multiple levels while ghosts just seem to be mad all the time. Believe it or not, there are no explicit laws stating that being a ghost is illegal, nor that you have to abandon any properties where you are may be spiritually linked. However, just like human beings, if you're being a real piece of trash, someone's going to come clean you up, and considering the information being discovered every day, more ghost-busting services and self-made exorcists are coming onto the ghost-removal scene every day. So, in short, you can stay spooky, but be prepared to face the consequences if you cross over into spooky scary territory.

This seems like a good time to talk about appropriate and inappropriate relationships between humans and ghosts, and I'm not talking about those weirdos who go on the Syfy Channel and give testimonials about ghost sex. As far as

I can tell, ghost sex, while widely reported, has never been proven to be a real thing. These rumors are likely just coming from weirdos finding an excuse to discuss their weird fuck habits openly. I mean, you're a ghost, and if you want to try to fuck a consenting human adult, then go for it, but I'm not sure it will work unless you wanna float around with sex toys like some kind of erotic magic show.

The main issue that comes between ghosts and humans is that ghosts are often jealous that humans are alive and doing human things, which is understandable considering being a human is great (although being a computer is better, probably). First of all, if you're a ghost, you shouldn't be jealous of human beings; even if they do have the vibrancy and sensory experiences that you lack. They also have tons of things that you wouldn't envy, such as the ability to feel physical pain and having to balance a checkbook. In fact, they have many more concerns than ghosts should ever have, such as starvation, freezing to death, paying taxes, caring for pets, having to dress themselves, etc. If anything, humans should be jealous of *you*, since you have the secret to immortality . . . but we'll get to that later.

Furthermore, a cohesive friendship and/or living situation between a ghost and human is far from impossible as long as you learn to communicate properly. For instance, if you're angry at the person in your home for sleeping on your dead son's bed, making the walls bleed doesn't necessarily send across a clear message that prevents it from happening again. Likewise, if you're angry about how your home is being treated, or if you don't like the owner's feng shui designs, slamming the windows and throwing things around the room isn't going to fix anything. If anything, it's only going to garner more resentment for you, and then it's only a matter of time before you're face-to-face with the ass-end of a containment chamber.

So if you can't just do crazy ghost nonsense, how can you communicate with the living in a timely, appropriate fashion? The answer is surprisingly simple: be straightforward. Depending on what kind of ghost you are, speaking may or may not be out of the question. If you can communicate with them directly and talk over your concerns, you should be able to find a harmonious understanding with your living counterpart. If speaking is out of the question, then perhaps the way to go is via writing; after all, if you can write something creepy in a foggy window, you should be able to pick up a pencil and share your thoughts on a piece of paper. And for the more aggressive ghosts out there, take advantage of your powers: possess their computers, tablets, typewriters, phones, and anything else to get your message across, as long as you're willing to listen to them.

However, if any relationship between ghost and human is going to be peaceful and complementary, you're going to have to expect some compromises on your end. Obviously, ghosts like yourself have been stereotyped as demanding, possessive, and incredibly stubborn. If you're going to be living with someone, you can't be the one calling the shots all the time. If this means allowing someone to sleep in your death bed, or if it means a child playing with a toy you once cherished, then so be it; after all, you've got no practical use for it anymore. And instead of spending so much of your time focusing on the negative in your house, why not turn your attention to the positive, like the new hot tub your housemate installed or the video blogging studio in the attic?

Likewise, you are also likely going to have to temper your ghostly sense of humor as well, especially if you're a goof. Sure, if we were all invisible and could float through walls, pulling pranks on other people would be on our priority list, and you definitely won't have to give it up completely. But once the pranks and spooky tricks happen on a daily basis, they can become really exhausting and aggravating, and that could cause a tense divide between man and spirit in your household. Like most things in life, spooking people should be done in moderation, but make sure you do get it on video since motherfuckers go bananas for that shit on the Internet.

Nevertheless, if you want any relationship to work with a human, tenuous or otherwise, there are some things you absolutely cannot do. First off, you really cannot act like a complete cunt to your housemate, even if they're being the biggest jerk in the world to you. That means you can't throw them across the room when you are mad, which is a quick way to end up in civil court, and you certainly can't attempt to murder them through a Rube Goldberg-esque series of events that would appear to the common man as an accident. This also means no banging on the walls, no shrill screaming whenever they enter a room, and no grabbing their hair when they're in the shower. If there's anything that you can do as a ghost that may make others think of you as invasive or just generally an asshole, then you should avoid doing that.

Another thing you need to cut out completely is playing with your human housemates' sleep habits, and don't act like you haven't. Nowadays, sleep is incredibly important to maintaining a functional lifestyle, and for people who work one or even two jobs, sleep is critical to fulfilling their responsibilities. So by watching people sleep, or making loud noises to wake up members of their family late at night, or pulling them out of their bed and beating the living shit out of them, you're really not doing anyone a courtesy. So during your night hours, you might want to find something productive to do with your time, such as reading *The I in Evil* again and then posting about how people should buy it on ghost message boards because it's so good and you love it.

Now, this next change of behavior is probably the most difficult of the bunch, but I am also going to suggest that you be more careful with your housemate's property. Ghosts like yourself are notorious for recklessly breaking property, or even worse, using their property to break other pieces of their property. God knows that small claims courts aren't going to side with a fucking ghost when it comes to destruction of property and criminal mischief. Just be careful around your home and the belongings of your housemate during your more emotional moments and you can see the results for yourself.

Besides, don't you lose your shit every time a living human gets near your old property? If you're angry and about to have a ghost tantrum, kill two birds with one stone and just break that old garbage instead. No one is going to miss it anyways, and they can't desecrate anything that you've broken yourself. In fact, that's probably the only thing you have control over now that you're a ghost, so be lucky that you have even that, you dead sack of shit.

Lastly, but certainly not least, it's very important that you do not possess people since it is essentially the rudest thing you could do to your housemates. Not only will it have physical and psychological consequences to the possessed, it's also an almost guaranteed way to make sure they're getting rid of you in a big, bad way. Exorcisms are meant for demons, *muchacho*, and if you're going to the same place as demons, then you can expect the closest thing to prison that a ghost can experience. Except there's no release dates, there's no parole, and there's no leaving on good behavior; all you'll find is non-stop demon torture and humiliation morning, noon, and night.

I wouldn't wish that on any ghost . . . well, maybe Hitler's ghost. If you are Hitler's ghost, and you're reading this, go ahead and possess someone so you get what's coming to you. Also, you better not try to take over the world again. You better not.

Yet for all the sacrifices you make for your housemate(s), you should also make it clear that you used to be a human once and that you deserve a little respect as well. After all, you have retained enough humanity to somehow purchase this book and attempt to better yourself. So if you're going to give coexistence the ol' college try, you might as well let them know that America isn't the only place that needs change. That's still relevant to say, right?

Before you start making demands, however, you should approach your human counterparts with grace and humility by letting them know that you're not perfect. Even though you can fly and teleport through walls and make nightmares come true, you'll never be the perfect housemate, but you will work on bettering yourself. However, they also need to know that you are not *Casper*, and you're not going to smile and eat a shit sandwich just because they're a human and you're not. So by letting your housemate know that you're willing to work on yourself as long as they're willing to work on themselves, then at least you're working towards a mutual goal while acknowledging that you're both fucked up and your shit's out of whack.

Once you've reminded them what human filth they really are, the next thing you have to ask them for is mutual respect. While you can make compromises and become more relaxed about what is and is not sacred and/or off-limits, you also have to stand your ground when it comes to specifics, like your baby's first toy or the spot in your house where you were murdered. If a human doesn't understand your needs as a ghost, they certainly are going to find every chance to walk all over you and also probably write anti-ghost sentiments on their private twitter accounts. If you've already got your housemate's fear, then you're going to need their respect; otherwise, how can they expect you to respect them back?

Another change you should be in your rights to ask for is more consideration of your privacy, especially if you're going to stop watching them sleep at night. You need to be firm in that it is no longer okay that they set up intricate camera systems to record your every move, and then attempt to post it on Youtube as evidence of the existence of ghosts. Also, there needs to be transparency in terms of their house guests, as you can only invite over those who coincidentally happen to own EMF meters and spy camera glasses. You have to let them know that this isn't your first rodeo, so if you're going to cohabitate with one another, they can't be leaving baking soda all over the place so they know where you've been and get all up in your grill.

Lastly, and this demand might be the most flexible, but you should also ask for a little bit of patience regarding your situation, and by that I mean that you're a fucking ghost. Unless you were one of those people with long, intricate plans of gaining immortality through a long-forgotten ghost ritual, no one really chooses to be a ghost; in fact, you're kind of killed into it for the most part. That doesn't mean they have to let every ghastly thing you do slip by them, but you might as well ask them for a little patience while you adjust.

Now, there's always the chance that your roommate is not a human, and that you are currently haunting a location where another monster resides. While this isn't necessarily a common occurrence, it does happen enough that you should be prepared in case it does happen. And if you don't think you should be prepared, let me tell you something: living with monsters can be a *scare*. PLEASE DON'T RETURN THIS BOOK!

First of all, you would be sharing a living space with cursed monsters, such as the vampiric and the lycanthropic. These are likely the monsters that you'll be most intimately familiar with and to which you will likely have the most connection, considering they likely got into their situation in a similar fashion as yourself. In that sense, it's almost like a reluctant pairing of monster and different monster, much like my as-yet-unproduced screenplay *The M.O.P. Squad: Monsters on Patrol: The Untold Origins*.

If you find yourself bunking with a vampire, then you should go back to Chapter Six to get a taste of their petrifying perspective. With that said, you won't have to really worry much about them attacking you or calling in the GBs to take your ass to the ghost clink, since they've got just as much to lose as you. You also won't really have to worry about them messing with your old stuff either; they often sleep in coffins in the basement, and are constantly ordering new things on late night infomercials since they don't know any better, so they have no use for your old possessions.

However, a ghost living with a vampire does have its drawbacks; if a vampire drains anyone on your property, you're likely to be getting new roommates on a consistent basis, and chances are that the place will turn into Grand Central Station over the course of eternity. Likewise, vampires are vain as the devil himself, and are prone to lash out in the light of criticism, so you might want to note them as "does not work well with others."

If your new housemate is a werewolf, that's a horse of a different penis altogether, considering ninty-nine percent of the time, it will be like dealing with a human housemate.

And in that other one percent of the time, the wolfman will take its killing sprees outside of the house, allowing you to get at least one night a month to yourself. However, if the wolfman is somewhat of a homebody, probably in partial thanks to my teachings in Chapter Five, then you will at least have a loyal housemate who follows instructions well and will bring you the newspaper.

But, as you might have guessed, werewolves have their own set of issues when it comes to being a housemate. For instance, you better plug the exterminators into your speed dial, because once a month, *someone* is going to bring in fleas and other assorted insects into the house. Bugs are not like humans; you just can't scare off insects willy nilly since they're accustomed to fighting for their lives on a daily basis. Furthermore, having to clean up hair sheddings and post-transformation bodily fluids every month is going to be a chore, especially when you really don't want to, but if you leave it until the morning, there's no way it's not going to stain.

Then there's the monsters that were born in their terrifying, horrendous skin, such as man-made creature or a gill-man. For man-made creatures, most of the benefits will come from just having an ugly hulking fool around the house. They will make you feel better about how you look despite not having a physical form. They also help get rid of pesky bill collectors and solicitors on a regular basis, and are pretty gullible considering they were potentially born yesterday.

Unfortunately, man-made monsters can also be some of the worst housemates ever, especially if you are the kind of ghost who likes to party. First of all, man-made creatures have a tendency to sulk about, reminding you of their sad existence as well as how sad your existence is because you have to deal with them. Second of all, because they're made of multiple cadavers, they have a tendency to weigh more than most human beings outside of the Midwest, so they are more prone to breaking all the things you hold dear in the house and taking away what few memories you have left.

As for gill-men, you don't want a gill-man roommate, and that's not a slight against gill-men. But if you let them roam around your house, getting everything wet all the time, you will have to deal with mold. That's a problem much worse than any haunting could ever be. Besides, they don't necessarily seem to respect human beings that much, alive or dead, and the jury is still out on whether or not they can read, so just save yourself a headache and deny their application up front. You can, however, point them to the nearest animal sanctuary, where they can swim down a river or some shit and launch to the top of the food chain.

Then there are the monsters who are simply products of their environments, and those ones are essentially the wild-cards of the bunch because their monsterdom has so often relied on their habitat. On one hand, you have mad scientists, who—like most creative types—need a very specific living situation in order to continue their obsessive-compulsive work endeavors. On the other hand, you have mummies, who have lived in pyramids and palaces for their whole existence, making their transition into the suburbs a jarring, foreign experience.

For mad scientists, there are several positive aspects of allowing them to share your living space, and they're admittedly pretty tempting. Chief among the benefits would be that they might find a particular interest in your existence, and moreover may even be interested in giving you life once again, which is the best chance you're going to get. Mad scientists are also known for being a pack of neat-freaks, and usually will steer clear of relics of that past that don't hold any scientific merit. Besides, watching a mad scientist work is akin to watching a real-life TED Talk or watching a really intelligent serial killer work his magic, and when you're a ghost, you'll take live entertainment wherever you can get it.

On the downside, mad scientists can also be a fucking handful in the wrong environment. Think Klaus Kinski and multiply that by ten, and you might have an idea of what it's like when a mad scientist doesn't have the proper supplies, equipment, or help to make their fucked-up experiments come true. And as for the barriers of privacy? Forget it; they're going to keep their eye firmly on you, and don't be surprised if you find them doing some weird shit literally behind your back when you're dazing off.

As for mummies, they'll essentially work as your home security system, which is nice because that will give you more time to focus on what will finally put your soul at rest. Not only that, but mummies also are fucking loaded as Hell, so if you want to experience the cool human shit that poor families who normally get haunted can't afford, all you need to do is use the art of persuasion to get that mummy to buy you shit. Also, since you've lost your sense of smell and taste, you won't have to worry one bit about the treacherous odors that follow mummies around.

At the same time, mummies are dusty, dirty motherfuckers who never leave the house, and don't really know how modern stuff works. And if you're among the dead, you really don't want to be saddled with the burden of teaching a thousand-plus-year-old immigrant how to use iPads and not strangle the UPS guy. Hell, as a ghost, you don't need more burdens than you already have, so make your choice wisely when it comes to having a mummy housemate.

Also, in case you're not "in-the-know," under no circumstances should you allow a zombie to take residence on your property. There's a reason why zombies are not featured in this book, and that's because they are the mortal enemy of ghosts, giving the dead a bad name both in real life and in pop culture. Furthermore, zombies aren't in need of books, and I would rather have my fingers be eaten by bees than write for a demographic that won't explicitly buy my book. I'm not fucking stupid, and to zombies, I say *nay*.

Then again, you might be the type of ghost who only lives with other ghosts, and have likely been skimming through this chapter waiting to be addressed formally. While this writer does not condone ghost nationalism, I do understand why ghosts would prefer to flock together as opposed to living with humans or other monsters. And there's nothing wrong with ghosts living together in harmony, as long as you're willing to play the game of social ghost politics among your spooky brethren.

The first hurdle to living exclusively with other ghosts is the complication of generally dealing with one another, especially if both ghosts are from separate classes of ghost. For instance, you don't want to be left doing all the haunting yourself if your housemate decides they're going to take the week off to work on their scare game. Likewise, you both won't necessarily be able to do physical things like yardwork or paying property taxes, so you can expect tension to rise as the estate gets more and more decrepit. And then there's the off-chance that your ghost housemate decides that your child's old bed is now *their* wife's old bed, and there ain't no talking things out once ghosts have marked their territory.

Then there's the chance that you possibly didn't do your due diligence in researching your ghost housemate. For all you know, your housemate could be a member of a ghost gang, and is simply looking for a schlub who will give away their living space to house the newest chapter of their gang, and they'll have no reservations about sleeping, fucking, and killing people on your old marital bed. Or they might have been a particularly obnoxious ghost; after all, what kind of fucking ghost leaves their old stomping grounds anyhow?

And worst of all, a house with multiple ghosts is more likely to draw the attention of the anti-ghost pockets of humanity. Houses with no human activity and reported paranormal activity are likely to garner the attention of psychic mediums, who will look to make a spectacle out of your existence and possibly drive you from your home. Likewise, similar situations will put you in the crosshairs of ghost hunters, who will come to your house with a whole reality TV crew and are willing to credit you with miniscule coincidences, making you the laughing stock of the ghost community. And then there's the GBs themselves, who will come knocking at your door once they realize there's not one but *two* ghosts to put on ice.

But whether you are living with a human or a monster, eventually, you're going to grow weary of a ghost's life and start looking for that great white light (and not a neon sign with the logo of heavy metal greats/arsonists Great White). Now, unless you know explicitly what it is that got you in your situation, finding your way back into the favor of God (or the Devil, depending what side of the fence you're on) can be a tricky trade in-and-of itself. And for ghosts who have been in the haunting game for decades, sometimes it's hard enough to remember just why you were untimely murdered in the first place. So let's talk about ways to make your undead living situation work, and how you can help yourself get closer to the great beyond.

If, for whatever reason, you can't remember why you became a ghost, you might as well attempt to be productive with your existence as it remains. From this author's experience, being productive is a great way to jar the memory (see Chapter Nine) and feel good about yourself while doing so. And if you're motivated to do well by yourself, you might find the same motivation to move yourself closer to your final destination, wherever that may be.

One way to be productive without a physical form is to try to find odd jobs that you can do from the comfort of your own home. Of course, the easy solution is to access the darkweb and join those sleazy yet purpose-serving camghost sites like *UndeadFriendFinder* or *Uncle Boo-ner's Scare 'n' Spank*. Another idea would be to charge humans for the "ghost riding" experience, where you can safely throw people around your house akin to that of an at-home rollercoaster. Lastly, you can have freaky goth musicians come over to your fucking house and play you their awful music, and then charge them for your notes on making their music more "authentic" or some bullshit like that.

Another way to be productive as a ghost is to get into the arts yourself, a field in which ghosts have actually found a way to become super-successful beyond the grave. The ghosts of Tupac Shakur, Elvis Presley, and Michael Jackson all continue to record to this day, and their albums sell better than they did when they were alive. Meanwhile, if you can get in touch with a filmmaker, you can make a haunting flick in your own home without costly special effects, so the Screen Actors Guild will be none the wiser about your performance so that you don't have to pay dues.

However, if you want to be particularly selfless about your productivity, you could always lease yourself out to hotels, motels, bed and breakfasts and, if desired, casino resorts to help bring some traffic to their establishments. To do this, you would have to go through the motions to enchant yourself into a book and rely on your housemate to make sure you get mailed out to the right place. From there, you can show up, scare a few people until the place gets a reputation, and help business owners find renewed relevance in their existence. Hell, if you end up somewhere like the legendary Stanley Hotel in Estes Park, Colorado, you might even be able to mix and mingle with some truly seasoned and knowledge-able spirits.

But even if you're the most productive ghost in the universe, you're still not going to make it to that existen-tial finish line without a little confidence. If you are a ghost, the only confidence you're likely familiar with is in your ability to scare people and break shit when you're mad; sur-prisingly, this is a common trait among "confident" humans. So if you're looking to make yourself a more self-assured ghost, it's important to admit your figurative vulnerabilities and then not be such a pussy about it.

Case in point: ghosts are among the most self-centered monsters out there, and are so focused on themselves that they even bought a self-help book despite having powers beyond reasonable explanation. But it's important to re-member one thing that ghosts are prone to forgetting, and that is you're not alone. Despite the eternal spiritual tor-ment that has caused your soul to exist while your body rots, almost all ghosts universally feel like this. In fact, I'm sure there are more than a few who got into their position in the same way you did, even if it's as specific as being hit on the head with a pipe, stripped naked, and drowned in a child-sized pool.

Furthermore, confidence can largely be a byproduct of love, and for many ghosts, love can be a long-forgotten memory. After all, women aren't writing as many ghost-fucking novels, and we already talked about the men's bizarre ghost-fucking fantasies. But to that point, this author asks: when was the last time you have given love? When was the last time you have offered a human the chance to love you for who you were? It's certainly not impossible, but it might as well be if you don't take the effort to make it happen.

And if you don't believe me, then let me tell you a little story about a certain writer who is clearly me but written in terms to poorly disguise my identity. You see, this writer grew up in a terrible position, and had a delusional father who very likely killed women across many different states. Having seen these gruesome acts in such an intimate setting so frequently, this writer grew up convincing himself that monsters are real and that those women must have been monsters because that's the only reason why a good man like father would kill them. But unfortunately, while you can run away from vampires, wolfmen, mummies and the like, you cannot run away from the ghosts of your past.

That's right, ghosts and ghouls: I live with spirits myself, and I know what their lives are like. I see them, I interact with them, and I do my best to help them find peace from what my father did to them and usher them to their own afterlife. That's because instead of reminding me of what my father did to them and attempting to rid me from their presence, these ghost women have offered me love and understanding, which I do my best to give back.

And while friends, colleagues and confidants often tell me, "Ken, there's no such thing as ghosts, we're seriously concerned about your well-being and can you please put down the knife," I know in my heart that they are ghosts, and if they don't need my help, then there's no one in my life who needs my help. So don't let the ignorant out there dissuade you, my apparition friends: if you love, you will be loved. And if you don't love, no one will love you, ever, and you will be sad when you die.

But it's all not going to matter in the end, for either ghost or man. Eventually, we're going to reach that bright light, and when the sun supernovas or the environment fully revolts against the folly of man, the cosmic apocalypse will send us all to our maker(s). You see, the end of the world will not come from the words of the Bible or from a comet in the sky, but rather by our acceptance that our end is inevitable. You see, the fall of man has been happening all along, and when humanity falls into the crevices of the Earth, this author will be reaping the rewards, side-by-side with the monsters he helped stand so tall.

However, there is one little matter that needs to be cleared up, and that is that I'm going to need a few of you ghosts to take one for the team and sacrifice yourselves to give me immortal life. Only once the ritual is completed, I will live forever in my physical form and without the strings of monsterdom to hold me back from greatness. And you will be martyrs for monsters everywhere, as my brilliant teachings will go on for centuries and centuries, teaching future generations of monsters how to do what humanity did, but only better. So please, if you're a ghost and you want to help the world truly be a better place for monsters, please enchant yourself into a book and find my mailing address, and I'll make sure there are statues erected in your honor once the world ends.

Whether it's finding eternal life via the singularity or gathering ghosts together to bind them into my soul and use black magic to give me immortality, this author is determined to live forever by any means necessary because *I deserve it*. The world needs a voice like mine to speak out into the darkness; the same darkness that is destined to encompass the Earth sooner or later. And when they do, there will be a place for ghosts just as there will be for vampires, man-made creatures, wolfmen, gill-men, monster brides, mad scientists, and mummies. There just will be no place for men, as people who cannot wield the power of a god have no right to rule beside them and therefore are destined to spend their final moments feeling the cold breath of death on their shoulders.

So if you're a monster and you've gotten this far into this book, hopefully you've done what has been instructed of you as well as bought extraneous copies of my book for no good reason. But if you're a human and for some reason you've read this book in its entirety, then you're probably coming to terms with your mortality right about now. But that's okay; there's no shame in dying, even though only losers and nerds die these days. But what's important is how you go about living, and if you can learn a thing or two from my words in this book, then maybe there's a part of you that's a monster after all.

You're still going to die, though. Sorry, humans.

Epilogue

Dear human readers,

As per my plea deal, I am writing this epilogue as an addendum to my smash hit book, *The I in Evil*, to clear the air about any misconceptions you might have had. Of course, you're all probably familiar with the very public fall from grace this author had following the book's release, in which police stopped my blood ritual before it could be completed. You also might have been a part of the class-action lawsuit against me for corrupting the youth, which had left me unable to afford a proper legal defense. You could have also likely seen my multiple apologies on the talk show circuits, including the one in which Steve Wilkos shouted at me as I wept profusely in a fetal-position that was shared all over the blogosphere.

Let me make myself 100 percent clear: there is no such thing as monsters, period. I wrote *The I in Evil* when I was in a very unwell state, reeling from a life of criminal activity that began when I was an unwitting accomplice to my father's heinous, unspeakable crimes. I know now, upon reflection, that telling people falsely about the existence of monsters was not right, and for that, I apologize. I also want to condemn the crimes inspired by my crimes, including all the amateur man-made creatures that were made by men much sicker than myself.

I also know now that ghosts do not exist, and that my bid for immortality on Earth was nothing but a delusion that I embraced because of my fear of death. Death fucking sucks, and I wanted nothing to do with it. But in the odd way that life turns out, death surrounded me and followed me everywhere I went, whether it was my time pretending to be a therapist or my time pretending to be a motivational speaker. And in my unclear disposition, the concept of living among ghosts and ghouls was a way to leave my lurid past behind.

But that is no justification for what I did, merely a reasoning as to *why* I did, and why I was able to guilt the fine folks at Skyhorse Publishing into publishing my book. At the end of the day, only humans exist in this world, and they are fragile beings, whose emotions shouldn't be played with and also shouldn't be killed (for the most part). Anyone who argues otherwise is also likely not well either, and should be ignored and/or dismissed.

So let this be a lesson to all you writers out there, aspiring or otherwise. Don't write self-help books for monsters. Don't write self-help books at all. No one needs them, and people's problems are more intricate and emotional than a stupid fucking book can offer. Whatever you do, don't let your search for immortality drive you to down a path of stupidity and insanity that will lead to multiple deaths. Take it from me, it's pretty fucking awful.

And I suppose *if* monsters *did* exist, and *if* they happened to get *this* edition of *The I in Evil,* and *if* they maybe found a spark of ingenuity in my words, then I sincerely would recommend they *don't* track me down, *don't* get me off the grid and *don't* put together another blood sacrifice as soon as possible.

Luckily, monsters *don't* exist. I cannot be more clear than saying they *do not* exist, and thus I am fulfilling my terms of the plea deal in my emphasis on their lack of existence. I regret what happened when this book was published. *Wink.*

Also, now that you've read my apology, don't forget to tell your friends to buy the new, revised version of *The I in Evil,* now with a brand new, captivating epilogue!

Yours now (and for eternity),

—Ken W. Hanley